WAVE

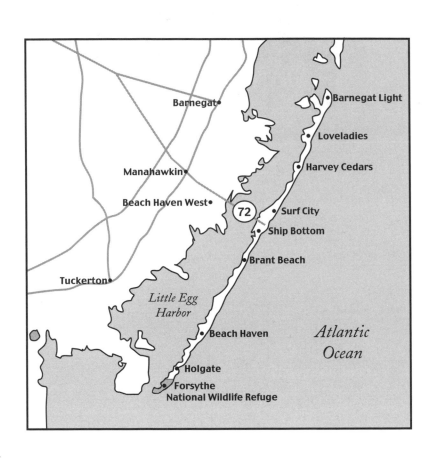

WAVE

Wil Mara

Plexus Publishing, Inc.
Medford, New Jersey

First printing, 2005

Published by: Plexus Publishing, Inc.
143 Old Marlton Pike
Medford, NJ 08055

Printed in the United States of America.

Library of Congress Cataloging-in-Publication Data

Mara, Wil.
    Wave / Wil Mara.
       p. cm.
    ISBN 0-937548-56-1 (hardcover)
    1. Long Beach Island (N.J.)--Fiction. 2. Victims of terrorism--Fiction. 3. Tsunami--Fiction. I. Title.
    PS3613.A725W389 2004
       813'.54--dc22
                                                    2004014018

President and CEO: Thomas H. Hogan, Sr.
Editor-in-Chief and Publisher: John B. Bryans
Managing Editor: Amy M. Holmes
VP Graphics and Production: M. Heide Dengler
Copy Editor: Pat Hadley-Miller
Book Designer: Kara Mia Jalkowski
Sales Manager: Pat Palatucci

Cover photo of Barnegat Light by Gordon Stull

Jacket design by Michele Quinn

To Francis James Mara, Jr.

1958–2003

†

"May light perpetual shine upon him."

ACKNOWLEDGMENTS

It would have been impossible to write this book without the help of some very fine individuals. I pray I haven't forgotten any of them.

First and foremost, boundless gratitude goes to John B. Bryans, my editor at Plexus Publishing, and my good and dear friend. He has been nothing short of amazing in his support and enthusiasm for this project. From the moment he received an e-mail from me saying, "Hey, I've got an idea for a book," to the very last red mark on the very last page, he has operated above and beyond the call. Every author should be so fortunate, at least once in his career, to work with an editor of this caliber. I sincerely hope the end of this novel does not also mark the end of our professional association.

Equal appreciation must go to the man who made sure all the facts about tsunamis were kept straight—Dr. Eddie Bernard, director of the Pacific Marine Environmental Laboratory in Seattle, Washington. Eddie gave so generously of his time and his knowledge that merely mentioning him in these acknowledgments does him no justice. He cared for this story as if it were his own, such is his passion for his work. I came out of the blue, hopeful yet hopeless, and never once did he treat me like a stranger. Sound scientific advice was also given by Dr. Stewart Farrell, the Director of the Richard Stockton Coastal Research Center. I thank him for his time, his energy, and his insight. If any errors in oceanographic factuality remain, they are either the product of intentional fictionalization or slipups for which I am solely responsible.

I must thank my wife, Tracey, and my three children, Lindsey, Jessica, and Jenna, for their patience and understanding. I tried my best to construct this book during the early hours of the morning, when I ran the least risk of absenteeism. But there were times when that just wasn't possible (e.g., weekend research trips to LBI). My family never complained, but I know they sometimes wonder why I didn't choose a more "normal" profession. (Answer: I didn't—it chose me.)

The late James J. Mancini, longtime mayor of Long Beach Township, spared several hours on a cold and rainy morning to talk about evacuation procedures, show photos of some of LBI's past disasters, and tell some very sobering stories. Those few precious hours mark the only time I ever met the man, but I came away deeply impressed and somewhat enamored—he had a charm about him that was impossible to resist. In that single encounter I could feel how much he loved LBI and its people. When I learned of his passing, I felt a genuine sense of loss. It would have been nice to visit with him one more time and give him a copy of this book.

Gloria "Mama" Palmisano, who has also passed away since I began writing this story, was kind enough to loan me her beach house in Manahawkin so I had someplace to lay my hat while I put this thing together. She is yet another example of overwhelming generosity that made this book much better than it would have been otherwise.

John Bryans's wife, Jenny, took the time to join John and me for dinner in the spring of 2003. She's a wonderful person and a delightful host. (Like me, John married "up.") Jane Bonnell was kind enough to read through the manuscript in its early stages and offer suggestions. I also spent some time pitching ideas back and forth with Peter Snell, Lisa Iarkowski, Sophie Papanikoloau, and Anne Garcia (a budding author in her own right). And I was fortunate enough to receive some superb feedback from Tom Hogan, Sr., President and CEO of Plexus Publishing, Inc., as well as Amy Holmes, Managing Editor, and Tom Hogan, Jr., Marketing Director. Dawn Messenger provided important input on technical details. These people probably don't realize how useful intelligent feedback is to a novelist. Reliable sounding boards are hard to come by; when you find one, you use it.

On a somewhat wackier note, I suppose I should thank the spammers out there in cyberspace for once again providing all the fictional names I needed for a story. By using the names that appear in the dozens of unsolicited e-mails that clog my inbox every day rather than tap my own creative resources, I almost feel it justifies the spam. So kudos to that branch of the loser nation for saving me the trouble— keep 'em coming.

Finally, I'd like to thank the many residents of Long Beach Island I encountered during my visits there. They were kind, courteous, and giving, just as their reputation suggests. LBI is a wonderful Jersey Shore community, and I envy all those who have the privilege of calling it home.

AUTHOR'S NOTE

Writing a fictional story about a real place is always tricky. The challenge is constantly put to you to decide where to remain in reality, and where to drift into fantasy.

Mark Twain promised to move entire towns and rivers in his stories if it fit his purposes. I didn't take quite so severe an approach, but I did exercise a handful of creative liberties here and there. Most are minor and will probably go unnoticed by most readers. One major overhaul, however, involves the geography of the Edwin B. Forsythe National Wildlife Refuge, located on LBI's southernmost tip: I made it larger and more complex, almost mazelike. You'll see why.

Also, a note to all naysayers who would scoff at the notion of a tidal wave coming to life in the Atlantic Ocean via the way I have described it. It is not only within the realm of the possible, it is *very* possible. When I first had the idea for this story, I promised myself I would write it only if I could make the birth of the wave *believable*. That meant, quite frankly, that "Hollywood-type crap" (e.g., an asteroid the size of Texas spins out of the sky and slams into the sea, or a giant brooding creature buried under the ocean floor for the last eight millennia finally awakens) was out of the question.

To make this happen, I hooked up with Dr. Eddie Bernard—one of the world's leading authorities on tsunamis, and a guest "star" on numerous tsunami documentaries, some of which occasionally run on the Discovery Channel. Between his wealth of tsunami knowledge and my plodding creativity, we worked out a scenario by which this could really happen. Just because we don't get tsunamis on the East Coast doesn't mean we *can't*. However, those of you who bother to do a little research of your own may soon realize that the science and the logistics presented here do not add up—that's because the conscious decision was made to underwrite these sections so, in a worst-case scenario, this otherwise innocent story didn't become a handbook for terrorists. In other words, if you compared it to directions on how to hot-wire a car, I left out steps two, six, and nine. But my God—how *easy* it would be.

Finally, I'd like to express a hope that, perhaps in some way, this little story provides food for thought to the civic leaders of relatively vulnerable seaside communities like Long Beach Island. It is far too easy to allow ourselves to be lulled into a false sense of "that-could-never-happen-to-us" security, much like the one that had numbed America prior to 9/11. I hope this story will support our already heightened vigilance toward the manifold dangers that infect our world—dangers that are not always the product of nature's wrath, but of humankind's too-frequent wrath toward itself. If the story makes just one person think a little harder about the "always be prepared" philosophy, then the effort put forth to write it cannot have been wasted.

Wil Mara
September 11, 2004

ONE

Sayed Zaeef shuffled along with the other passengers toward the boarding gate. The woman at his side, whose name he had come to learn was Aleida, was still talking. She'd been going nonstop for nearly a half hour. He didn't mind a bit. She spoke in her native Dutch, the official language here in the Netherlands. He'd learned it over the last three years, along with another native tongue, Frisian, but hadn't mastered either. All the better that she was dominating the conversation.

Zaeef had picked her out of the crowd shortly after arriving. She was among about two-dozen passengers who had come early and were hanging around, waiting. Some watched the giant airliners out the windows while others tried in vain to catch some rest on the torturously uncomfortable contour chairs. Aleida was one of the plane-watchers. She stood with her arms folded and spoke to an elderly woman sitting nearby whom she obviously did not know. She was the type who would talk to any stranger. Perfect. He set his shoulder bag down and moved alongside her, saying nothing. He adopted a look of almost childlike fascination as the planes came and went, mimicking her expression. Eventually, as he expected, she peered over and found him there. When she did, he returned the glance and smiled. She remarked how amazing modern technology was, and he agreed. Their conversation soon moved from airplanes to other matters—the weather, current events, and, ultimately, personal issues. She found him attractive, he could tell. And he was attractive. A handsome Syrian in his early thirties, his smile could charm a dying man out of his last heartbeat. The women were particularly easy, he thought, and this appeared to be a prime example.

As the line moved along, she started offering cutesy little anecdotes about her husband. He nodded and laughed in all the right places. She was probing him now, he knew, gauging his reaction to the fact that she was married. On the outside she was the good and faithful wife, but if the right, discreet opportunity came along, she'd stray. He cultivated the flirtation. For the other passengers, to see him with this woman would create an aura of acceptability. How could you be suspicious of someone who was so intimate with one of your own?

The little American flag-pin on his lapel sealed it. He'd figured this out quickly enough after September 11, 2001—Americans and other westerners were far less likely to pay you any mind if you had a flag of some kind on your clothes, flying from your car, or hanging outside your home. He found the gullibility amazing.

They reached the counter and handed over their tickets. The uniformed woman greeted him with a smile, which he returned. A man in a matching uniform stood behind her. Zaeef avoided eye contact. It was important to appear casual. The woman removed something from the envelope, then handed it back and said, "Have a nice flight, Mr. Qari." He nodded and thanked her. Aleida was still talking. Something about her flowerbeds.

They went down the rectangular tunnel and reached the door of the plane. Five more employees stood waiting—two female flight attendants and three pilots. They were all smiling, very happy to see everyone this morning. They locked on Zaeef as soon as he appeared, but he pretended not to notice. When he reached the threshold, he laughed out loud and said something in Dutch to his new friend. He appraised the crew with a single, fleeting glance and made his evaluation. The female flight attendants were of no concern. Aging wannabe-models with too much makeup, nail polish, and unjustified arrogance— about as dangerous as houseflies. The pilots had an ex-military scent about them. They kept their hair short and their faces smooth. They would've been equally at home in business suits and ties, sitting in a boardroom with their briefcases on the floor beside them. Two were small, a little paunchy and out of shape. They'd be no problem, if it came to that.

It was the third man—the captain—that made Zaeef nervous, as nervous as he was capable of being. He was older, probably late fifties, with a bronze tan and thin, steely eyes. They were watchful, intelligent. This was a man who was not easily fooled. His motto could have been, "Earn my trust *first.*" And in spite of his age, he looked fit and able. He stood with arms akimbo, his hands ready. A deep, primal instinct that had saved Zaeef's hide before told him this man could be trouble. As they started down the aisle, Zaeef felt his eyes boring into him, studying him.

Aleida found her seat first. Checking Zaeef's ticket for him, she realized he would be more than ten rows back.

"Maybe I can come back and see you once we are in the air," she said in Dutch.

"That would be nice."

He moved on, inwardly thankful to be away from her for awhile. He made a point of looking carefully at every number on every row, hoping to appear a little helpless and vulnerable. He found his seat and scanned the area. A heavyset white-haired woman was in the seat on the opposite side of the aisle, reading a copy of *People*. She looked at Zaeef the way most people look at snakes in a zoo. *This is an American*, he thought. "Hello," he said with a quick nod.

As he expected, she did not reply. Instead, she shrank back slightly and brought the magazine a little higher, as if using it as a shield.

Ignoring the slight, he opened the overhead compartment and stuffed in his green shoulder bag. Then, in another calculated move, he took off his suit jacket and set it carefully in the adjoining seat. He wanted the people around him to see that he was concealing nothing—no knives, no boxcutters, no plastic explosives. They were all appraising him, he knew, even if they were trying to appear as though they weren't.

He took his seat. The plane was almost full now and would be in the air in a matter of minutes. It would take nearly nine hours to reach Washington. He glanced at his watch; it was just after six-thirty A.M. A personal thought crept in—*I'll never see another six-thirty in my life*. He pondered this for only a moment before the years of training and mental discipline kicked in and erased it.

The plane shuddered as it pulled away from the dock and began a slow taxi toward the runway. A single electronic note rang through the overhead speakers, and a disembodied voice reminded everyone to buckle up and turn off their cell phones and laptops. People around him began chatting with their neighbors. Idle talk, useless talk, the talk of the small-minded.

As soon as they were in the air, he set the seat back, closed his eyes, and folded his hands across his stomach. Then another personal thought crept in, and it surprised him—he remembered the time he had spent a Sunday helping his mother make bread.

4

Back in those days in Damascus it was not uncommon for a mother to make bread for her family, but it was unusual for a son to help. Young boys in Syria were not supposed to busy themselves with domestic chores. But for some reason he had wanted to help her that day, and what was strange was the fact that his mother hadn't seemed the least bit puzzled or surprised. She rarely showed any emotion, but he had hoped he would see something then. Less than a month later she was gone, the victim of an American bomb meant for an ammunitions warehouse that had gone astray.

Surely she would approve of what he was doing now.

TWO

"This is for Patrick, but only if he eats everything else first," Karen said, holding up a small container of chocolate pudding. Brown hair, medium height, attractive enough although not to her own satisfaction. She wore a cream-color business suit, one that never seemed to fit quite right. "I made him a baloney-and-cheese sandwich, which he likes, at least this week. There's also some milk in here, a bag of pretzels, and a nice big—" She rummaged frantically through the bag, then her shoulders drooped. "Oh no...I forgot the orange. I'd better go to Acme right now and g—"

Nancy took her arm. "We've got oranges, sweetheart. Don't worry."

"Oh, no, you already do so much for—"

"Karen, we've got plenty."

Karen finally relented, but Nancy knew it would bother her for the rest of the day. She would probably bring two oranges tomorrow—one for Patrick, and one to replace the one Nancy had given him today.

"Okay, well there's also some money in here in case the ice-cream truck comes around. And I packed their swimsuits just in case Bud wants to take them on the boat."

The two boys bounded into the sunny Holgate kitchen, bursting with springtime energy. Patrick, four, was the older. He was as skinny as a rail and as fair-skinned as a ghost. Michael, three, was dark-haired, pudgier, and wildly freckled. He considered his brother something of a god and shadowed him ceaselessly. This didn't seem to bother Patrick in the least.

"What are we going to do today, Mrs. Erickson?" Patrick asked, grabbing hold of Nancy's floral dress and jumping up and down. Michael did likewise.

"Boys, boys…" Karen pleaded.

Nancy smiled and looked down adoringly at her charges. "Well, your mother brought your swim trunks along, so I guess you'll have to go out on the boat at some point."

The boys cried gleefully—Karen was amazed at how much noise two small children could make—and jumped some more. Nancy beamed down on them, not the least bit put off by the intensity of their enthusiasm, while Karen thanked God once again for bringing Nancy Erickson into her life. She was nothing short of an angel.

The women had met in 1979, when ten-year-old Karen walked into a Beach Haven Elementary School classroom on the first day of sixth grade. Teacher Nancy Erickson was writing her name on the blackboard (which was actually pea green) as Karen slid quietly into a seat in the second row. Their mutual fondness was instantaneous—Karen was a well-behaved, hard-working student, and her new teacher was patient, gentle, and nurturing. Karen cried when the school year ended and she had to move on to another grade, another room, and another teacher. After college she moved away from LBI, but, like so many others, she eventually returned.

She spotted Nancy at Holy Innocents Episcopal Church, on Marine Street, shortly after she got married, and the two women essentially picked up where they'd left off. Having lost her mother to breast cancer two years earlier, Karen adopted her former teacher as something of a surrogate. Nancy accepted the role without hesitation.

Nancy started watching the boys sparingly at first, when Karen and Mike were in a jam and needed someone quick. She soon found that after almost ten years of retirement she not only missed the interaction with youngsters but looked forward to Patrick's and Michael's exuberant presence. She and Bud had three children of their own, but all were grown and had long since moved off to build their own worlds. Only one of them, a son who designed industrial-application software in California, had children, and visits were infrequent. Patrick and Michael filled an emotional void.

When Nancy first proposed the idea of watching them all four days a week that Karen worked at Tarrance-Smith Realtors, just a few miles past the Causeway on the eastbound side of Route 72, Karen resisted. She was concerned that the boys would run the couple ragged. Nancy was in her late sixties, Bud over seventy. But Nancy would hear none of it—she said she felt as fit as a cheerleader. That was only part of the truth. The rest was based on an opinion that she and Karen shared—that daycare just wasn't what it used to be. Nancy wanted to make sure these two boys that she had grown to love received a solid foundation. Under her care they never sat zombie-eyed in front of a television set. Instead, they were taken on nature walks and slow rides around the bay behind the house in Bud's little motorboat. They were given basic lessons in math and spelling.

For Karen and Mike, Nancy and Bud were a dream come true. They were overjoyed to the point of guilt. Karen insisted on paying Nancy at least the same amount she would have paid to put them into daycare. Nancy refused the money at first, but agreed to take it once she realized Karen would have it no other way. She had taught Karen to be proper and decent, and she had taught her well. In fact, Karen was still uncomfortable referring to Nancy by her first name, which Nancy insisted on. In her heart, Karen could not think of the woman as anything other than "Mrs. Erickson." Most of the time she simply formed her sentences and questions in such a way that using a name was unnecessary.

"Okay, I've got to go," she said, looking at her watch. "Mommy's going to be late." She crouched down and opened her arms. "Come give me a kiss."

The boys charged over and nearly knocked her down, smothering her with affection.

"I love you guys."

"Love you, too, mommy," they replied in an uneven chorus.

"We'll walk out with you," Nancy said, following the ritual.

Karen stepped out into the bright spring day. "Call me if you need anything," she said, pulling the keys from her purse as she walked away, backward.

"We'll be fine," Nancy told her. The boys were already waving. They looked perfectly happy. Maybe too happy, Karen thought. *Aren't they supposed to be sad when I go?* They certainly were when Mike left for that meeting in San Francisco three days ago. They cried until she had to distract them with ice cream and a Disney movie.

She climbed into her Nissan Maxima and waved back through the windows. She continued waving as she pulled away. Watching the three of them grow smaller in the rearview mirror, she felt the sting of tears that hadn't diminished even slightly over the last two years.

*   *   *

In the brightly lit office of Long Beach Township Mayor Donald J. Harper, a trio of attorneys sat in their conservative suits and waited. On the opposite side of the enormous, L-shape desk, Harper was hunched forward, elbows on the glass, hands together, forefingers raised like a church steeple. He paid his guests no mind. It was as if he'd forgotten they were there.

They sat like a judgment panel, left to right, in three chairs. At one end, a young man with dark hair and GQ features was reviewing some papers that had nothing to do with the mayor's case. As far as he was concerned, Harper was yesterday's business. He knew a lost cause when he saw one, and J. Quentin Taylor—a third-year attorney who already owned a new BMW and a 32-foot yacht—didn't waste his energy on lost causes. He had come today only because due process and professionalism demanded it, but in his mind this was nothing more than the final viewing of a corpse.

Next to him was the only female in the group. Susanna Graham had been with the firm less than a year, had in fact been out of law school less than two, but she already knew how to carry herself like the frigid corporate bitch she'd always longed to be. With one leg crossed over the other, she stared down Harper and wondered why an elite firm such as hers had ever gotten involved with such a loser.

Jay Bennett was the senior member of the coven, a full partner in Thomasen, Smithfield, Bennett, and Clarke. It was one of the largest firms in South Jersey, handling everything from divorces to personal injuries to criminal litigation. Forty-nine and in perfect health, Bennett had silver hair and wore small, round glasses set in tortoise-shell frames that cost more than most people made in a week. He was single, had no major vices, and was so introverted that people who had worked with him for years had no idea how he felt about anything. That was just how he wanted it.

Bennett allowed another moment to pass, and then, realizing they might end up sitting there all day if someone didn't say something, offered, "Mr. Mayor, Judge Hadley will be expecting a decision on our plea in about—"

"You know," Harper interrupted, "there was a time when I wouldn't have taken a paper clip that wasn't mine." He let out a little laugh that seemed more like a cough.

Taylor removed a silver pen from inside his jacket and scribbled something on one of his papers, apparently unaware his client had spoken. Graham rolled her eyes and repositioned herself yet again. Bennett nodded noncommittally and studied the beige carpeting.

"Did you know I installed the first direct sewer line to Vol Sedges? That's right. They said it was impossible. Others tried to do the same thing and failed. I got it done in less than a year, nearly half a million dollars under budget, and I was only thirty-one at the time." He was glassy-eyed and dreamy. "The schools were a mess, too. The board was run by tired old people with no ideas or enthusiasm. The textbooks were ten years out of date, the best teachers wouldn't submit resumes, and the students' test scores were in the twentieth percentile statewide." He smiled and straightened up slightly. "I changed all that. In two years we moved up to the seventieth percentile, renovated both buildings, got all new books, cleaned out the board—and no one's taxes went up a cent. Not one cent."

Harper fell silent again, wrung his hands, and stared into space. The smile faded as he returned to whatever mental hideaway he'd been in all morning. For weeks, in fact.

Graham shot her boss an urgent look. Bennett cleared his throat. "Mr. Mayor, you really do need to tell us what it is you want to do. If we don't contact the judge by day's end, we run the very serious risk of—"

"My dream—my ultimate dream—was to go to Washington. Did I ever tell you that?"

"Yes, I knew that," Bennett replied. "I think we all knew that."

"That's what I wanted more than anything—to be a U.S. Senator. The best senator the Garden State ever had. A legend. The kind of politician who was grudgingly admired even by those who hadn't voted for him. It was a big dream, probably an impossible dream, but it drove me. It gave me the strength and the passion to do things I wouldn't have been able to do otherwise. Have you ever had a dream like that, counselor?"

As he looked to Bennett for an answer, he realized it was the first time he'd made eye contact with any of these lawyers today. Bennett didn't reply, didn't appear as though he had a reply. Harper laughed again and appraised Bennett's colleagues, then shook his head. He knew about the dreams of people like this— to acquire as much wealth and power as possible while leaving a trail of human casualties in their wake. *What a group*, he thought. *Three Stooges.* And then, from someplace deeper, *How did I ever get mixed up with this crowd? There was a time when I wouldn't have given them a second glance.* Finally, and most chillingly—*Thank God my father isn't alive to see any of this.*

The Harper family had a broad and varied political history on LBI, spanning four generations and more than a hundred years. Donald Harper's great-grandfather had been the mayor of Beach Haven, one of LBI's larger towns, before ultimately reaching the state legislature. He authored the state's first environmental laws, some of which were still in effect and had created a power base for New Jersey's conservation groups. Harper's paternal grandfather, while never holding an elected office, was an influential local businessman who had played a key role in early railroad lines to and from the island. His other grandfather had sat on the numerous city councils for more than three decades, while his father, Roy Allan Harper, was the only mayor elected to serve more than one LBI town—two terms in Barnegat Light and one in Long Beach Township. When he died of a massive heart attack in June of 1997, nearly five hundred residents and luminaries attended the funeral.

It seemed only natural that Donald, the oldest of three children, would carry on the legacy. There was tremendous pressure, considering the family's gloried history, but he accepted his role without hesitation. As a young boy he would stand in front of his bedroom mirror and give mock speeches, tirelessly trying to emulate the dramatic gestures of heroes like JFK and Winston Churchill. He joined the student council in sixth grade—the earliest it was permitted—and was president within a month. In high school he won popularity through charm, intelligence, and a fanatic devotion to preparedness. During the debate for that presidency, he crushed his opponent so overwhelmingly that the hapless victim received only nineteen votes.

Harper left LBI to attend Colgate University, went on to claim his master's degree in political science with a minor in civic management, then did a four-year stint in the Air Force, where he reached the rank of captain. It was during this brief military service that he put the finishing touches on his already considerable leadership skills. When he returned to his hometown, he was ready.

He won his first race for mayor, but it was close. His opponent, a popular moderate Democrat named Brenda Morrison, preyed on his youth and inexperience. But she went overboard and ended up looking like a bully while Harper earned voters' respect by keeping cool under pressure. The residents also remembered his father, some even remembered his grandfather, and they just plain liked the nice young man with all the fresh ideas. Morrison knew her stuff, but she had passed her prime a few steps back and seemed more interested in winning the job than actually doing it. Harper discussed the issues and—perhaps most importantly—appeared to know what was going on in people's minds. Morrison didn't.

Not long after Harper took office, the voters discovered their new mayor also had a gift for numbers. He announced there would be no increase in local taxes and, after some number-crunching and cost-cutting, managed to bring the township budget out of the red for the first time in recent memory, giving the town an actual surplus.

In the years that followed, one success led to another, and Harper's influence and popularity grew to the point where people started calling him the "Mayor of LBI." The other mayors, knowing it was to their advantage, rallied behind him. By the time Harper hit forty-five he had the island in his back pocket and began seriously thinking about going after his Holy Grail— a senatorship. He had the record, the support, and the financial commitments. In Washington, incumbent Senator William Lacey was on his way out, having announced his intention to retire after his current term. The New Jersey Republican wheels were already sniffing out Harper as a potential candidate, and they liked what they saw. Republicans traditionally had a tough time in New Jersey, especially on the senatorial level, but Harper had developed a following among moderate Democrats and was considered a potential crossover candidate—something the conservatives hadn't enjoyed in the Garden State in ages. All in all, the current seemed to be flowing in Harper's direction.

And then Gus Riggins entered his life.

Riggins was a slovenly, foul-mouthed creature who had spent his professional life in the construction business. He didn't trust people who wore suits, and felt most of the human race was essentially valueless. He bragged about the fact that he never finished high school yet had more money than anyone he knew who'd graduated from "one of those so-called institutes of higher learning." After fifteen years as a laborer, he'd started his own business, Riggins Builders, Inc., and cultivated it into the second largest construction company in South Jersey, overshadowed only by the almighty Hovnanian empire.

Harper and Riggins were aware of each other and kept their distance through the years. Harper thought Riggins was dangerously ambitious and was glad they never had any direct dealings. Conversely, Riggins felt Harper was just another Ivy-League prick who'd been born on third base and had no clue what hard work was really about. But when the town announced they were going to build a new shopping center on a prime Sixth Avenue lot that had previously been untouchable due to a litany of legal snafus, Riggins decided, come hell or high water, that the contract would bear his name. And the Honorable Donald J. Harper was the one man who could make it happen.

His first thought was of that business chestnut known as blackmail; it had yielded good results for him in the past. So he did some digging. He hired a small band of sleazy detectives and sank a little money into a Dun and Bradstreet report. One month and three thousand bucks later, however, he was forced to swallow the fact that Harper was as clean as fresh snow— there was nothing, absolutely nothing. All this did was inspire him to double his efforts.

He considered threats, then realized that would be too risky. A guy as popular as Harper had allies everywhere; he'd likely pay a hefty price without reaching his objective. Bribery appeared to be out of the question, too. So what was this man's weakness? Which button needed to be pushed?

Riggins decided to utilize a tool he despised—charm. He had it but didn't like to use it. It was a little too close to butt-kissing, and Gus Riggins was no butt-kisser.

But in this case he was willing to make an exception. He paid Harper a visit on a sunny summer morning wearing a suit and tie he'd bought off the rack the night before. His hair was swept back in lush, greasy strokes and his face was smoother than it'd been in years. His immediate objective was to shatter whatever negative image Harper had built of him through rumor and reputation. He wanted to show this upper-crust Boy Scout that he had not one, but two sides to his character—the rough-hewn, blue-collar side that had enabled him to claw his way through the cutthroat ranks of the construction industry, and the classier, urbane side that made him every bit as refined as any-one in Harper's world.

Much to his surprise, Riggins found himself actually liking Harper. As easily as Riggins could play the role of an elitist, Harper could curse like a millworker and produce jokes that were so off-color they'd make a hooker blush. Riggins soon realized what this man's true gift really was—he could connect with anybody. And it wasn't all smoke and mirrors, either—somehow, he really knew. By the end of their first meeting, Riggins felt Harper was someone he could deal with.

And best of all, he'd found the Achilles' heel he'd been look-ing for—Harper loved money.

The first trip Harper took to Atlantic City on Riggins' tab occurred less than a month later. Riggins had done some work for a number of smaller casinos and was friends with all the owners. He went out of his way to make sure the mayor had a grand old time—free room, free meals, thousands of dollars in credit, a few shows. Harper brought his wife on the first trip, but afterward he always went alone, usually with the aid of a pair of sunglasses and a baseball cap. He was a smart gambler, able to stay afloat longer than most, but in the end he always walked away a loser. That didn't matter ultimately—Riggins kept send-ing the cash, and Harper kept accepting it. He lost track of the grand total after awhile. Some of it went to AC, some straight into his pocket. It seemed to be flying around everywhere. Riggins even taught him some of the basic principles of creative accounting, and Harper, to his own shock and surprise, found himself occasionally making use of his new talents. It was like an addiction over which he had no control. The sickness was always there, but he had managed to keep it at bay on his own. Once Riggins appeared, that resolve was stripped away. Part of Donald Harper hated himself for what he was doing, but another part was having the time of his life.

Four months after their initial meeting, Riggins got the contract. Subsequent deals followed, and Harper continued to enjoy himself. Years later, in hindsight, Harper realized Riggins had slid the knife in so skillfully that he wasn't even aware of it. By the time word of their little arrangement leaked out, it was too late to deny it.

The local media picked up the story first. Initially they kept direct allegations to a minimum and buried the text in places where it would be generally overlooked. When some of Riggins's enraged competitors pressed for more information, however, Newark's *Star-Ledger* became interested, and the beginning of the end was at hand.

Like any seasoned politician, Harper denied all charges until there was no other choice. When that time came, he declined to issue any comments and hired a legal team. His wife, embarrassed and humiliated, left him and went back to her parents in rural Pennsylvania. They had no children, so there was no messiness on that front. The public, feeling confused and disillusioned, unplugged themselves from the debacle and simply waited for a successor. After awhile most people weren't even sure Harper was technically still in office, he maintained such a low profile.

Now, six months and a string of follow-up articles later, on the eve of what surely would be his last significant appearance, he was being asked to sharpen the blade for his own professional execution. It was the only option left. At least the media and the courts didn't find out everything, he thought. Yes, he would lose his job and maybe end up indicted, but he was certain he would go down for much less than he had actually done. And even now, a part of him was still genuinely baffled by how it all could've happened in the first place.

Once again Jay Bennett, Esq. shook him out of his daze.

"Mr. Harper, we have to have a decision," he said firmly, showing more emotion than was usual for him.

Harper paused for one last, precious moment, savoring the position he'd worked so hard and so long to achieve. Then, with a heavy sigh, he wrote the first word in what surely would be the darkest chapter in his family's political history.

Leaning back in the leather chair of an office he knew he would not occupy much longer, he said, "Tell the judge my plea will be 'guilty.'"

"Thank you, Mr. Mayor."

*   *   *

News of Harper's plea traveled like lightning along the following path: First it went to the courthouse, where it was entered into the public record. Two minutes later it traveled from the municipal clerk through a phone line to the home office of E. Gordon Davis, III, attorney-at-law. Davis lived in LBI's upscale town of Loveladies, in a fairly intimidating three-story monstrosity overlooking the ocean.

Davis did not answer the phone when it rang. Instead it was picked up by one Thomas T. Wilson. Small and bookish with neatly combed dark hair and round glasses that added an air of intellect to his otherwise boyish face, Wilson was, technically, Davis's political advisor. He had no formal degree in politics, nor did he have any firsthand political experience. He was commonly known as a "natural"—one who possessed an innate gift for knowing what worked and what didn't in a particular field without the aid of any official training or education.

Wilson had been Harper's right-hand man since the day Harper's name first appeared on a ballot. Outwardly, Wilson hated everything political—he hated the underhandedness, the sleaze, the corruption, and the rampant, unchecked incompetence. He favored no party, only truth and honor. To that end he resented any elected official for not using his granted power to inject more good into the world. Anyone who had the opportunity to do something decent and chose not to, he felt, should be stripped of their power and humiliated. He was as honest as the day was long.

Wilson was willing to work as an advisor for Harper because he felt Harper had similar qualities and beliefs, and because local history suggested Harper's family did likewise (his personal theory was that the Harpers never rose above a modest local level because New Jersey's corrupt upper echelon intentionally kept them down). He believed Harper possessed the seeds of greatness and, with his help and a little luck, could reach dizzying political heights. In truth, deep down, he loved the political system of America because he believed it was the only one where a person even had the chance to do great things; in other systems such opportunities simply did not exist. He never considered running for any office himself, for he knew he didn't have the required traits. It simply wasn't part of his destiny.

Harper, on the other hand, had them all—he was handsome, commanding, sure of himself without being cocky, a scholar, and a reassuring leader. He was also an excellent speaker with tremendous public presence and charisma. Women liked him; men wanted to be like him. He came from a solidly middle- to upper-class family: He wasn't too rich. He was active in extracurricular activities during his school years and retained close friendships with people from a wide variety of backgrounds and races. He worked hard and didn't complain about it. In short, he was blessed with what most called the "X factor"—that indefinable quality that makes people follow and believe in you. Politically speaking, he was built for speed.

The two men fit together seamlessly. Wilson covered Harper's blind spots, and Harper covered his. They trusted each other, and their egos never clashed. They were comfortable in their respective roles, and both focused on the same objective— getting Harper into the U.S. Senate.

When the scandal first reared its head, Wilson didn't believe it. He was sure one of Harper's political rivals had fabricated the story. When bits and pieces of what appeared to be solid evidence began surfacing, Wilson decided it was an elaborate setup, and that Gus Riggins had been a plant.

Then the night came when Harper, alone with Wilson late in his office, confessed that it was all true, every word of it, and that he had no explanation or defense for his actions. He said he got caught up in a current and was unable to free himself. Wilson was stunned, speechless at the ugly fact that his idol was not only human after all, but no better than the legions of crawling maggots who polluted the current political scene. He was just another one of Them.

Wilson stormed from the office and never spoke to Harper again. He drifted for awhile, unsure of everything he had ever known. Ten years of his life shot to hell. How could Harper have done this to him? How could he be so evil? (Maybe he did still have a bright political future, Wilson thought—he was, after all, obviously a master of deception. In today's political climate, he'd fit in perfectly....)

Harper tried repeatedly to contact his old friend, tried to make amends and attempt to explain himself. Wilson wanted nothing to do with it. He didn't want to hear Harper's story because Harper had had plenty of time to compose it. It would be good, for sure, but it wouldn't be honest. It'd paint him in a sympathetic light, somehow make him out to be the victim. Wilson believed he was the only victim here—he and all the people who had believed in Harper and given him their support. On an island that was largely Republican but still had its fair share of Democrats, Harper got nearly eighty-six percent of the vote. Eighty-six percent. It was a record, and a confirmation of Harper's mass appeal.

What did the electorate think now?

Roughly three months after their last conversation, Wilson decided his future. As he had played a key role in putting Harper in power, it was his duty to the people of Long Beach Island to take him back out. In addition, he had to make sure some other lowlife didn't take Harper's place. He had to find someone with genuine integrity, someone who was already high-profile enough to slip painlessly into the job.

Elliot Davis became the man. Davis was small and heavy, with a charming, impish way about him. He smiled easily and enjoyed the company of others. He had been the president of Continental Savings and Loan for nearly ten years and was active in community affairs. He had earned a reputation of unprecedented decency and compassion as a bank president, working out cautious but generous loans for private citizens and businesses after they'd been rejected everywhere else. He seemed to be a shining example of the now-famous "compassionate conservatism" ideology, which appealed to much of the island's populace. He most assuredly did not possess Harper's many other, smaller political gifts and certainly would never get anywhere near the U. S. Senate in this or any other lifetime. But he would be an easy replacement for Harper. He would competently mind the store while the people of Long Beach licked their wounds. At least this was how Wilson envisioned it.

Davis was amenable to Wilson's plan because, as Wilson knew, he had often flirted with the idea of running for mayor. He was born and raised on LBI and loved every inch of it with all his heart. Davis knew Harper well and felt genuinely bad for him when his career began to unravel. He knew nothing of the details aside from what was printed in the local papers, and Wilson never offered any. So he simply accepted the situation and went forward, letting Wilson be his guide. This guy had a proven track record, after all.

Wilson, perched on the edge of Davis's desk, snatched up the phone when it rang on this sunny spring day. He'd been staring out one of the windows at the back of the house. Sandy Island was hazy but visible in the distance.

"Elliot Davis's office. Yes? Oh, hi, Freddie. What's up?"

Davis leaned forward, his eyebrows raised. Wilson held up a finger.

"Really? Are you certain? Okay, thanks. I'll talk to you a little later."

Wilson's expression did not change. In fact it rarely ever did—he was as stone-faced as they came. If you were to draw a picture of his mouth, a short, straight line would be more than sufficient.

Davis was about to crawl out of his pants. "Well?"

Wilson permitted himself a rare smile in this instant—one side of that short, straight line curled upward almost a millimeter.

"Congratulations, Elliot. You're going to be our next mayor. Our current one just figuratively tipped over his king."

Davis stood and shook Wilson's hand.

"Great, Tom, just great. Sad that it had to happen this way, but..."

Wilson nodded, tried to appear empathetic. Inside he was savoring the victory.

"Yes, very sad. Very sad indeed."

* * *

Mark set the cell phone gingerly on the passenger seat and pressed the foam-covered bud into his ear. The microphone hung about six inches farther down the coated wire, bouncing off his neck. He worked the tiny buttons without taking his eyes off Bay Avenue, cruising past Marine Street in central Beach Haven. Jennifer picked up on the first ring.

"Hello?"

"Hi, sweetheart."

"Hi!"

Warmth flooded into him, a nourishing, soul-caressing warmth. He had grown addicted to the joy in her voice whenever she picked up the phone and found him on the other end. That unabashedly I'm-so-glad-to-hear-you tone that made him feel like he was truly wanted. They'd been together nearly a year now, and it was still as bright and sincere as ever. *I love her so much*, he thought.

"What's going on? Are you almost there?"

"Yeah, almost. I just wanted to call and say hello, tell you that I loved you, and make sure everything's still on for later."

"You bet it is. I wouldn't miss it for anything."

"Great."

"And I love you, too, Mark."

He paused, stiffened slightly. His foot went to the brake pedal on its own as he drew too close to an elderly woman puttering along in a rusting red something-or-other from the sixties.

"You do?"

"Uh-huh."

"Really? I mean...really?"

"Yes," she said through a laugh that sounded more like an attempt to clear dust from her nose. "You silly, of course I do."

He relaxed, smiled. "Okay. Sorry, I don't mean to be so needy."

"That's all right."

It is? Are you sure about that? The words were there, in that echoey place in his brain where all his words were manufactured. But he clenched his teeth and kept them in. He didn't want to push, didn't want to turn her off. If he pushed too much she might...

Disappear like your dad did? Or maybe just stop loving you like your mom? Stop loving you and pretend you're not even there? No...please God, no. Not with Jen. Not that. Anything but that. Anything...

"Uh...what time? Twelve-thirty?"

"Right, twelve-thirty," she said. "I'll bring the food, you just bring your wonderful self."

"Great. I'll see you then."

"Okay," she replied, kind of singing it—o-KAY-ee.

"Bye."

He pressed the button that disconnected all calls and removed the bud from his ear. He tried to return his attention fully to the road as he entered Holgate, but it was hopeless. For nearly twelve months he had examined and re-examined the mystery of why a girl as sweet and as wonderful and as...normal as Jennifer King would want to dispose of her precious hours with the likes of him. She came from the kind of sane, stable world he only dreamed of—a nice home in a middle-class town, with parents who were still together and, from all outward appearances, still in love with each other. She was "good stock," a girl any mother would want her son to marry.

And him? Well, we know all about that, don't we? We know this bubble's going to pop sooner or later. You'll wake from this dream and find yourself back in reality, chump. You're so far out of her league it isn't even funny. You've got some nerve—carrying this thing as far as you have. Why waste the time? Why waste her time? If you really love her so much, do her the favor of her life and cut it off now. Give her a chance to find someone who deserves her.

He knew she'd have a fit if she got wind of these thoughts. And he felt bad keeping them from her—they had agreed not to keep secrets from each other, and for the most part he'd kept his end of the bargain. But these feelings of inadequacy were proving harder to shake than a shadow. Jennifer had a mother and a father who doted on her. He had a mother who barely noticed he was there, and an overbearing brute of a stepfather who wished he wasn't. She had a good education and a bright future. He had a high school diploma and six credits at Ocean County College. She had an older sister she spoke with almost every night. He had no relatives he could stand, much less communicate with. He couldn't suppress the notion that he wasn't *contributing* anything to the relationship, that he brought nothing to the table. She had so much, he had so little. The disproportion riddled him with guilt. And depression. And, most of all, *fear*—the stark, white terror that one day she would wake up, realize she could do so much better, and toss him like a toothpick. *What was I thinking?* she'd wonder as she walked off, arm in arm with someone else. *Just what in hell was I thinking?*

He shivered at this image and doubled his determination to concentrate on his driving. The entrance to the Edwin B. Forsythe National Wildlife Refuge came up at the end of Long Beach Boulevard. He eased into the parking lot and discovered, with a certain selfish pleasure, that he was the only one there. *Makes sense—how many other people would be visiting an LBI wildlife refuge on a weekday morning in May?* He grabbed his camera bag from the back seat and got out, not bothering to lock the tired '92 Honda Accord that served as his sole mode of transport. And she drives a 2004 Camry. Another way she out-classes me hands down.... He slung the bag over his shoulder and began to walk.

The air was warm and sweet. He loved nature, loved being in the middle of it. He spent the first few moments just looking and touching, feeling and admiring. Then the professional side of him remembered why he had come, and he took out the camera. It was a basic model—Pentax K-1000, the camera high schools give to their Photography 101 students—but it was all he could afford. Much to his surprise, it had served him very well. It had no automatic features, but he came to love that. Having full control gave him more room to express himself, and the dependency forced him to stretch his abilities to their limits.

He brought the camera to his face and turned it sideways. All shots would be taken this way today—portrait instead of land-scape. They needed covers back at the *SandPaper*. Mark's boss, the paper's photo editor, told him to shoot at least a hundred. The theme was spring, with a nod toward the coming summer. Mark had worked there for nearly two years now, as both a writer and photographer. The exposure had made him some-thing of a minor local celebrity.

He spotted a prothonotary warbler atop a little shrub. It was the first one he'd seen this year. He attached a zoom lens and eased toward it.

When he felt close enough, he brought the camera up and twisted the lens into focus. Through the viewfinder he found a beautifully composed frame—the animal's primary yellows against the burning blue of the morning sky. He was awed by the sheer austerity of it and found it impossible to click the shutter for a moment.

The bird took flight when his cell phone twittered. He tried to get the shot anyway but he knew he'd missed it. He pulled the phone from his belt and flipped it open, then closed it when a voice on the other end asked if he'd be interested in having his kitchen remodeled. So much for the National Do-Not-Call List.

As if to punish the device for disturbing his work, he turned it off.

* * *

Ricki Lake would be on first, then Sally Jessie. And then, best of all...*Jerry.*

BethAnn Mosley thought Jerry Springer was a god. He wasn't exactly a celebrity in her mind. He wasn't cute enough, like Tom Cruise or that hunk of all hunks, Brad Pitt. (She in fact had several pictures of Pitt stark naked, and in suggestive poses, on her computer. She'd downloaded them from the Web and wasn't even sure it was really him—they might have been faked, with his head imposed on someone else's body. Nevertheless they sufficiently served her purposes.) No, Jerry Springer was a god because his show had the best content, the best conflicts, the best...*hate.* Even though she would never admit it to anyone, she *loved* hate. It was as addictive as the Doritos, Coca-Cola, and Ben and Jerry's ice cream that formed her staple diet. This was to say nothing of marijuana and, when she could afford it, a bit of ecstasy.

Sometimes she would tape Springer, and if it turned out to be a particularly violent episode, she'd watch the explosive moments over and over. She loved the enraged look on people's faces when their resolve finally gave way and they tried to kill each other. God, how she loved that. Why didn't that happen more often in real life? She supposed it did, but not in *her* life. She liked pushing people's buttons, liked trying to get them to those heights of irritation, but even in her best moments she couldn't seem to inspire the kind of rage Jerry provided. She'd heard somewhere that a lot of his shows were scripted, so maybe that was why they seemed so perfect. She didn't care. The pleasure she harvested far outweighed any concerns over artistic integrity.

The Ricki Lake Show paused for a commercial break, so she raised the remote and began flipping. To her right was an open bag of Fritos. To her left, a pint of Chunky Monkey with a spoon sticking out of it. A can of Coke was trapped between her flabby legs. The rest of the six pack was in an ice chest on the floor, awaiting its fate. All the curtains in the trailer were drawn, all the windows shut tight, both doors locked. A giant metal cocoon.

Ricki ended ten minutes later and BethAnn sighed. It would be exactly four minutes and thirty seconds until Sally started her monologue. She glanced down at the cordless phone and felt a familiar sense of dread. She'd put this off as long as possible. There were no spare minutes left.

Brian picked up on the second ring. "Hello, Beach Haven Acme, this is Brian Donahue, how can I help you?"

"Brian...it's me."

She sounded feeble, elderly. An old woman on her deathbed imparting her final thoughts.

"BethAnn? You sound terrible."

The sincerity was still there, she thought, and that was good. She'd held onto this job for almost fourteen months now—a personal record. Most of her other employers caught on pretty quick. But not this guy. He seemed utterly clueless.

"I feel terrible. I've been throwing up, and I've had diarrhea, and—"

"Well, just stay home then. We'll hold down the fort."

Hold down the fort. What a Brian phrase that was. So gung-ho, so all-American.

What a schmuck.

"Thanks, I really appreciate it. And I'm sorry."

"Don't be sorry. We don't have control over these things."

"I just feel bad because it's inventory day. There's so much work to be done."

"Don't feel bad. Just feel better."

Another Brianism; her stomach knotted. She wanted to choke people like this.

"Thanks. I'll call tomorrow."

"Righto."

She turned the phone off and tossed it aside. It landed at the other end of the couch, buttons up. If it rang she'd ignore it; she wasn't expecting any other calls today.

She smiled. It was a horrible, demonic smile. She knew who Brian would call to take her place—Jennifer King. Jennifer was the only other person in the store who knew how to use the inventory computer. That damn thing was ancient. Monocolor screen (black with glowing amber characters) and so slow to respond to commands that half the time you wondered if you had entered them correctly. But Jennifer went to the trouble of learning how to use it. Didn't complain that it was out-of-date or that it was slow. Just sat in the lunchroom in the back, on her own time, and read the manual over and over until she'd mastered it. Another gung-ho schmuck. Her and her nonstop talk about her beloved boyfriend, the hotshot writer and photographer for the *SandPaper*. She was another one who should be choked to death.

She tried to envision the sinking look on Jennifer's face when Brian broke the bad news. She knew Jennifer was supposed to meet Mark for lunch today at Forsythe. She knew that because *everyone* knew it. Jennifer was always giving updates; the Mark and Jennifer newsletter. This would shatter those plans. Jennifer would be sad, but she wouldn't complain. Nope, not her. All-American girls like her never did. She'd just carry on like a trooper and keep the disappointment to herself. But it would be there, and knowing that was good enough for BethAnn Mosley.

Sally finally came on. Then the Fritos ran out. BethAnn cursed and got up with a groan. She kept her stash in a chest-level cabinet so she wouldn't have to bend or stretch. It was jammed—potato chips, pretzels, popcorn (all three varieties—plain, cheese, and caramel). This was one of the practical advantages of working in a grocery story. She chose Munchos this time.

Jerry was next, so it was a good thing she got the new bag when she did.

THREE

aeef kept his eyes closed and his hands folded the entire trip. He thought about many things, but mostly about the paradise that awaited him. What fools these people were. If they only knew. They cherished and clung to their mortality as if it possessed true value, never suspecting there was a better world waiting on the other side. *This* was the hell and the purgatory. Obliterating the non-believers was Allah's work, Allah's will. The Americans were the greatest heretics. They not only clung to their lives, they clung to their money and their material goods with equal fervor—sometimes more. They were soulless and godless. Zaeef believed this with every ounce of his soul and felt no remorse for what he was about to do. In fact he felt excited about it. Excited and eager. This was the high point of existence. It would earn him passage into the great kingdom. It would exalt him in the eyes of the Almighty. Once the videotape he left behind—the one where he explained what he was doing and why—was found and played on news channels across the world, he would also be a hero of his people. Not that heroism interested him. Well, that wasn't completely true—it interested him inasmuch as it would encourage others to choose a similar course. That was something to be thankful for. But he could not dwell on it for long.

The plan was so simple and yet so powerful. Smuggle a radioactive device onto a plane bound for Washington DC and detonate it upon landing, rendering the city uninhabitable for a few decades. They believed their biggest challenge would be getting the device on board, but it turned out to be ridiculously easy—they simply bribed an airport employee to do it for them. They'd searched for months for just the right candidate and finally found him when the Schiphol Airport laid off nearly a hundred people in a cost-cutting move. Employees were given a month's pay and three weeks to find work elsewhere. With so many embittered workers, the stage was set. An offer of ten thousand dollars and a story that the box contained a hundred pounds of cocaine was all it took. They even gave the guy some as a "bonus." Airport security in America had tightened like a vice, but that didn't mean it had tightened everywhere else. The Americans could increase their control over planes that left their soil, but they couldn't do much about the flights coming in. Great Britain and a number of other high-profile U.S. allies had increased their security, but the Netherlands was chosen for this operation because it was relatively easy to overlook. No one would suspect a flight from Amsterdam posed much of a threat. Once again the devil would be caught with his guard down. Zaeef smiled at this and allowed himself the very mortal sensation of personal gratification. He had watched tapes of terrified Americans reacting to al Qaeda's victory of September 11, 2001. Thinking it would happen again, and that he would be the cause of it, was very gratifying indeed.

He opened his eyes and checked his watch—just after eight. The pilot had announced a few moments earlier that they were expected to land about ten minutes ahead of schedule. That suited him just fine. *The sooner the be—*

The plane rocked violently and Zaeef was almost thrown from his seat. Others tumbled into the aisles. A woman screamed, compartment lights flickered, and then a second and more violent jolt came. Overhead compartments flew open, vomiting their contents.

Zaeef had purposely left his carry-on bag unzipped. The plan once they'd landed in Washington was to simply get up from his seat as soon as they stopped moving, reach inside, and press the button on the detonator that had been disguised as a can of shaving cream. The bag now rolled out and fell onto his head, then to the floor, spilling items everywhere.

He cursed in Arabic and lunged for the can. Some of the other passengers forgot about the turbulence and trained their eyes on him. For a flicker of an instant the personal charm was gone and the terrorist stood before them.

No one moved. Time dragged and warped, became meaningless. Zaeef knew his cover was blown, knew it was time to improvise. But he waited anyway, just in case. If there was a move to be made, he wanted one of them to make it first.

Someone did—one of the fashion-model flight attendants. She'd been at the far end of the aisle helping an older woman to her feet. She rose slowly and, keeping her eyes locked on the Syrian, knocked on the cockpit door. She had a brief exchange with someone on the other side, then the door opened and the captain appeared. *The only one who looked like he had a brain in his head,* Zaeef thought bitterly. The man studied him for only a moment, but in that moment Zaeef could see the intelligence working, the years of training being accessed. He also noted that one of the copilots was on the radio, no doubt sending a distress call to the ground.

The captain approached cautiously. He didn't appear to have a weapon, but Zaeef sensed danger nevertheless. There were people all around him, many of them Americans who would be more than happy to take part in a heroic effort. He had no intention of letting that happen.

The revolver he pulled from the bag was a modified Glock, the notorious "plastic gun" that had had anti-firearms activists in a state of perpetual frenzy for years. Made from high-tech polymers, and easily assembled and disassembled, this type of gun was often used by government agents working undercover. Although typically some of the internal parts were metal, plastic parts could be substituted where a weapon would only be fired a few times. This was the case with Zaeef's gun, which could pass undetected through virtually any airport security system.

There was a collective gasp and more screaming. Everyone near Zaeef backed away. The captain, whose nametag identified him simply as "Casey," froze as if he'd been hit with some kind of stun ray. Zaeef's eyes were wild, insane. He aimed the gun at the nearest window.

"Everyone back," he shouted twice in passable English, "or I'll shoot it out!"

He had the shaving cream can in his other hand, held against his chest with his thumb on the button. The fear in the captain's eyes reassured him, made him feel in command of the situation. If he could control this guy, his instincts told him, he could still carry out this mission. Inspired by this, a new plan fell together in his mind.

"This is a detonator!" he said, holding the can up. "I push this, the plane goes!"

"I don't see anything here large enough to be a bomb," Casey said calmly. "I think you're bluffing."

"With the luggage, in the plane's belly, you stupid fool." Zaeef permitted himself a tiny smile. "Getting it on was so easy."

A few passengers were crying, convinced the end was at hand. One elderly man in a plaid jacket went down on his knees and began praying. At the very back, a boy of five watched with a mixture of curiosity and confusion. His mother, an attractive brunette in her thirties, held him close, drawing as much comfort as she was giving.

Casey was watching and waiting. Zaeef could tell what was going through his mind—*Just give me one chance. One chance and I'll take care of this little bastard.* A John Wayne type. A real American hero.

"Turn around," Zaeef snapped, motioning with the gun. When Casey refused to comply, he took aim at the window again. His was the perfect poker face because there was no bluff—Casey had no doubt this lunatic would be more than happy to get sucked out the window if it meant taking everyone else with him.

He turned around.

"Back to the cockpit. Anyone moves, I kill them."

They began moving forward, roughly ten feet apart. The copilots, who had been watching through the narrow rectangular perspective of the open doorway, looked up into their captain's face as he reached it.

As he approached them the captain said under his breath, "Tony, empty the cargo bay."

A brief pause.

"Captain?"

"If he has a bomb let's drop it here."

Tony nodded.

Zaeef appeared at the threshold just as Tony initiated the opening of the cargo doors. Within seconds there would be hundreds of suitcases falling from the sky. Zaeef peered inside and motioned angrily with the gun. "I want to see all of you. Stand up!"

The men obeyed, standing alongside each other as if posing for a group photo. Except there were no smiles. Just thinly contained anger and obvious hatred. No fear, though, and that irritated Zaeef. *Arrogant American bastards.*

"Take off your jackets and turn around slowly."

Again they obeyed. The sight of the three grown, uniformed men revolving like ballerinas would have seemed oddly comical under different circumstances.

None were armed, Zaeef observed, and a feeling of relief flowed through him. "Get back to the controls and keep flying."

The pilots exchanged silent glances that transmitted the same message: *He doesn't know how to fly the plane.* Reading their faces Zaeef realized his blunder, and felt an overwhelming desire to detonate the bomb. To kill all of them then and there.

"The controls!" he screeched.

The captain looked him straight in the eyes and said, quietly yet firmly, "No."

"I will shoot you dead and your passengers will all die!"

Zaeef's small audience offered no response, which served only to enrage him further. The captain put his hands in his pockets, a smug expression on his face.

It was their easy willingness to die for their principles that pushed Zaeef to the breaking point. He took aim at Tony and fired. A splash of blood leaped from his chest, and he slammed into the controls.

Amid the screams of the other passengers, Zaeef said, "You will be next! Fly the plane! Fly the—"

An arm slithered around his neck like a tentacle. It was thick and hairy, and very powerful. The owner, whoever it was, tried to pull him backward. But Zaeef was experienced in close-quarters combat and managed to stay on his feet. He brought the gun up and shot blindly over his shoulder. More screams, and the arm lost its strength and fell away. Zaeef didn't bother looking back and would never know who the attacker was.

During this brief scuffle, the captain took his chance. One of the last cognizant thoughts the Syrian had was that Casey moved with remarkable speed and agility for a man of his age. He came through the door and brought his hands up in one fluid motion, as if he'd practiced it a hundred times. Maybe he had. Regardless, he wasn't quite fast enough. Zaeef swung the pistol back around and fired again, aiming for Casey's head. It was a foolish move, as the torso was a much bigger target, but he was possessed by hatred now and wanted to see the man's face disintegrate. Instead the bullet strayed left, missing its target entirely and blowing out one of the cockpit windows.

The sudden depressurization forced the plane into a dive, the terrified screams of the passengers blending with the sound of violent air displacement to create a deafening symphony of horror. Tony's body went out first, then Casey's. The third pilot—a man named Adam Rodas who was making his first international flight—went along with Zaeef. Both hit the frame at the same time and looked for a second like two kids emerging from the sunroof of a limousine. They were already unconscious and would die in minutes. Their bodies left blood stains and strips of flesh around the frame where they had dragged against the jagged edges.

The cockpit door slammed shut with near-sonic force, and for a moment it appeared as though this segment of the nightmare was over. Then the door began to bend like a deck of cards and finally snapped off its hinges, zoomed through the window, and spun into oblivion. Since the plane had been flying at twenty-six thousand feet, unconsciousness occurred in less than a minute. If they'd been cruising a bit lower—say, fifteen-thousand—some people, with the aid of the oxygen masks that now dangled over their seats like snakes from a tree, might have been able to do something.

More bodies went out. One by one, those who hadn't remained in their seats with their belts on sailed down the aisle along with empty soda cans, magazines, napkins, and paper plates. Aleida, the woman who had befriended Zaeef at the airport, went out at one point. Her head struck the cockpit doorway with such force that the skull cap was sheared clean off. It took nearly three full minutes for the depressurization to complete. Of the original one hundred and twenty-nine people who boarded the plane, ninety-one remained.

Continuing its kamikaze run, the 747 broke through cloud cover at three thousand feet. Minutes later, against the paradoxically beautiful spring sky, it drove into the Atlantic Ocean and exploded into bits. The bodies inside evaporated as if made of papier-mache, while those that had been sucked out of the plane before impact were spread far and wide, and eventually consumed by sea life. When the NTSB personnel combed the crash site weeks later, they would find no trace of the aircraft or any of its passengers.

A few miles away, a well-packed wooden crate weighing more than a hundred and fifty pounds and bearing the stenciled words "BONE CHINA AND SILVERWARE—PLEASE HANDLE CAREFULLY" hit the ocean and went under. It seemed in no hurry as it moved through the sun-stippled water, down and down into darkness. When it reached a depth of about two hundred feet, the pressure caused the poorly constructed bomb to detonate. The core of it was an eight-kilogram sphere of Pakistani-bought plutonium about the size of a baseball. It was crudely refined—what was popularly referred to as "dirty"—but packed enough explosive force to create an uninhabitable radius of about twenty miles.

A water column filled with hot gases and bomb residue shot up more than 3,000 feet and grew to nearly a full mile in diameter. Shock waves traveled through the sea in every direction. Most eventually shrank to a whisper, but those that moved downward were met by an unstable barrier—a sea slope nearly four miles long. As in any other instance when one force meets another head-on, a battle for dominance ensued. In this case there were no winners—the inhuman power released by the bomb would eventually be absorbed, but not before jarring a great portion of the slope loose, which triggered an undersea landslide.

According to the laws of physics, when one solid object in a tightly confined space occupied by other solid objects changes position, the position of the relative objects must also change. As the rocks and sediment began their violent journey downward, an equal parcel of the Atlantic Ocean was, in essence, drawn down, and it chose the only available direction to go— up. When the sea level rises, another law of physics states that it must eventually fall again. For that to occur here, the excess had to find a place to settle...

At 8:34 Eastern Standard Time on the morning of May twenty-fourth, a massive tsunami was born roughly six hundred miles off the Mid-Atlantic coast of the United States. Then it began radiating in all directions.

FOUR

*I*n Control Tower B at Washington's Ronald Reagan National Airport, four men in short-sleeve shirts and ties stood in a small huddle around the radio and waited. They'd heard nothing from American Flight 334 for nearly fifteen minutes.

"Play the last one back," one of them said. He was slightly overweight and had a harsh, gravelly voice from years of smoking. Ken Dawson had worked in the airline industry his entire professional life, starting as a baggage handler in 1967, and was now less than a year away from purchasing that big boat and heading down to the Keys.

One of the others pushed a button on the control panel, and the late Tony DeFranco's voice came through the tiny speakers along with a rash of static: "We have a situation here…a man with a gun and an object he claims is a detonation device. He appears to be in his early thirties and of Middle-Eastern descent. Captain Casey is in the cabin attempting to deal with him."

And then Dawson's voice, loud and clear: "Understood. Are you able to shut and secure the door of the flight deck?"

DeFranco said, "I believe I can do th—wait...no. The Captain has turned around and is coming back. The passenger with the weapon is behind him. I—"

Then silence.

Dawson shook his head, "Jesus, what's going on up there?" He consulted his watch; a cheap silver job wrapped around a beefy, freckled arm. "We'll give it another minute, then we've got to contact the NTSB per procedure. Have you got their current position?"

"Yes, they're roughly six hundred miles off the central New Jersey coast, heading southwest."

Then someone asked: "Can I run to the can, chief?"

Justin Malone was the youngest and least experienced of the crew. Twenty-six, slim and handsome, he still gave off the vibe of the wild college boy he'd been back at Loyola, respectable post and formal attire notwithstanding. He was so exuberant and irreverent that the others still weren't sure if they loved or hated him.

Dawson didn't take his eyes off the control panel. "Yeah, go ahead."

"Thanks."

Malone hustled out and hit the stairwell running. Two flights down he entered the quiet ground-floor hallway and went to a door at the far end. Behind it was a bathroom so tiny there was barely enough space to turn around. He told his colleagues he preferred it over the larger one upstairs because it reminded him of the bathroom in his parents' trailer, which, inexplicably, he'd spent countless hours in as a child. His coworkers laughed and told him to just make sure he kept it clean.

He locked the door and flicked on the light. The ceiling fan groaned into life. The fan was the real reason he came down here—it was so loud it smothered all other noise.

He sat down and took a small cell phone from his pocket. Then he tapped in a number that he knew by heart but didn't dare enter in the phone's memory. Someone answered after the third ring.

"Hello?"

"Hi, it's Justin."

"Hey, what's up?"

"There's something going on here."

The person on the other end—whom he had never met but, judging by the voice, couldn't have been much older than himself—listened patiently, then asked a series of questions. Sometimes Malone felt like he was betraying his employer; Dawson in particular, who wasn't a bad guy and sometimes treated him like a son. He rationalized all this by reminding himself that the media needed to know what was going on in the world, had a First-Amendment right. The fact that he was feeding information to CNN, of all places, was also too cool to ignore. And, of course, he was being well-paid for his troubles. He received cash on a per-call basis, and every penny helped when you no longer lived with your parents and had a growing collection of CDs.

"I'll give you a call back when I know more. Shouldn't be long. Just wanted to give you a heads-up now."

"Much appreciated. I'll talk to you in a bit."

"Right."

He replaced the phone in his pocket, opened the door, and hit the switch for the light and fan off. For the sake of authenticity, he flushed the toilet.

* * *

Some days, Dave Dolan needed a few extra cups of coffee. Oceanographic field work wasn't exactly a night out on the town, but he still loved it. It wouldn't lead to riches or fame but he could honestly say he was doing something he enjoyed.

He sat in a long, brightly lit room in the Rutgers Marine Field Station in Tuckerton, New Jersey, a bank of computers and monitors running along one wall. Every item worth more than ten bucks had a sticker featuring a bar code and the legend "Property of the Woods Hole Oceanographic Institution." Some of it was cutting-edge and worth a small fortune, and the WHOI expected it to be properly maintained. He had no problem with that; he was grateful for the opportunity to use it in the first place, and equally grateful that Rutgers had joined up with Woods Hole on a few joint projects—general studies on climate, pollution, and underwater sea life. All part of the state-funding game—you couldn't conduct just one study, you had to be economical and do them *en masse*. The fishing industry wanted to know where the fish were. The DEP and EPA wanted to know where the pollution was. And the National Weather Service wanted to know what was brewing out there. Woods Hole had instrument arrays in shallow waters, intermediate waters, and in the deep, hundreds of miles out, some sitting at this very moment on the ocean floor, thousands of feet below the surface, in darkness and stillness that would drive a human mind beyond its limits.

A good portion of Dolan's duties involved simple data collection and logging. Not terribly interesting, but the professional experience—especially with all this cutting-edge equipment—was priceless. Real-time feeds via the Iridium satellite system. It was beyond incredible, a true luxury in a field where study methods were archaic just five years earlier. Dolan didn't consider himself "driven," and that didn't bother him. His immediate plan was to finish his master's, then go for his doctorate. Once that was in the bag he'd secure a comfy teaching post at some respectable coastal university, and eventually he'd retire to an obscure spot in the Pacific where he could spend his twilight years watching the sea life with a mask and a snorkel.

Curled up in an ancient desk chair that tilted back way too far, Dolan reviewed the readings from the previous day. The Doppler was an autonomous and self-registering instrument that measured the speed and directions of sea currents. A second instrument, known in the vernacular as a tide gauge, reported the distance from the sea floor to the water's surface. These instruments, along with a few others, were clustered together in sets. Each set was spaced roughly fifty miles apart, and the string of clusters ran about 700 miles out, well beyond the Continental Shelf.

He yawned and rubbed his eyes. The coffee was helping, but not enough. He glanced at his watch and decided it was still too early for a Coke. Maybe he'd head over to the Dynasty Diner and get something to eat.

He also decided he wasn't going to spend the bulk of his morning sitting here listening to the equipment beep, gurgle, and belch. He took an oversized textbook from his knapsack and set it on his lap. The glossy cover featured a photo of a huge wave curl. Along the top was the title *Oceanographic Geology, Volume 4.*

Dolan had just removed the playing-card bookmark and begun to read when one of the alarms went off. It was unfamiliar to him—he'd heard others in the four months that he'd been here, but not this one. He looked up and found an unusual tide-gauge reading—a swift and sudden ocean rise of about four feet.

"That can't be right." He leaned forward to get a closer look.

"What was that?" a voice asked. Dr. Sarah Collins came into the room. She was thirty-two, single, neither attractive nor unattractive, and the leader of this two-person project. Her affiliation with Rutgers began two years earlier, but her ultimate goal was to secure a full-time position with the Woods Hole organization. Most of her colleagues believed—some of them grudgingly—that she had the necessary skills to reach such an exalted position.

"The tide gauge," Dolan said. He tapped the LED glass lightly. "It says the water just rose four feet, but that can't be right. I mean, it's not impossible, but…"

"That's from unit seven, isn't it?"

"Umm…yeah. Number seven."

"That one's due for a checkup." She shook her head, annoyed. "It'll take a full day just for the team to get out there, and who knows what's wrong with it?"

"What should I do about the reading? Should I record it?"

"No, don't bother. Just note in the log that it needs maintenance right away. And run a diagnostic when you get a chance, just so we have the information."

"Okay."

She lingered for another moment, giving a cursory inspection to the rest of the equipment. All other readings appeared normal. *Four feet in open sea. Yeah, right.…*

She returned to her office—a tiny antechamber with an aging desk that had been given so many coats of glaze the wood was mummified—and sat back down. There was a cube fridge in one corner and, on top of it, a small television set. The TV was on, tuned into CNN with the sound turned down. She sifted through some paperwork, occasionally glancing at the screen. Somewhere in the back of her mind she noted that Bill Hemmer was talking above the BREAKING NEWS banner, but she dismissed it because rarely a day had gone by since September 11, 2001 that CNN, MSNBC, and FOX News didn't use this visual gimmick. It seemed like *everything* was "breaking news" now. What struck her as particularly ironic was the fact that something considered breaking news one day could be forgotten the next.

If the press continued to cry wolf like this, she thought, eventually nothing would be able to grab the public's attention.

What finally made her take the remote in hand and turn the sound up wasn't the file photo of a 747 or of the Schiphol Airport in Amsterdam, but the long, running shot of the open ocean. Anything related to the ocean grabbed her; it had been this way since she was a child.

At first she thought it was a commercial and was about to dismiss it. Then CNN switched back to Hemmer and his BREAKING NEWS banner, and this time she read it—Commercial Airliner Goes Down In Atlantic Ocean. Possible Act of Terrorism.

" ...shortly before eight-thirty this morning. The plane was a Boeing 747 with one hundred and eighteen passengers and a crew of eleven. It left the Netherlands bound for Washington DC and is believed to have gone down roughly eight hundred miles off the northeastern coast of the United States. We have been told that a message was sent by one of the pilots saying a passenger—a man who appeared to be of Middle-Eastern descent—claimed there was a bomb on board and was threatening to detonate it."

A map of the Atlantic came up with a highlighted area and a caption box that read "Possible Crash Site." Collins scrambled out of her chair and went back to the monitors. "David, where did you say that reading came from? It was unit seven, right?"

"Uh-huh."

Papers flew as she dug through a sheaf of maps.

Dolan replaced his bookmark. "Hey, what's up?"

"Go look on the TV in my office."

She reached the bottom of the pile—or what was left of it since most of the papers were on the floor now—and said angrily, "Where are the damn geo maps? David?"

Dolan's reply was dull, lifeless. "In the ... the file cabinet." Then, much quieter, "Holy shit."

Collins yanked the drawer back. When she finally found the map she wanted, she unfolded it quickly and spread it across the top of the cabinet. David came alongside her.

"This is where they said the plane went down," she said, tapping the spot with a stubby, unvarnished fingernail. "And look at this." She slid her finger to a tiny icon, and underneath was the legend, "Unit 7."

"My God. Do you think...?"

She stared into his eyes; her own had become glassy with fear. "No, I doubt even the most powerful bomb in the world could elevate the open ocean that high. But what a bomb *could* do, just maybe, is this...."

She went into the next drawer down and finger-walked through the hanging folders. This second search was less frantic, as the contents were better organized and rarely referenced.

The second map portrayed the same general region. It boasted a variety of primary colors and bore the legend, "Geological Instability Survey #774."

Pointing again, she said, "That's what I thought."

Dolan may have been nearly a year short of his master's, but he knew enough to get what she was talking about. "It's prime landslide area," he said.

"That's right. This is one of the regions the Garrett Group was concerned about in '99, remember? That's where this map came from."

"But...it's more than five hundred feet down. Wouldn't a bomb have to—"

"If it exploded on impact, nothing would happen. But if it exploded well below the surface the shock waves could trigger a landslide." She shook her head. "It wouldn't even have to be a particularly powerful bomb."

They looked at each other, awash in the faint hope that this was nothing more than wild speculation; an academic exercise.

"I'm gonna check the readings one more time."

"Okay. You didn't run the di-ag, did you?"

"No, not yet. Let me do it right now."

He turned the unit back on. Green LED characters came to life, at first in meaningless formations while the receiver waited impatiently for a signal from a satellite that floated thousands of miles above them in frigid space. He ran the diagnostic, which took no more than a minute. As they both feared, the unit appeared to be working just fine.

And then the tide gauge reading arrived—confirming the wave's four-foot spike.

Dolan's face paled as if all the blood had been drained out of it. "Christ, that's just about right, isn't it?" When he received no response, he said, "Sarah?"

She was back in her office already; he heard the sound of a wooden drawer being opened.

He found her at her desk with a tiny pocket calculator. She mumbled to herself as she tapped the keys and worked out the numbers. Then she stopped.

"My God," she said, her voice merely a whisper, "the waves will begin striking in about two and a half hours."

FIVE

Sarah Collins had always prided herself on her ability to remain calm in tight situations. As a youngster, she awoke one summer morning to the screams of her mother when the tall stockade fence that surrounded their backyard had somehow caught fire. She called the fire department and held the blaze at bay with a garden hose until they got there. When she was just thirteen, she successfully applied the Heimlich to an elderly man at a restaurant. And at twenty she not only saved a small boy from drowning off the beach in Point Pleasant, but also the inexperienced lifeguard who had gone out to rescue him.

But those incidents were meaningless compared to the crisis that lay before her now, and she knew it. For the first time in her life, she had to expend a conscious effort to locate the required calm within herself. She thought of her late father, who had the ability to turn stone-cold when necessary. He had told her, "If you find yourself in the heart of the storm, you must be the one to lead." She focused on that—on the notion that it was her duty to take control. And her objective was obvious—tell as many people as you can.

She took her cell phone from her purse.

"What's that for?"

"I'll tell you in a min—Danny? It's Sarah."

Dr. Daniel Kennard had been Collins's professor when she was pursuing her doctorate. Like so many students before her, she eventually fell in love with him, platonically. He had white hair, a kind and grandfatherly manner, and a seemingly endless supply of patience. He gave generously of himself and treated his students as equals. Collins cried the day she left him to return to the East Coast, but they never lost touch.

His voice was groggy and confused. "Sarah? Sarah Collins?"

"Yes, Danny. It's me."

"What the hell time is it?"

"It's just after nine o'clock over here," she replied, not bothering to add that that meant it was just after six Seattle time. "I'm really sorry to call so early, but there's a tsunami heading toward us."

He sounded immediately alert. "What did you say?"

"There's a tsunami coming. Right now!"

"You're in New Jersey?"

"Yes!"

For a moment there was only silence. Collins became aware of the triphammer thumping of her heart, plus the fact that she had begun to perspire.

"How do you know this?" Kennard was stern now.

She sacrificed thirty seconds to recite the story.

"Oh God," was his reply. There was a dreariness to it that made Collins's stomach twist.

"There aren't any advance warning systems out here, are there?" she asked. But it was more of a statement than a question.

54

"No, none." Another pause, and then, "You'll have to do it the hard way."

With a calm that surprised even her, she said, "Okay." She set the cell phone down, picked up the receiver on the Nixon-era desk phone, and dialed 911.

* * *

As the rest of the nation became slowly hypnotized by the story of the latest terrorist attack, Long Beach Township Mayor Donald J. Harper hid in his now-darkened office, voluntarily isolated. There was a time when he'd leave the shades open all day and admire the view of the Atlantic. Not today. This had turned into nothing more than a waiting game, a long and tantalizing delay until the ax fell. He had given the nod himself, not that there was any choice. He had never felt so useless in his life—there was simply nothing to do. No objectives, no focus.

He sat behind his desk in a slouch, a most uncharacteristic position for him. Until recently he had always made a point of sitting bolt-upright, regardless of where he was or what he was doing—at the office, at a restaurant, at home. You never wanted to give the impression of disinterest or dereliction. If you were in politics it was important to appear awake and alert at all times, ready for anything. Amazing how deeply the training had been rooted, the years spent preparing for a life of public service. And how easily all that could be thrown away....

He slouched because he felt like slouching, and he remained in that position for awhile. The air-conditioner switched on and off at least a dozen times. The shades were drawn; the only light in the room coming from between them. At one point he wondered if this was what Howard Hughes' world was like during his final days, in that hotel room in Acapulco where his withered, ninety-pound body lay under a layer of filthy bedsheets as his "aides" stood by with the next shot of codeine, one of which would eventually put an end to his surreal existence.

He took note of a small pile of papers Marie had left on his desk to sign. Well, it was something to do, he thought. He leaned forward, grabbed a pen, and began scribbling. He didn't bother reading any of them; after all these years he only needed to glance to summarize the content. There was nothing of great substance here. Was that by circumstance or by design, he wondered? Had Marie, always one of his most faithful employees, already begun preparing for the regime change? Was she hiding a second, more substantial group of papers somewhere else?

He didn't know and wouldn't be able to find out, and this only augmented his depression. In his heart he didn't want to believe it—she'd been loyal from the beginning, but who knew anymore. After recent events, even the deepest loyalties began to falter. Was there anyone left in his corner? Any believers left in the parish? He supposed not.

He finished, rose, and went out. Marie was at her desk in the next office, typing at her computer. She was small and aged, kind of wispy, but she had the constitution of a teenager and, at times, the tongue of a viper. Today she was wearing a blue polka-dot dress and a string of pearls. The paradox amused Harper—she always looked like the classic "little old lady," but underneath lay the soul of a warrior.

"These are signed," he said.

She looked up, startled. Or maybe she just pretended to be.

"Hmm? Oh, thank you, Donald." She set them aside and turned to her notepad. "You also had two calls. One from Mickey Blake, and one from Allison Cauldwell."

He nodded noncommittally. Blake owned an auto-repair shop on the mainland and was pushing for a second, in Spray Beach, but needed the zoning permits. He and Harper had gone to high school together. He was a nice enough guy and ran an honest business, so Harper had been planning to help him. Allison Cauldwell, on the other hand, was a little bitch who had taken over her late father's three-office real-estate business and wanted to grow it to fifty. She was absolutely off her rocker, obsessed with becoming New Jersey's next Diane Turton. Turton wasn't any less driven or ambitious, but at least she had some finesse. Cauldwell had a set of lead-pipe sensibilities that would make a stampede of elephants look like a ballet recital.

"Okay, thanks." He ran a hand through his hair and headed back to the cave.

He blanched when Marie's phone rang again. This is how it was now—*Could this be The Call?* he wondered every time. He paused at the double oak doors, half-hoping for the worst just so this nightmare would come to an end.

"Donald?"

He tried to act as though he hadn't been listening but it was an exercise in pointlessness; they both knew he had.

"Hmm?"

"A Major Gary Oberg for you. Says it's urgent."

What would Gary be calling me for? Harper wondered. To offer condolences?

A mild nausea came over him. Old friends and familiar faces would be emerging from every direction with wan smiles and words of tender reassurance. *This has to be the worst part of it.*

Oberg was a genuine friend, one of the few people he trusted implicitly. Small and thin, with dark, almost Mediterranean features, he was a career military man who believed in the sanctity and fundamental goodness of the United States of America. He was old school, a product of the Greatest Generation, and slightly at odds with modern times. Harper met him in 1974 when they were assigned to the same base in Virginia, and they'd kept in touch after Harper left the service following his four-year tour of duty. Oberg was reassigned to the National Guard base in Sea Girt, New Jersey, in the spring of 1992, and since then the two men got together fairly regularly.

Harper took the phone. "Hello, Gary." He was aware of how tired he sounded but didn't have the will to mask it.

"Don, have you heard about the tsunami?"

No preamble, no small talk, which was very unlike the man. Suddenly Harper felt uneasy.

"Tsunami? What tsunami?"

"Don, listen. You've got to get everyone off the island, and you've got to do it *now*. We just received an emergency call from Rutgers about a tidal wave that's moving in your direction."

"Come on, Gary."

"No joke. You know that plane that went down this morning? The flight from the Netherlands?"

"Yeah, I heard about it on the radio."

"There was a bomb on it. Part of some new terrorist plot. It was bound for DC, so they think that was the original target. But something went wrong and the plane went into the drink. The bomb exploded and somehow triggered this thing. I don't know the details."

Harper absorbed every word and calculated the scenario instantly. He knew a little bit about oceanography, having been as enamored with the shore as millions of his fellow residents.

"Jesus Christ. Are you certain, Gary? Absolutely *certain?*" The words sounded far away, as if they were coming from someone else's mouth. Harper's body had gone numb. Not cold, just... nothing. It was as if everything from his neck down was no more than a wooden prop for his head. A sufficiently surreal morning was developing into a trip through the Twilight Zone.

"Yes, I'm positive. Some Rutgers scientists in Tuckerton spotted it. They've checked and rechecked and there's no doubt. It all adds up."

"My God...."

"Don, I have to go. We've got a million things to do here. But I wanted to let you know because every second matters now. You've got to get everyone out of there, and fast. We'll contact the Coast Guard from our end. They'll clear out all the marine traffic."

"Okay, how long do we have?" Harper asked.

There was a pause, and in that instant he knew the answer was going to be horrifying. He braced himself.

"About two hours."

Inside Harper's tall, broad-shouldered body—in fact, inside his very soul—every function paused.

"Two hours?"

"Yes."

"But that's not enough," Harper said in a whisper, more to himself than to his friend. "We're almost into Memorial Day here. There are thousands of people on the island. I can't guarantee we'll get everyone off in just two hours!"

"Don, if you need me, call me. And remember—you're still the mayor, okay?"

"Yeah, sure. Thanks."

"Good luck, pal," Oberg said, clicking off.

* * *

What happened next took all of about fifteen seconds, although inside it seemed like hours. Harper's mind downloaded an image of himself standing at the bisecting point where two long country roads met. It could've been someplace in the South, like the Carolinas or maybe Georgia. There were no road signs, no cars, no people around. Just him, standing at a crossroad in the middle of a sunny and otherwise undeveloped area.

He looked down each road, wondering which one was best. They all seemed about the same—that was the hard part. No real indication of which one he should take. For a flicker of an instant he felt angry, felt like he was being treated unfairly. There were no outward clues for him to follow. How could you be expected to make a decision without information?

Then it occurred to him—the decision was supposed to be purely instinctual, supposed to be based on what was inside, not outside. That was the whole point. Gary had said it perfectly—*Remember, you're still the mayor.* At first Harper didn't understand why he'd thrown that in, but now it made perfect sense. He had to make a choice. The right road would become obvious after he decided what he really wanted to do with himself. He thought he'd lost that right. He thought everything had been stripped away, but it hadn't. He saw that now, saw what it meant in the big picture.

And he saw an opportunity, too.

* * *

At the Schooner's Wharf in Beach Haven, Tom Wilson sat in a quiet corner of the Gazebo Restaurant with Elliot Davis and plotted Davis's glorious political future.

"NJN began covering the story when it got too big to ignore," Wilson said over a plate of neatly cut waffles. "I know the producer over there pretty well. He's asked me a few times what I thought would happen once Harper is gone."

"What did you tell him?"

"I was playing it cool at the time, but I'll be calling him later today. The guy covering the story will want an update. That's when I'll mention you. They may want to talk to you at some point. In fact I'm sure they will. Now that Harper is on his way out, they'll be looking for someone new to focus on. You should make yourself available. Can you do that?"

After a pause, Davis said, "I believe so." This was technically only a half-truth—he had a packed schedule in the coming weeks and had already cancelled a sailing trip with his eldest son. How was he going to work in press appearances?

"Good, very good. Would you prefer they come to your office, or do you want to meet them outside, in the front?"

"Is the bank a good place to meet? Didn't you once say there was a danger in that? Something about me being too closely associated with money?"

Wilson nodded. "I did worry about that at first, but I've changed my mind. Most of the people in this area are pretty conservative, even the Democrats. And everyone already knows you're a bank president. If we try to hide that, it'll make it look like we're trying to hide it. That'll suggest a crime where no crime exists." He took a sip of coffee and waved his hand. "No, I've got a better idea. We'll go ahead full-throttle with your image as a banker, but we'll soften it. We'll play up all the decent things you've done, all the high-risk loans you've given out, the late payments you've let slide. You've been a pretty fair and decent guy in a position where others have not. Let's take advantage of that."

There was a scream in the next room—a woman's scream. Similar sounds quickly followed—gasps, cries, and "Oh my Gods."

The two men exchanged a puzzled glance, then rose quickly and hurried from the table. The adjoining area was dominated by a long counter. The waiter on duty looked like the all-American boy working his way through college. He and some customers were trained on a television hanging from a high corner. On the screen, a woman from NJN was breaking the news of the oncoming disaster.

"...predict the tsunami will strike the coast in approximately two hours. Governor Mayfield immediately declared a state of emergency, and all residents of the Jersey Shore from Belmar to Cape May are urged to move inland at once. Again, if you're just tuning in, all residents of...."

The restaurant cleared out at record speed. Keys jingled as they were pulled from pockets and handbags. The collective hum of group chatter rose to a meaningless cacophony as the herd migrated to the front exit. The waiter, apparently not loyal enough to go down with the ship, put one hand on the countertop and leapt out of his enclosure with graceful athleticism.

"Jesus Christ, Tom," Davis said hollowly. "We've got to get the hell out of here."

He turned to his political advisor and, in one of the most unpredictable moments of his life, found him smiling.

"No, Elliot ... not yet."

Davis's face crumpled with confusion. "What? What are you talking about? We've got less than two hours—we've got to go! I have to go home and get Helen. She'll be—"

He turned to leave, but Wilson caught his arm and held him.

"This is your chance, Elliot. This is *it*."

"What? I don't—"

Wilson pointed to the screen.

"The people are going to be looking for a leader right now. They're going to need someone strong, someone commanding. Harper's credibility is shot, so they'll be looking for someone else. Every major news channel is going to be on this, so you'll get exposure from coast to coast. Just as Giuliani's name will be forever linked with New York City and 9/11, your name will be linked with this. Don't you see?"

Davis looked back at the screen. NJN had added the scrawl along the bottom—ALL RESIDENTS ALONG THE NEW JERSEY COASTLINE FROM BELMAR TO CAPE MAY ARE

ORDERED TO LEAVE THEIR HOMES AT ONCE AND MOVE AT LEAST TWO MILES INLAND. COMMUNITIES TO THE NORTH AND SOUTH MAY ALSO BE EFFECTED BY THE TSUNAMI. NEW JERSEY GOVERNOR JIM MAYFIELD HAS DECLARED A STATE OF EMERGENCY....

Davis swallowed hard into a dry throat. Every muscle in his body seemed to have turned to stone. "Well, okay. What do I need to do?"

"Come on, I'll show you."

SIX

*B*ethAnn Mosley was happy. *Springer* had been a blast, an absolute blast. A group of teenage girls admitted they'd dabbled in prostitution in college—on campus, specifically, in order to make money for booze and drugs. Some of their former customers were there, too, waxing nostalgic about what an unforgettable time they'd had. What ol' Jerry didn't tell them, at least at first, was that all the girls' fathers were also there, off-stage, listening to every word. Whenever the cameras went to the fathers, sitting there kneading their hands as they stockpiled homicidal thoughts, a charge went through Mosley. There was no word for it, no name for it, but she knew she was hopelessly addicted to it and always would be. When the fathers were inevitably released from their cages and the hunt began, Mosley actually clapped like a delighted child and jumped up and down on the couch. When the fathers began beating on the boys and the cameras swayed around crazily, she leaned forward so she wouldn't miss anything. One of the boys ended up with a broken nose that bled like a burst pipe. Another lay on the glossy studio floor, just off the riser, and moaned as he drifted in and out of consciousness. It was glorious. When it was over, she felt spent, exhausted.

There was a commercial break—a top-of-the-hour commercial break, and that meant nearly ten free minutes. In spite of her undying devotion to television, she hated commercials; she didn't have any money, so what good were they?

She got up and ambled into the kitchen. Time for a snack. There was a frying pan in the sink from last night submerged in the basin. The water was skim-milk cloudy, and bits of something-or-other from the previous meal floated on the surface like pond scum.

She "washed" the pan by holding it under a stream of cold water for a second, then shook it dry. The remaining moisture sizzled when she set it on the glowing coil. She smeared a blob of butter over the scoured teflon surface, then set down four slices of Taylor pork roll, which had been involuntarily donated by Acme.

The TV sang—a single note sustained for about ten seconds. She glanced over with only partial interest while she ate, standing at the sink so the crumbs wouldn't fall onto the floor. A message crawled across the bottom of the screen. She didn't bother reading it, for she'd seen them, and heard the familiar beep, a million times. A storm warning of some kind. Thunderheads rolling in, maybe a rising tide. By pure luck, this mobile-home park had been built in a low-risk flood zone, and her particular unit had been propped on four rows of cinder blocks. The unit originally had been set on only one row, but Kenny had insisted on spending a small fortune to install three more. It would dramatically reduce the risk of flood damage, he claimed, while increasing the property's value when it came time to sell it. BethAnn had argued with him about the expenditure, not because it didn't make sense, but simply because she enjoyed arguing about things. But he'd been right—in the eight years she'd lived here, there had been no water damage. A few close calls, but the increased height made all the difference. She'd hated the fact that he'd been right and punished him for it in small ways. After he reached his emotional breaking point and left her for good, she decided to hate him in a more complete way. The fact that he was a good guy at heart and that she was the reason he wasn't around any longer only served to enrich this hatred.

Little things like storm warnings made her think about him. As she munched her way toward an early heart attack, and the mid-morning breeze made the curtains over the sink dance and sway, she wondered if he was still "out west." That's where he had said he was headed. She knew he'd been ambiguous on purpose. She saw him only once after that, when they signed the divorce papers in his lawyer's office. She thought about getting a lawyer of her own, just to give him a hard time. But they didn't have any children or savings, and he'd already decided to give her the trailer and all its contents. What would she fight for? All he wanted was his freedom, and she knew why.

She finished the sandwich, wiped her hands on her T-shirt, and went into the bathroom, leaving the door open. The fart she ripped as she slid her sweatpants down sounded like a dry towel being slowly torn in half.

As she sat reading a rippled copy of *Alfred Hitchcock's Mystery Magazine*, the TV sang again, this time followed by a garbled announcement. Somewhere in the back of her mind she noted that an actual voice message was unusual, even for the shore—

This is an emergency broadcast from the National Weather Service. All residents along the New Jersey coastline from Belmar to Cape May are required to leave their homes at once and move at least two miles inland. Again, all residents along the New Jersey coastline from Belmar to Cape May are required to leave their homes and move at least two miles inland. A tidal wave has been detected roughly six hundred miles offshore and will strike the coastline in approximately two hours.

At first she thought she'd misheard it, similar to the way a song on a radio sounds slightly different if you're far away from it. She jumped up and hurried out, still clutching the digest-sized magazine with her thumb acting as a bookmark. There was another long beep, followed by a repeat of the recorded message, which would obviously replay hundreds of times this day. The scrawl at the bottom of the screen, an amateurish superimposition but no less effective, was almost identical—

...>> URGENT <<...ALL RESIDENTS OF THE BEACH AREA FROM BELMAR TO CAPE MAY ARE REQUIRED TO LEAVE THEIR HOMES IMMEDIATELY AND MOVE AT LEAST TWO MILES INLAND. A TIDAL WAVE WILL STRIKE THE COASTLINE IN APPROXIMATELY TWO HOURS...>> URGENT <<...

"Holy *shit!*"

She grabbed the remote and switched around for more information. The same message was running on every channel, originating from the local cable company. It occurred to Mosley that there was a small chance this was some kind of error or maybe even a practical joke; perhaps a recently released employee ("disgruntled" was the word that entered her mind) had set it up to run automatically, long after he or she had high-tailed it out of there.

Then she landed on CNN, where two reporters—one male and one female—were sitting at the news desk, looking grave and earnest. The BREAKING NEWS banner under them alternated between "Commercial Airliner Goes Down In Atlantic Ocean. Onboard bomb detonates." and "Tsunami Approaching Southern New Jersey Coast. Tidal Wave Expected to Strike In Less Than Two Hours." As they spoke, the screen switched to a generic map of the state, and in the light blue area that represented the water was a series of concentric circles in pulsing red, representing the radiating movement of the tsunami.

At that moment it became real to her. The fact that the best known news channel in the world had picked up the story made it impossible to deny. It wasn't April Fool's Day.

This was really happening.

* * *

Tarrance-Smith wasn't the largest real estate company on the Jersey Shore, but it was one of the oldest. Started in 1919 by Samuel Tarrance and his business partner, Neil Smith, the company grew slowly but steadily, amassing a loyal customer base through four generations, two world wars, and nearly a full century. There were eight offices, all within the Garden State. The one in Manahawkin on Route 72, where Karen Thompson worked, was the smallest.

She sat in a long, brightly lit room with five colleagues, each with their own desk but without walls or dividers. It was vaguely reminiscent of the secretarial pools from the 1950s. Only Scott Tarrance, great-grandson of Samuel, had an enclosed office with an actual door.

Karen made a point of keeping her workspace neat and tidy. On a practical level she found it easier to keep track of everything that way. From an emotional standpoint it made her feel more organized. And in terms of PR value it was priceless—a customer considering the purchase of a beachfront home that might cost anywhere from a half to five million dollars wouldn't want to deal with a salesperson who couldn't find a Post-It or a paper clip.

She kept all of her pens and pencils in a Tarrance-Smith coffee mug on the left side, which was within easy reach as she was left-handed. Next to it was a stapler and a tape dispenser.

On the right was a tray containing the day's files, which she always prepared at the end of the previous day. At the back was a little desk lamp, and flanking it on either side was an ever-growing population of framed family photos. It looked like a miniature city, with the lamp acting as some sort of peculiar centerpiece to the downtown area. There were numerous shots of Patrick and Michael—some with their father, some with their mother, some with both, some neither. One picture showed them playing their first round of miniature golf at Thundering Surf, in Beach Haven, another had them eating Italian ices at Bay Village. With the exception of Karen and Mike's formal wedding shot (the happy couple standing alongside their silver Rolls-Royce limousine) all the photos were of the boys.

She looked at these pictures often and drew strength from them. Most importantly she drew motivation. Each time she saw their round, smiling faces, fresh pangs of guilt would alight in her stomach. She cursed herself for not being able to spend more time with them, *all* of her time with them. She worked because she had to work, because just about all mothers had to work now. It was part and parcel of the modern age—both parents worked, and someone who had absolutely nothing to do with the children's organic existence raised them. She hated this, hated it so much that it sometimes made her mildly ill. She only worked part-time—four days a week, about seven hours a day—but she hated every moment. The fact that the Tarrance family treated her well and that Nancy was the greatest babysitter in the world didn't make a difference in the final sum of things—nothing erased the pain of being apart from her kids.

For nearly ten minutes after she got behind her desk this morning, Styrofoam cup in hand, she stared at the photos. She summoned all her strength and reminded herself again of The Plan. She and Mike had sat down one evening at the kitchen table after the boys had gone to bed and worked it out on paper.

Provided neither of them lost their jobs and Mike continued getting a yearly salary increase of at least three percent, she could quit working altogether in another five years. Patrick and Michael would only be nine and eight then, which left plenty of time before they packed their bags and headed out into the world.

Five more years, she thought bitterly as she tore her eyes away and forced her hands to pick up the pile of manilla folders that cried for her like a nest of starving sparrows. *It's like a prison sentence.* It wasn't the first time that thought had surfaced, either. If she didn't think it would arouse suspicion among her coworkers and her boss, she'd hang a calendar on the wall to her right and start marking the days with big Xs.

She was reviewing a rental contract for a property in North Beach when she first heard about the downed airliner. Scott had come in, dressed in dark tweed slacks, a crisp white shirt, and a navy tie, with his favorite coffee mug in hand. It was simple white porcelain with THE BOSS printed in a plain font across the visible side; one of many gifts his staff had given him over the years. He was tall and thin with a slight but unmistakable forward lean that no doubt wreaked accumulative havoc on his spine. He was always clean-shaven and kept his dark hair conservatively cut and impeccably groomed. He smiled easily and had a soft, gentle voice that, as far as Karen knew, had never been raised in anger.

"Did you all hear about the latest terrorist attack?"

Three of the other five real estate agents were in the office, too. Everyone looked up.

Myra Gates put a hand to her chest and said, "Oh my God, no. What happened?" Forty-three, single, and still youthfully pretty, she was a veteran of the Jersey Shore social scene and spent the bulk of her weekends with a group of close friends in Atlantic City. She and Karen were galaxies apart in terms of lifestyle, but they got along well. Myra loved when the boys visited and always brought little gifts for them on their birthdays.

"They hijacked a flight to DC, but something happened on the way and it went down in the ocean."

"Jesus..."

"About six-hundred miles offshore, they're saying."

"Off *our* shore? Right here?"

Tarrance nodded. "Yep." He shook his head. "Incredible, isn't it?"

Karen shook her head, too. She almost never used profanity in her speech, but her inner voice said at that moment, *What a fucked-up world this is.* Then, in a moment of irony that she couldn't possibly be aware of, she thanked God they lived in such a quiet, relatively overlooked place. They'd have to get out the snowplows in Hell before any terrorist group decided to descend upon Long Beach Island—too low-profile a target with too small a potential body count.

A short time later Tarrance reappeared. "I have some bad news," he said in a steady, quiet tone, eyeing his staff earnestly. His face was pale, the coffee mug was gone. "It appears there was a bomb on the hijacked plane and when it went down it somehow triggered a tsunami—a huge tidal wave. And it's coming this way."

Karen was aware of the gasps and the "Oh my Gods," but mostly she felt the frost settle over her body; first on the surface, and then down to her very soul. In a flicker of an instant she somehow knew what was coming next.

"They've started evacuating LBI. If any of you have any friends or relatives there you better call them now."

His gaze fell on Karen; she stared back, a hundred thoughts flowing between them. He was very in touch with what was happening in his employees' lives and he knew her boys were on the island. His expression seemed to say, *It's going to be*

chaos getting off the island. Two little boys and a retired couple won't have much of a chance. I'm sorry, Karen. I'm so sorry.
"If there's anything I can do to help, let me know. I'll be right here. I've got three phones and a car."

He started to say more, but Karen wasn't hearing it. She up-shifted into a strange frame of mind that was somehow both alien and familiar. She'd heard about out-of-body experiences, where people were aware of themselves from a third-person perspective and able to function at the same time. It was kind of like that. She watched her hand yank the phone from its cradle and her fingers tap out Nancy's number at blazing, almost comical speed. But she wasn't *feeling* any of it. Utter and complete numbness, pure objectivity. An overload of emotions so massive that she was unable to connect with any of them.

As the call was going through, she had a wild idea about what she would do if the boys didn't make it.

It was the ugliest thought she'd ever known.

*　　*　　*

Jennifer King didn't like listening to the radio. She had a pretty extensive collection of cassettes and CDs, so she figured she'd have a better chance of hearing a song she liked with one of those.

When she bought the car two years ago (actually her parents had covered half, and she was paying them back in installments of two-hundred dollars a month), it already had a cassette player from the factory. The addition of a CD player was easy—she simply velcroed a Sony Discman to the dashboard; a dummy-cassette adapter connected the two units. The Discman had been a Christmas present from Mark. Unlike many males she'd known, he had a knack for picking the right gift.

The drawback to ignoring the radio, she knew, was that she was isolating herself from what was going on the world. Her father, for example, got his daily news fix during his hour-long commute. Sometimes she'd get to work and hear everyone discussing some current event that she hadn't a clue about, and it made her feel ignorant. From time to time she'd promise herself she'd try to be more aware in the future, but somehow it never happened. She liked music too much and, at this stage in her life, cared about world events too little.

The first public announcement concerning the tsunami came over the radio only moments after she got into the car. Others followed, of course, but she never heard any of them. She was too busy singing along to Simply Red's *Home* album.

She parked around the back of the Acme and used a steel door marked FOR EMPLOYEES ONLY. She was one of four employees who had their own key. Brian had given it to her when she was coming in at odd hours to familiarize herself with the inventory computer. She knew it was a sign of trust, and she felt privileged and flattered. Others had to ring the bell to be let in.

With her Acme apron still rolled up in her hand, she stepped out of the sunny morning and inside the dim and cluttered bowels of the old building. She took her timecard from a diagonal slot and set it into the punch-clock. The outdated machine stamped it with brute force.

She went into Brian's office to say hello, but he wasn't there. This struck her as odd. He was a highly organized and regimented individual, and at this time each day he took care of paperwork. He hated it, she knew, and always wanted to get it out of the way first thing. It was unthinkable that there wasn't any. Maybe he was dealing with a customer complaint.

With a sigh she tied on her apron and went into the stockroom. Ancient sodium lights hung from the high ceiling in conical aluminum cages, accentuating the cold, warehouse feel of the place. The cement floor between the aisles had been worn to a dull shine. In the corner near the giant delivery bay was a small table, and on it was the dreaded computer. At least the chair was cushioned, she thought as she settled into it. She turned on the system and waited. It would take a few minutes to warm up. She always found this funny—the computer her family had at home (in the living room so everyone could use it) was ready to go in about thirty seconds. It had a 17″ flat-panel monitor, Windows XP, and an Athlon processor. Comparatively, this thing was a fossil. The mere fact that it still served someone's purposes was amazing.

Brian had left the master list for her, and she started into it immediately. Time passed—ten minutes, twenty, thirty. She got into what she called "The Zone"—a near-hypnotic state induced by intense concentration combined with a lack of distraction. When someone came through the paired swinging doors that separated the back area from the sales floor, she was only vaguely aware of it. The keyboard continued chattering under her swiftly moving fingers.

"Who's there?" said a voice. It sounded frantic, forceful.

Jennifer turned and saw Brian peeking around the end of the aisle. She was momentarily surprised—it hadn't sounded like him at all.

"It's *me*, Brian! Who do you th—?"

He came down the aisle fast, not jogging but almost. He had his hands out as if two people, one other either side, were about to slap him five.

"What are you doing here?" he cried. "You've got to get out!"

"What? Why?"

"Don't you know?"

He emerged from between the towering, steel-girded shelves and came alongside her. His face was red—not from overwork like it usually was, but from fear. Jennifer realized in that instant that something was terribly wrong.

"Know what?"

"About the tidal wave. Come on!"

He took her by the arm—gently but firmly—and pulled her from the seat. She went willingly, carried along mostly by her trust of this man.

"What are you talking about? What wave?"

He shook his head. "You and your CDs. There's a tsunami coming."

"A tsunami?"

"Yeah, a *tidal* wave."

Through the yellowish dimness she could see the satiny shine of perspiration on his forehead. Some had run down his face, leaving glossy tracks.

"*What*? No way!"

"Yes way. You've got to get out of here, and *fast.*"

"Oh my God, Brian. Tell me you're kidding. Tell me this is a joke."

They rounded the end of the aisle and came back to his tiny office. Through the glass windows Jennifer could see the mess of paperwork that had been left undone on the desk. Now she understood why.

"I wish I could, I really do."

Brian opened one of his desk drawers and put a few things in a plastic shopping bag. They were personal items, Jennifer noticed—a penknife, a keychain, his lucky silver dollar. Then he began ripping down the pictures of his kids and his wife. There were no frames—they had been taped to the wall. While he did this, Jennifer fired a litany of questions at him—when would the wave strike, what had caused it, how were people getting off the island? Brian answered as many as he could, but the truth was nobody had all the answers at the moment.

His last act was one of pure nobility—he went to the store safe, worked the dial with remarkable calm, and removed all the cash. Jennifer had no idea how much was there, but she could see it was a lot—stack after stack of neatly wrapped bills; he left the coinage behind. The thought occurred to her that a person of weak morals could make a fortune at a time like this—take it all, hide it, and claim the store was looted or the money was lost in the destruction. But she knew Brian too well—he would return it later, every penny. He was smart like that—his integrity would get him farther than the cash would. The company big-wigs in the main office in Idaho would have a record of every penny. When they learned that he'd made the effort to protect it, they'd remember him for it. For all she knew, he also made a point of having her there so he'd have a witness.

"Okay, let's go."

He left the office door open, which he never did—always locked tighter than Fort Knox—and the lights on. For some reason this scared Jennifer. Systems were breaking down, rituals were being ignored. The glue that held her world together was melting.

They stepped outside, and the door shut behind them with a hydraulic thump.

"You have your car, right?"

"Uh-huh."

"Okay, get in it, and get out of here! What about your family?"

"I'm going to call them on my cell phone right—"

She stopped, turned white. Somewhere in the distance, a siren began wailing. The eerie synthetic scream somehow made the terror all the more palpable.

"What? What's wrong?"

"Oh my God!"

"What's the matter?"

He had taken a few steps away from her, toward his own car. Now he took those steps back.

"Jen, what's wrong?"

She looked up at him, her eyes reddening. "Mark."

"Have you heard from him?"

"No, not since this morning."

She took her cell phone from her bag and dialed quickly.

"He's got a phone, too, right?"

"Yes, but he always—"

The number rang just once, and then a pleasant recorded voice said, "We're sorry, the person you are trying to reach is not avail—"

Jennifer terminated the connection. "He turned it off. He always turns it off when he does a photo shoot." Tears began streaming down her face. "Oh my God, he probably has no idea. He doesn't even—"

Brian took her by the shoulders. "Hey, hey. Shhhh...calm down, just calm down. Now, where is he? Didn't I hear you say he was going to the Forsythe Wildlife Refuge?"

"Yeah..."

"That's not far. Let's go."

He had been frantic only moments earlier, but now he was calm—utterly and completely calm. His voice was comforting, reassuring. She felt a little better, felt like the situation was still under control. Crazy and scary, but still under control.

"Okay," she said through a sniffle.

They ran to his car. Other cars were starting to accumulate on the Boulevard, heading toward the bridge.

They were going in the other direction.

* * *

Mark wasn't having such a great day, photography-wise. He'd gone through only two rolls, and knew that most of those shots weren't *SandPaper* cover material. He didn't want to resort to stills—flowers, trees, shrubs, etc.—unless he had to. To him photos like that were dull and unchallenging. Wildlife shots were his thing.

The path he'd been following had narrowed considerably. He was well off the beaten track now, possibly on a trail used only by local wildlife. He had a sense that it would simply end at some point and he'd have to turn back. But he couldn't be certain—this refuge was a dizzying array of twists and turns that, as far as he knew, had never been properly mapped. One moment you found yourself high on a ridge, able to see across the Atlantic to the horizon, and another you were in a damp, forested area with little sunlight and no clue how to get out. Natural hallways created by dense hedgerows closed in on all sides, mixed with vine tangles so thick you needed a machete to cut through them. For a diehard naturalist it was a heady experience.

Suddenly realizing how tired he was, he sat down to rest for a moment. He closed his eyes and tried to wipe his mind clean. Total relaxation, total refreshment. He still had a lot to do and wasn't anywhere near ready to leave. If he went back to his boss with the pictures he had now, he wouldn't be asked to do another cover shoot for a long time.

He checked his watch—9:30. Jennifer wouldn't be here for some time; plenty of time to get some good shots. He took stock of his general surroundings and observed that he was literally in the middle of nowhere, enveloped by walls of scraggly shrubs on all sides, solid earth underneath, and an endless blue sky overhead. There were no clouds today, per se—just a few vague brushstrokes. The only signs of civilization were the sound of a distant siren—typical LBI noise pollution—and the faint groan of what sounded like a small plane. He tuned the noise out. He felt the growing warmth of the sun on his face and smiled. He could stay here forever. It was so peaceful, so calm.

Nature had its own special order to it, in Mark's view. His mother and stepfather could never understand that, could never enjoy and appreciate nature the way he did. He felt pity for them rather than anger or resentment. In some ways they were so empty and always would be.

When he felt rested enough, he got back up and continued along the narrow trail, willing it to terminate in a clearing rather than a wall of hedges or a tangle of thorns. He fished through the camera bag for the water bottle and took a long, greedy swig. As he replaced it, his fingers inadvertently rediscovered his cell phone. He had no regrets about leaving it off, but he wondered momentarily if he should check his messages. It would only take a second.

He took it out, turned it on. The rubber numerical pads adopted an eerie greenish glow, barely visible on such a bright morning.

Before the phone had a chance to lock onto a signal and check in with the voice mail system, Mark switched it off again. His reverence toward nature overrode his more modern desire to be "in touch." It could wait, he decided. These opportunities were too rare. Once he got back to the real world he'd be in touch around the damn clock. Yes, it could wait.

He put the phone back in the darkened corner of the bag to which it had been assigned and moved on.

* * *

The plan fell together in Donald Harper's mind with a neat click. It was one of those moments of divine inspiration. He saw every detail, every dimension. It was complete, devastatingly simple, and flawless. In his gut he knew it would work. He *knew* it.

"Donald, what's hap—?"

"Marie," he said, and his deep, resonating voice—what he called his "boom voice"—suddenly returned. It surprised him. It wasn't a conscious effort of his part, it was just there, like a cat who'd run away and then turned up on the doorstep a week later. For the first time in weeks he felt like a leader again, in command. The balance of power had returned to its old and wonderful shape.

The mayor was back.

"There's a tsunami coming. You know—a tidal wave. It'll be here in about two hours. I'll need your help getting the word out. We've got to get everyone off the island. Call Andy Truman over at WKRZ right now. Use my name. Meanwhile," he took his cell phone from his pocket, "I'll call the National Weather Service people down in Cape May and have them issue a warning over the television and the NOAA weather radio."

"Holy Jesus. Um, okay."

Harper retreated to his office. She continued watching him while she tapped in the number with a trembling hand. He left both doors open and pulled up the shades. The symbolism was impossible to miss. As he spoke into his cell phone, he picked up the desk phone and placed another call. Marie's desire to drop everything and get the hell out of town was overwhelming, but she fought it. What struck her as strange was that Harper didn't seem to be suffering the same battle of nerves. He was so outwardly calm it was intriguing. In fact he seemed to actually be...*enjoying* himself. The irony was almost a tangible thing—when it came to a scandal, he was so listless and dispirited that he seemed like a cadaver. But now, facing a natural disaster and the possibility of death, he seemed more alive than ever. The reality was that Donald Harper, plain and simple, thrived on challenges. Crises were the lifeblood of his soul. That came from a variety of factors, one being his naturally restless personality, another his years of military training.

As he got back behind his desk, this realization brushed across his mind like a loving hand. The one that immediately followed was, *If you'd only realized that before Gus Riggins came along.* It wasn't the temptations that Riggins carried with him that lured Harper from his integrity; it was boredom. Pure and basic, the same variety suffered by millions of people every minute of every day, some for countless years, some for most of their miserable lives. At the time Riggins entered his life nothing of great note was happening. There were the normal demands as the mayor of Long Beach Township, and of course certain challenges went along with that. But he'd been managing them for so long and was so overqualified for the position that they weren't really challenges anymore. He could've phoned in his duties. He possessed the necessary skills to be a goddamn *senator*, after all. Whiling away the hours as a mayor in a place like this was downright painful.

He wiped these thoughts away; consciously cleared them from his mind like clearing off a table with one broad sweep of the arm. This was the first step in the focusing process, something else he'd picked up during his years of military training.

The current objective was clear—*Evacuate the island.*

* * *

01:33:00 REMAINING

At a convenience store in West Lafayette, Indiana, more than two-dozen customers had gathered around a television perched high in a corner to watch CNN's report on the developing story. In Times Square, hundreds crowded the sidewalk to follow it on the giant 26' x 34.5' Panasonic Astrovision TV screen. And in Tupelo, Mississippi, two millworkers who were on strike and already half-drunk so early in the day started a betting pool where the winner would be the one who came closest to guessing the eventual number of fatalities. They would get nearly a dozen entries. CNN got hold of a recording of the final transmissions from the cockpit of the airliner that went down. Some kid in Virginia had picked it up on his ham radio, recorded it, and sold it to them for $5,000. It would eventually come to be considered part of the "soundtrack" of this historic tragedy, like WLS Chicago reporter Herb Morrison's quavering voice as he cried, "Oh the humanity!" when the Hindenburg fell, in flames, at Lakehurst's Naval Air Station in 1937.

To calm a jittery public and an even more jittery Wall Street, the President of the United States made a statement just after nine o'clock. He told the country that the incident appeared to be isolated and not part of a broader terrorist attack. No other planes were grounded, much to the relief of the airline industry. He assured the nation that government forces were doing everything in their power to assist in the coastal evacuation. When asked specifically about Long Beach Island, he gave a wholly honest reply—he had never heard of it. He quickly added that he was deeply concerned for everyone who lived there.

All along coastal New Jersey, towns were being evacuated at a frenetic pace. Red lights swirled and sirens blared. Although teams of experts were certain the path of the tsunami would carry it to LBI first, surrounding communities such as Seaside Heights to the north and Margate to the south were emptying fast. Casino owners in Atlantic City cringed at the thought of losing all their customers, even if only for a few hours, but had little choice.

Back on the island, the first of the New Jersey National Guard troops began rolling in, their camouflage fleet forming a long, pulsing convoy along both sides of the Garden State Parkway and down Route 72. They brought all the large vehicles they had, the plan being that they would go onto the island and bring back as many people as each could carry. The designated dropoff spot was the enormous parking lot of Home Depot, on 72's eastbound side. The commander of the operation prayed to God that it would be far enough inland. The Rutgers people said the tsunami's waves would roll in and then draw back, so, theoretically, there would be very little flooding, especially since there was a bay on the other side of the island to act as a barrier to the mainland. But still.... Against the urgings of his advisors, he refused to bring the residents any further. Doing so would take more time, and in the end if it turned out he missed saving just one more truckload of people because he had taken the others farther than necessary he would have to carry that burden into eternity.

Traffic swamped the Causeway within minutes of the first public announcements. Local police stood in the roads frantically waving their orange batons and yelling for people to keep moving. Whenever some idiot would stop to ask a question, the cop, under strict orders, would shake his or her head and reply, "No questions, keep moving!" Every vehicle was ordered to carry as many passengers as possible, and those with children were always given the right of way. Strangers suddenly became close friends. If you had a car or a truck with an empty seat, you had the chance to be a hero.

Three of the four lanes on the bridge were designated outgoing—two on the westbound side, and one of the two on the eastbound side. The other eastbound lane was kept clear for incoming rescue transports, which had to be empty and ready to take another load at one of the designated pickup points along Ocean Boulevard. When they got down to the last fifteen minutes, this lane would revert to another outbound route. It was doubtful anyone would be willing to go in at that point anyway, under military orders or not.

Every police officer from every town in Ocean and Atlantic Counties had been called in for duty. While some managed the traffic, others were dispatched to comb their respective neighborhoods in search of residents unable to get themselves out. The older and more experienced cops were given this assignment. They'd know who was too elderly to have a driver's license, who was handicapped, and who worked at night and slept during the day with the phone turned off.

LBI residents were informed with brutal honesty that they should not expect to see their homes again. "When you're deciding what to take and what not to take, remember that," Mayor Harper announced over the radio and on television. Most residents acted sensibly and simply left, realizing they weren't so much running a race against a tsunami as against time. Across the island, they gathered up their loved ones, pets, and a handful of cherished personal items and jumped into the most reliable vehicle they owned. If there was a choice, Harper instructed, clunkers were to be left behind. "If it might break down and cause traffic delays, don't drive it." He asked that families stay together in one car rather than add to the number of vehicles on the road. He encouraged the use of motorcycles and bicycles, as they could cruise along shoulders and on sidewalks. And he instructed people to leave coat hangers on the front doors of their homes so police officers driving by would know they had been fully vacated.

Not surprisingly, some people seemed to lose their get-moving-now rationality in their panic. One middle-aged woman in Loveladies wouldn't leave until she'd picked out just the right outfit. A retired man in North Beach didn't bother telling his sleeping wife about the emergency until he'd loaded his beer-can collection into the back of his pickup truck. In Spray Beach, a nineteen-year-old high school dropout who had already told his mother he'd left the house was in fact trying to find a suit-able hiding place in his rusted '89 Cutlass for the marijuana crop he'd so lovingly cultured in their old shed for the last six months. And in High Bar Harbor—one of the highest-risk areas due to its distance from the bridge—a thirty-something couple who had already been on the verge of divorce wasted almost ten precious minutes arguing over whose car would be left behind: his Jaguar or her BMW. In the end they left separately.

Most business owners were willing to leave their wares behind, but many found the time to take copies of their insur-ance policies. Some had no insurance. One man who had invested almost ninety thousand dollars in a video-rental shop in Brighton Beach a few months earlier called one insurance company after another in the hopes of getting a quick policy together. He had no luck, and when he finally jumped into his car he was crying like a baby.

News of the oncoming disaster spread first through the rest of the Garden State, then throughout the northeast corridor, and finally across the nation.

America watched and waited.

* * *

Karen let the phone ring at least a dozen times. It was about ten more than necessary—Nancy picked up right away when she was home. Karen couldn't leave a message, either, because they didn't have an answering machine. Neither Bud nor Nancy cared for them.

She was certain that if they had left LBI they would have called her first. Where could they be?

Next, she tried to call Mike on his cell phone, knowing how early it was on the West Coast. When she got an "unavailable" message, she hung up, frustrated.

She grabbed her keys and her bag and got up. Then she paused for a moment, wondering if she should take along all the framed photos, too.

"Will the water reach where we are?" she asked no one in particular. Only Scott Tarrance, Myra, and a forty-something divorcee named Alice who'd been with the firm just a few weeks remained. Karen hadn't even noticed the departure of the others.

"Not the wave," Scott said. "But there could be some flooding."

She nodded and, without further reflection, began to load her personal items into the bag. There wasn't much beyond the pictures, and there was no time to take them out of the frames.

She froze as her gaze fell on one photo in particular—a formal posed shot of Patrick and Michael that had been taken on the observation deck behind the James J. Mancini Municipal Building. The boys were wearing identical outfits—navy blue cotton slacks, white button-down shirts, dark shoes. Patrick also had a white sweater with a navy stripe around the collar. He looked like a real Ivy-Leaguer. His hair was a little too puffy on one side and mussed up in that way it always was. But he obviously didn't care. He and his brother were smiling in the bright, happy way some children do when they're being photographed.

The delicate innocence captured in that image combined with the crawling reality that they might not survive fell on her like a pallet of bricks. The tears came so quickly they felt as though they were being force-pumped. As her hands went to her face, Myra came over and put a comforting arm around her shoulder. She said nothing, for she was wise enough to know there was nothing to say. Scott Tarrance came forward but was unsure what to do. His instinct was also to touch her, but he held himself back because he lived in an age when making physical contact with someone of the opposite sex in the workplace, regardless of context or intention, was a gamble.

"I've got to go," she said, pulling her bag onto her shoulder. The inclusion of all her personal items had given it considerable weight and bulk, but she didn't appear to notice.

"Good luck, honey," Myra said, rubbing her back.

Karen pushed the front door aside and headed for her car, first in a brisk walk, then a moderate jog. She wiped the tears away, leaving dark mascara streaks in their wake. The bag was thrown into the passenger seat, the rattling keys jammed into the ignition. The engine roared to life, and she thanked God her husband was diligent about car care. Mike wasn't a mechanic but he could've been if he'd chosen to. He could fix or build anything. He took care of all the handy-work around the house and was more or less fanatical about making sure everything ran at peak efficiency. Karen sometimes teased him about his anal behavior, but inside she was comforted by it. She had scores of girlfriends whose husbands had to be goaded, bribed, or outright threatened to do anything around the house.

As soon as she pulled onto Route 72 she saw them—the two thick lines of traffic on the westbound side. There was a traffic light about a hundred feet up, and it had been turned off. A cop was standing at the intersection, urging everyone forward. His patrol car was parked next to him, lights swirling.

She suddenly noticed a car on her side of 72 coming toward her. For a second she was nearly paralyzed by confusion. Then she moved into the right lane and saw that there were others behind it. *They're using the eastbound lanes to get people out, too.* For some reason that made it more frightening; here was further confirmation that systems were breaking down, that the glue that held this community together was beginning to melt.

She became acutely aware of her place in all of this—thousands of people pouring off the island while she headed back to it. Her heart pounded and perspiration broke out all over her body. She lowered all the windows because it was suddenly too hot and difficult to breathe.

She wiped more tears from her eyes and, perhaps a little cruelly, forced all thoughts of Patrick and Michael aside. They would distract her, and right now she needed to concentrate. If she got into an accident—Jesus, she didn't even want to think about that. What would Mike say? What would he do if she didn't get back in time?

She decided it was time to try calling Mike again. Without taking her eyes off the road, she reached into the bag for her cell phone. When she was blocked by the profusion of personal items she'd stuffed in there, she turned the bag over and shook everything onto the seat. In direct support of Murphy's Law, the phone was the last item to fall out. She snatched it up and, using only her thumb, hit MEMORY and then 2. She knew it was illegal in New Jersey not to use a hands-free headset when making calls on the road, but there was no time for that now. She cradled the phone between her chin and shoulder and waited.

At first there was only silence. Then a cheerful female voice said, "We're sorry, all lines are busy. Please try your call again later."

She tried again but got the same message.

As she approached the intersection, the cop who had been directing traffic spotted her. He was tall and heavy, with a gut that bulged like a full-term pregnancy. He wore his cap low, like a drill sergeant, and had a dark mustache. Karen watched him—watched and waited for the inevitable reaction. He moved to her side of the highway and started waving his hands.

No, please don't. Don't walk out into the road to stop me.

She wondered what she'd do. Run him down in cold blood? If not—if she stopped—how much time would be lost? Would it make all the difference? Would she regret it later? Would the day come when she wished she *had* run him down?

Mercifully it never came to that. The cop couldn't make it to her lane because too many cars were speeding by in the other westbound lane. Just before the car at the front of the line—a pearl-white Lexus sedan—reached her, the driver stuck his arm out the window and jabbed a finger westward. *You're supposed to be going that way, stupid!* was obviously the message. He was honking his horn, too. In fact, she noticed for the first time, a lot of people were honking. She glanced at the cars on the normal westbound side. Almost every face in every vehicle was staring at her. There were other finger-jabbers, too.

"I'm going to get my children," she said through clenched teeth to no one driver in particular. "So you can just stuff it."

She crossed the intersection, and the cop screamed over the roof of a passing car, "Stop or you'll be arrested at the next checkpoint!"

She kept going.

The cop yelled, "Hey!" again, and she could see him in the mirror, pointing and blowing his whistle. Then, to her horror, he took his walkie-talkie from his belt, never once taking his eyes off her. She couldn't remember the last time she saw someone who looked so pissed off.

She turned back to the road, and her heart jumped into her throat—some idiot trying to play policeman's little helper had moved his ancient Ford pickup into her lane to act as a barrier. The driver stepped out—tall and lanky, long golden hair with a full beard and mustache. A young dark-haired woman was in the passenger seat and looked utterly terrified. But her boyfriend/husband/whatever was grinning in that way only a man can when he's sure he's going to get the best of someone.

Karen registered all this in a span of maybe two seconds. That left about two more to react. She jerked the wheel clockwise, driving off the pavement and onto a sandy area that acted as a makeshift shoulder. The car bumped around like a ride at an amusement park. She screeched a few obscenities and prayed, internally, that she wouldn't hit the idiot who had forced her to do this. She was vaguely aware of him as he passed by the open window, could hear him yell a few expletives of his own, and saw him jump back to avoid being struck.

She twisted the wheel and returned to the road. It was worse than getting off—new pavement had been set down less than a month earlier, creating a rough-hewn lip of nearly three inches. She heard a loud knock, then an angry metal scrape as the undercarriage dragged across the hard surface.

The car fishtailed into position, and she jammed the pedal to the floor. The engine screamed in protest. *Tough shit,* she thought cruelly. *Now's the time I need you the most.* The urge to look in the rearview mirror itched like a rash, but she resisted it. She had to be on the lookout for others who had heroic aspirations. Once word got around, she realized, there'd definitely be others. For a second or so this frightened her, but then the fear faded, as if it had been tossed in a tray marked "For Later." Some kind of liquid strength—cold and potent— flooded into her.

Let them come, she thought as she passed the pizza place where she and her family had eaten just a few weeks ago. *I dare them.*

* * *

BethAnn wasn't sure what to take with her, and her mind was spinning so much stark fear that it was almost impossible to concentrate. She had virtually no book-learning skills to speak of—she'd finished up high school with a glowing D average—but she had a natural cleverness about certain things. She knew enough, for example, not to bother with the television set. It was old and outdated, and the insurance money would cover a new one anyway. (This kind of excited her, actually—she fantasized about what kind she'd get, and decided one of the flat-screen, high-definition models ought to suffice.) Same with the fridge and most of the furniture. There was almost no jewelry, and what she had was cheap costume crap. Her engagement ring (which Kenny had given her at the Carousel Ice Cream Parlor, in Barnegat Light, buried in a banana split) and her wedding ring were both history, sold on eBay for about five percent of their original price. The money was long gone.

That left only a small collection of family photos and the videotapes. She was sure she wanted the former, so she hustled down the hall into the bedroom. The stench hit her like a boxer's punch—the dirty clothes that formed a small mountain in one corner, the empty food containers. On the nightstand was a plate with orange streaks of hardened cheese sauce. A fork was welded to the surface. Over the bed, the one and only window in the room was covered by a piece of cardboard that partially bore the logo for Tide laundry soap.

The folding closet doors were already open. She dropped to her knees and dug madly though the rotting sneakers until she found a shoebox with a rubber band around it. It weighed no more than a couple of pounds, but it was still an effort for her to pull it out of there and heft it onto the bed. Sifting quickly through the contents, she rediscovered different stages of her life. The deeper she dug, the farther back through history she went.

She found a shopping bag under the kitchen sink and slipped the shoebox inside. Then she grabbed three bags of junk food from the cabinet over the fridge—cheese doodles (crunchy,

not puffed), caramel popcorn, and pork rinds. She knew she'd
want something to munch on while she was in the car. It would
keep her from chewing her fingernails down to the skin.

She went into the living room, the bag slung over her shoulder like she was some kind of Bowery bum or maybe a Santa
Claus wannabe. The TV was still on, CNN's Bill Hemmer still
giving up-to-the-minute reports on this latest world event. The
headline along the bottom now read TSUNAMI EXPECTED TO STRIKE
SOUTHERN NEW JERSEY COAST AT APPROXIMATELY 11:30 A.M. BethAnn
consulted the clock on the wall—two brass strips on a slab of
jagged-edged wood forever trapped in about eighty coats of
clear glaze—and gasped when she saw that it was almost ten.
Her first impulse was to *run*—just jump in the car, hit the gas,
and keep going until the Causeway was nothing but a shrinking
shape in the rearview mirror.

But the tapes, the videotapes she had amassed and cata-
loged over the years ... what to do with those? She had been so
meticulous that she even surprised herself. She'd buy blanks in
bulk—packs of five, six, sometimes ten. Then she'd insert one
into the VCR and set the timer. After a show was successfully
taped (she always thought of it as "captured"), she'd write the
information (name, subject, date aired) on the label affixed to
the side. Her handwriting had always been damn near illegible,
but for some reason she went out of her way to write neatly. As
the collection grew into the hundreds it became one of the few
aspects of her life she took pride in.

Did she really want to throw that all away now?

There wasn't enough room for the tapes in the bag she had,
so she went back to the kitchen and got another one—a dark
green garbage bag that was large enough, she hoped, to carry
the entire load.

She kept the tapes in a tall cabinet next to the TV. She'd
bought it at the Wal-Mart in Manahawkin and put it together

herself. It took almost a full day because she had no patience when it came to reading directions, and it was a bit crooked because she had no mechanical skills, either. It had cost her $69.95, and she didn't really have the money to spare, but three weeks of careful skimming and creative accounting at Acme had covered it.

She tried to pull the doors open, but they were locked tight. Then she remembered—the previous Friday, after she'd come home from a grueling six-hour shift, she had wanted to watch a particular episode of *Jenny Jones* she'd taped awhile back, but couldn't find the key. She had planned to do a trailer-wide search but never got to it.

She wrapped all ten fingers around one handle, set her foot against the opposite door, and...

"One...two...three!"

The staple-shaped handle ripped free of the wood, and BethAnn went sprawling. She tried valiantly to maintain her balance, flailing like an alarmed chicken, but her legs gave way and she plowed into the end table next to the couch, sending the contents of a large Tupperware bowl—a two-day-old supply of party mix—flying.

Cursing loudly, she scrambled to her feet with uncharacteristic nimbleness, grabbed a wooden chair from a set of four that surrounded a circular table, and began beating the cabinet with it. She was running on pure adrenaline, pure fury. She aimed for the lock at the center but would be just as satisfied if one of the doors simply crumbled. She could hear the tapes clattering inside, tumbling from their shelves in what amounted to a major earthquake in their little world.

The tantrum ended when there was nothing left of the chair, and one of the cabinet doors had split down the center. Then, like a contestant in a shopping spree, she grabbed everything in sight. The bag quickly became too heavy, so she dropped it to the floor and began using both hands. It took almost two full minutes to retrieve all one hundred twenty-four tapes.

Before she turned to go, she spit into the empty cabinet and told it to go fuck itself. She wanted to give it a brisk kick and knock it over, too, but she was too winded.

She knew she wouldn't be able to carry both bags, so she decided to bring the tapes to the car first. She expected them to be heavy, so she tried to mentally prepare herself. She got to one knee, wrapped the bag's yellow tie-loops around her hand, then turned herself so they were over her shoulder. One thing she'd learned from doing inventory at Acme: Let your legs do the work, not your back.

She rose slowly, and the moment the bag left the ground and the full weight of it became her burden, an unbelievable dizziness overwhelmed her—she had no idea they'd be this heavy.

She staggered around like an exhausted dancer, trying to maintain both her footing and her consciousness. Then, without warning, the bottom of the bag split and the tapes gushed out. They bounced and slid in every direction, some of them disappearing under the couch.

Already trembling with anger from the confrontation with the cabinet, BethAnn willingly gave up her remaining hold on sanity. She let the deflated garbage bag fall away and grabbed another chair. Instead of directing her rage on the tapes themselves (which had caused the problem) or on the bag that had broken (how do you hurt a goddamn garbage bag?), she simply began swinging at anything that looked like it could be damaged in a satisfying way. A tall bamboo shelf with a rounded peak that she'd always hated became the first victim. It had been in Kenny's dorm room the one year he went to college. As she hit it broadside it folded like someone taking a blow to the stomach. When it toppled over in agony, she proceeded to beat it until it was nearly flat. All the cheap little porcelain figurines that had been on it were reduced to sharp white crumbs on the gold carpet.

Next came the glass-topped coffee table that Kenny had found at a factory tag sale for about ten bucks. She had always claimed she hated it, but what really steamed her was the fact that it actually looked pretty good with the rest of their furniture. She thought of herself as the interior decorator in those days and didn't appreciate the way he'd invaded her turf. The smoked glass shattered into a billion tiny, glittering pieces on the first shot. The frame, more pressboard junk, also yielded with minimal resistance.

The round table that she and her ex-husband had eaten hundreds of meals on (and twice had sex on) broke neatly in two after the third blow, as if it'd been chopped in half by a martial-arts expert. The two pieces fell forward and were left leaning against one other.

She paused for a moment to find the next target. When she spotted Paula Zahn on CNN, her blood began boiling. *Another little princess with straight white teeth and no hips.* There was a speck of hesitation, though—did she really want to smash the TV? Then she remembered that the insurance company would get her a new one, and the light in her head went from red to green. A smile stretched across her doughy face.

She ran sideways, bringing what was left of the chair back like a baseball bat. She had never participated in sports in school and hated gym class with a passion, but she did have some natural ability. The swing in this case was perfect. Broad and powerful, it made contact at just the right spot in the arc. The great glass eye exploded in a shower of sparks, and smoke seethed out from all sides, bleeding through the plastic vents like steam from a city sewer grate. She wrenched the chair from the hole and struck again, this time on top. That took out the cable box, which was fine with her; their service always sucked anyway. The third and final blow, on the side, knocked the set from its perch. It tipped over with comical dramatic slowness. As it hit the floor, it yanked the plug from its socket, which BethAnn took as a sign of surrender.

Furious energy was still surging through her, but she was finished with the destructive aspect of the tantrum. She tossed the remains of the chair aside (where it landed only inches from the last one) and went back to the kitchen. This time she took not one but three garbage bags from the cabinet under the sink, tripling them up so there'd be plenty of support.

She dropped to her knees and gathered all the tapes she could find. She decided not to waste any time counting them; if she got the bulk of them, that'd be enough. When the bag was full, she hefted it over her shoulder, got to her feet, and went to the door. It was locked, of course. She didn't want to take either hand off the bag, so she gave the door a hard kick. It swung back violently and banged on the wooden handrail. The sunlight was fierce. The heat, too, poured in with a vengeance, as if it had been waiting for the chance to get in there. She loaded the tapes into the trunk of her ancient Toyota Celica, then went back for the second bag.

She paused at the doorway for the briefest moment. She appraised everything once, quickly scanning the catalog of memories she'd amassed since buying this place. She realized she had absolutely no emotional attachment to it. She was leaving with more or less exactly what she had brought six years ago—a box of photographs and her physical self. The tapes were simply a by-product of a personal interest that could've been administered anywhere, anytime. Six long years she'd been here, and virtually nothing had changed. At least nothing for the better.

Leaving the door wide open, she turned and left.

* * *

"Have you spoken to your parents yet?" Brian asked. Then he answered his own question—"I don't think you have."

"No," Jennifer replied, her cheeks glazed with tears. She had been silent during the ride thus far. "I'll call them now."

She tried twice but couldn't get through.

"Keep trying," Brian said. "Just keep hitting redial."

She got through on the fifth attempt.

"Mom? It's me."

"Thank God! Where are you?"

"I'm with Brian, my boss. We're in his car."

"Good, get home *right now*. We've got to go!"

After a moment's pause, Jennifer said, "Mom...I can't."

"What? No, Jennifer. No nonsense. Get over here now."

Carolyn King's voice was sharp and powerful, and Brian had no trouble hearing it from the driver's seat. He peered over at Jennifer, curious as to how she would handle this, as a line of houses in South Beach Haven blurred past them. He wanted to have his own definite feelings on the matter, wanted to be able to provide guidance if necessary. But the truth in this case was that he just wasn't sure. He understood and empathized with both points of view.

Jennifer's tone quickly became pleading. "Mom, Mark's missing—he's not answering his phone. I don't know where he is!"

Unlike Brian Donahue, it took Carolyn King all of about one tenth of a second to decide her stance on this.

"Jennifer, you listen to me. You get home *right...now.*"

Jennifer felt a raw, burning anger come alive inside. Like virtually all young women in love for the first time, she desperately wanted her parents to like the person she brought home, and her mother had always been nice to Mark—very polite and proper. Up to this point she felt sure her mom had accepted

Mark, perhaps even felt a little love for him, too, though there were still isolated moments of doubt. Moments when she got the impression her mom thought of Mark as somehow inferior —not quite good enough for her little girl. Every now and then she got the feeling her mom quietly hoped the relationship would fizzle out. She had no tangible evidence of this, nothing she could hold in her hand and say, "Look, here's the proof." It was just a feeling—abstract and unfocused—but it was a strong feeling nevertheless. And now, when the situation was tight and the pressure was on, the truth was finally coming out.

"No, mom. I'm going to—"

"JENNIFER!"

This came out so shrill and harsh they both jumped, and Brian thought he was going to have a heart attack. He'd seen Mrs. King in the store dozens of times, had a pleasant if somewhat formal relationship with her. She was always well-dressed, and very proper, and carried an air of haughtiness—although he would never offer that opinion to her daughter. To witness this nasty, forceful side of her—which he had always suspected lurked below the surface—was frightening, even if only over a cell phone.

Jennifer began crying again, and she shook like she was having a mild seizure. Brian tried desperately to appear as though he wasn't listening, was only paying attention to the road and the long line of cars flowing past them in the opposite lane—and wondering just where in hell that line ended, since that's where they'd have to get on eventually.

"Mom, please...."

"Jennifer, if you don't come home right now, you'll be *very* sorry!"

There was a pause. Jennifer stared through the windshield, her eyes red and swollen. Clearly she wished she hadn't made

the call in the first place. Brian felt a twinge of guilt for sug-
gesting it.

She set the phone on her knee, kept staring dumbly into
space.

"*Jennifer!* Put your boss on! Put him on that goddamn phone
right—"

Jennifer pressed a button to disconnect the call, then
another to turn it off.

* * *

"And I want all the helicopters you've got.... Yes, that's right,
colonel. Every one. We'll be getting back to you with some spe-
cific landing points but for now I don't care where you land
them—in the streets, parking lots, on the beaches. Anywhere
your pilots see groups of people. Please get them moving
now—we're down to about an hour and a half here." *And we've
got more people than we can possibly evacuate in that time*,
Harper thought as he replaced the receiver in its cradle.

He rose and went back out. Marie was at her desk, flipping
through a phone book.

"Did you hear from Frank?"

"He's on the way. Said he's on the Boulevard and should be
here in about ten minutes."

"It must be a parking lot."

"According to Frank it's slow going but it is moving. Putting
all those extra officers out there to keep the traffic flowing was
an excellent idea."

Harper smiled and briefly considered how long it had been
since he'd received a compliment for something he'd done as
mayor. "I appreciate you staying and helping out, Marie. Most
people would've hit the road by now."

"I'm not staying any longer than necessary," she said flatly.

"I don't blame you."

He turned to go back into his office, but stopped when she said, "Oh, here—a few more of these calls came in."

She stood to hand him a paper-clipped pile of small pink sheets. The heading "PHONE MESSAGE" was printed across the top of a miniature form with fields for everything from when the call came in to a synopsis of the message. Harper had often opined that anyone who had the time to fill the damn things out had more free time than they knew what to do with. But Marie insisted on using them and while she didn't fill in every space, she came close.

He returned to his chair and browsed through them. He only looked at the names, amazed—NBC, ABC, CBS, CNN, MSNBC, FOX News.

It crossed his mind that if this had happened a year ago, it would've been his ticket to the top—his big break.

He would've been a hero, and everyone voted for heroes. George Washington became President almost entirely because he was a hero—he didn't even want the job. Neither did Grant or Eisenhower. But when the public loves you, you have little choice but to heed the call. It was such a tantalizing line of thought that, for just a flicker of an instant, Harper felt that old ambitious glow in the hollow of his belly—he could legitimately run for the U.S. Senate, and probably cruise into the job. His party would back him all the way. He'd be remembered as the guy who'd saved LBI from the tidal wave—and voters wouldn't forget it when they saw his name on the ballot. *That's the guy who saved LBI, remember?* They'd recall his heroism, his brilliant handling of the situation, his calm and commanding manner, and the way those who looked to him for guidance and reassurance were not disappointed. This was the kind of man you wanted to represent you and your state. He had proved his devotion. He had *earned* the job.

Senator Donald J. Harper.

He could hear the masses cheering, could envisage them clapping as he rode out of town, waving, on his way to Washington. They'd have a ceremony, and the press would be there. Reporters would ask about this day, and he would take the modest route and downplay everything. He'd sign autographs and kiss babies. And then he'd be gone...gone from this little stretch of nowhere to a permanent place in American history.

"Here's another one," came the voice that snapped him from his daydream. Marie walked in, let the pink sheet drop from her fingers, and went back out. It seesawed gently to the blotter, and she never noticed the faraway look in his eyes.

He had a flash of panic—how many priceless minutes had he just blown on his little daydream? He looked to the gold-framed lucite clock on the desk and was relieved to find only a minute had passed. In that minute, however, the vision of what might've been was clearer than ever before. *This day...this day would've done it. After this everything would've been different. You would've had your wish. But now....*

The desire to cry, to let it all out at last, came over him, but he swallowed it and snatched up the latest message.

Adela Callendar it said, and there was a number underneath. Under that Marie had written, *Personal cell phone.*

Like most other Americans, he was familiar with Callendar, the MSNBC reporter with the high cheekbones and piercing blue eyes. He had always liked her style, the way she balanced all the right elements—humanity, dignity, sincerity, toughness, and just enough humor to make you like her. She was clearly among the best of the new breed, and he wondered how many of her colleagues who carried the curse of mediocrity resented her.

He knew what she wanted, what they all wanted—the exclusive interview from the eye of the storm. By now they would've heard about his scandal, would know that he was on his way out. But that could be spun to add intrigue to the story.

He flipped open his cell phone, paused as a faint ripple of fear went through him, then tapped in the number. As the call went through, he got up and quietly closed the doors to his office.

Just before he got back to his chair, a voice said, "Hello, this is Adela."

"Ms. Callendar?"

"Yes?"

"This is Donald Harper. The mayor of Long Beach Township?"

"Mr. Mayor. Thank you for returning my call. I know you're very busy."

"Yeah, this has been quite a day so far."

"Would you mind if I asked you a few questions?"

"Not at all. Are we on the air right now?"

"No, not yet. We will be in a few minutes if that's okay with you."

"That's fine." He paused. "Um, how many people will be hearing this, if you don't mind my asking?"

"Let's see...." Harper heard what sounded like pages being flipped. "I'd say anywhere from two and a half to three million."

That bit of information went into him like a lance. He couldn't even picture three million people.

"I see." This wasn't a particularly intelligent thing to say, but it was better than saying nothing. If he did that, he might as well print the word amateur on his forehead.

"Now, the broadcast will be live, so don't curse or anything."

He laughed. "I'll try to control myself."

"We'll be running a small head shot of you while you're on the air."

Another blade sliced into him. *Which one were they going to use?* he worried. He was generally photogenic, but certain angles were less flattering than others.

As if reading his mind, Callendar said, "Don't worry, it's a good shot."

He laughed again; he couldn't help it. Her gift for sensing and easing tension was remarkable. "Okay, if you say so." The facade had crumbled so quickly—she knew he was green, but she also knew how to handle it. He wondered how much she really knew about the scandal, about how close he was to the end of his career. For some strange reason he didn't want her to know. He wanted her to think he was still on his way up, still on his way to being a Somebody, a Player. He wanted to impress her. The stark reality was much colder. *If only this had happened a year ago,* he thought again with a mix of anger and sadness.

"Mr. Mayor, are you ready?"

He pushed his emotions aside and refocused. "I'm ready," he said, surprised by the confidence and control in his voice. *You would've made a helluva senator,* came the bittersweet thought.

"Just a few more seconds," she told him. "Okay, here we go...."

SEVEN

$\mathcal{A}$t the Rutgers Marine Field Station, Sarah Collins remained glued to her seat, the ever-faithful Dave Dolan standing behind her. Fresh readings were fed from the instrument clusters via satellite every few minutes—as close to real time as anyone could desire. The problem was that the clusters lying out there on the sea floor were spread roughly fifty miles apart, so nothing of note would show up on the monitors until the wave passed over them.

The reading on the tide gauge jumped to four feet, then dropped to minus the same amount.

"You see that?"

"I did," Dolan replied, writing it down. Then he did some quick math, which Collins had already finished in her head.

"It's traveling at—"

"Roughly 200 miles per hour," she said.

"Yep. Damn."

Collins nodded, waiting for the next reading, which would be in about ten minutes. And it wouldn't come from the wave the instruments just "saw"—it would come from the one that followed.

She now had the unenviable task of telling the governor of New Jersey that the typical tsunami consisted of not one wave but many, the first four being the most destructive, with each more powerful than the one before it.

* * *

Karen reached the point of Route 72 where it went over Route 9. More people heading west honked helpfully, some with the added emphasis of their middle fingers. Someone had called her a "dipshit," another a "dumb bitch." She was developing a very thick skin. At least the tears had stopped. For now.

As the Causeway came into view, so did the military vehicles. They were clustered at the base, and Karen could see the men in their camouflage uniforms and jackboots directing traffic. These were not the local police, she knew—these were hard men, men in peak physical condition who kept their heads shaved and purposely forgot how to smile. They were not beer-bellied morons. They wouldn't wave their hands and yell. They would resort to more effective methods. They were trained to Get Things Done.

As she drew closer, she noticed some of them were holding rifles. She didn't know one model from the next, but they looked exactly like the ones the Secret Service brought out when they surrounded the White House during the terrorist attacks on 9/11. Those, she remembered from the news reports, were semi-automatics. Clearly it was the weapon of choice among the authorities. And that was very likely because, like the people who used it, it Got Things Done.

Would they really shoot a defenseless woman?

She decided not to find out. The first man to spot her stood in the center of the lane and came forward with his hand up. The butt of his rifle bore a hook that ran around his elbow. His face was devoid of expression, his eyes locking onto her through the windshield. His body language spoke volumes—there was no room for negotiation here. You were being ordered to stop, so you stopped. Veering off the road like Burt Reynolds in *Smokey and the Bandit* wasn't an option this time.

She came to a halt a few feet from him, and he came around to the side. A fire truck, its lights swirling madly and its horns bellowing, zoomed by.

"I'm sorry, ma'am, no cars are allowed through except emergency vehicles and military transports. You'll have to turn around."

"This is an emergency, corporal," she said, noting the two chevron shapes on his sleeve. She knew the rank from watching *M*A*S*H* as a child with her father. Radar O'Reilly had been a corporal and had the same insignia. "My two children are being watched by a friend who lives in Holgate, and she hasn't been answering her phone. I don't know if they got off the island yet."

The corporal, whose last name was Moreland according to the patch above his shirt pocket, paused, apparently unsure what to do. Karen judged him to be in his early twenties. He was a good-looking kid, hardened by his training but still boyish in subtle ways. He probably had no children of his own and therefore couldn't really relate to her predicament on that level, but he would understand that this problem could not simply be dismissed.

"Please wait here, ma'am."

He walked over to one of his superiors, an older man who was speaking to a guy in an aging, faux wood-sided station wagon. A woman, presumably the driver's wife, was in the passenger seat, leaning over to take part in the conversation. Two small children were playing in the back seat, blissfully unaware of the magnitude of the situation. Behind them, in the cargo area, was so much crap you couldn't see into the windows.

The two soldiers conferred for a moment, then the corporal turned and came back. Karen smiled optimistically.

"I'm sorry, ma'am," he said. "My sergeant said no one is allowed to pass."

"But corporal, I have to—"

"But what I can do, ma'am," he continued as if she hadn't interrupted, reaching behind himself, "is try to call your friend with this."

He produced a small cellular phone made of hard black plastic that, Karen knew upon first glance, wasn't a model available on the consumer market.

"What's the number?"

"Corporal, I've been trying to get them for the last ten minutes," she said, holding up her own phone. "All the lines are busy."

"That won't be a problem, ma'am," he said, the tiniest smile crossing his lips. It wasn't arrogance, it was the supreme confidence of the well-conditioned military mind, a confidence that comes from devoting all your time and energy to creating situations where things worked, things happened. And, she sensed, there was a bit of pride, too, as if this kid thought there was nothing cooler than having access to high-tech equipment.

"Okay, it's 555-4347."

"Area code 609?"

"Yes."

Moreland dialed. As he waited, he surveyed his surroundings, returning to his original assignment rather than waste the few seconds unproductively. Distantly, Karen marveled at the discipline, the focus. She also realized for the first time that, in spite of the catastrophic danger that was headed this way, he didn't seem the least bit frightened.

A few seconds passed, then a few more. Moreland bowed his head and stuck a finger into his other ear as if he was having trouble hearing.

"Did someone answer?"

Without looking up, he replied, "No, ma'am. It just keeps ringing."

Karen's stomach sank. "Dammit."

"Doesn't your friend have a machine?"

"No, they consider them annoying modern devices."

Moreland nodded as if he understood completely. He turned the phone off and reattached it to his belt.

"I'm sorry, ma'am, but that's the best I can do. I'll try again in a few minutes."

"Thank you. Should I wait here?"

"No, please pull over there." He motioned toward the shoulder at the base of the bridge. Nothing more than a narrow, gravelly margin separating the blacktop from a stretch of reedy wetland. The southern branch of Barnegat Bay lay beyond, the gentle ripples twinkling like broken glass in the mid-morning sunlight.

"Thanks."

He nodded and left.

The option of simply sitting there, waiting, while the precious seconds ticked away and that giant wall of water moved ever closer to Patrick and Michael never entered Karen's mind. Perhaps the young corporal really did care about the fix she was in—she still couldn't tell for sure—but the bottom line was that, at the moment, he wasn't doing anything about it, and neither was she. That was unacceptable. Doing anything was immeasurably better than doing nothing.

For the time being she followed his orders and pulled to the shoulder, perhaps thirty feet from where the Causeway began its ascent. She could see across the bay, could just make out the rough shape of the famous "clam shack"—once a serviceable shelter for clammers and fishermen, now little more than a dilapidated novelty slowly being consumed by the unyielding force of the elements.

She knew Moreland expected her to turn the engine off, but she didn't. Instead she sat and carefully watched him and his superior, Sergeant Whoever. Moreland was still scanning like a human security camera. The Sergeant was too distracted to engage in such activity, trying futilely to keep the cars moving while, invariably, someone stopped to asked one idiotic question or another. The elementary concept of *keep moving* was apparently too difficult for most people to grasp.

Moreland glanced in her direction every thirty seconds or so. She was sure this hadn't been part of his routine—he simply wanted to keep an eye on her. Once she realized this, she grew irritated by the lack of trust. *Of course*, an inner voice said, *he has good reason not to trust you, doesn't he?*

At that moment a large military transport pulled up and Moreland approached it. Karen thought this might be her chance to ease away, but the young soldier remained vigilant. He talked to the driver from the passenger side rather than going around and letting her out of his sight. Nevertheless, each time he turned his head away she removed her foot from the brake and allowed the car to inch forward.

Moreland hopped down from the running board and started toward her. The truck rumbled away, the transmission groaning as it began the laborious climb. The corporal's face appeared to have reddened, the jaw set tighter than before. He fixed her with a cold, pissed-off stare that sent fear shooting through every vein. *He noticed*, she thought. *He's seen the car moving, knows exactly what I'm trying to do, and is going to tell me to turn around and leave.*

As he reached back toward his service pistol, a 9mm that could blow a hole through a concrete wall, Karen felt all the blood drain from her face.

"555-4347, right?" he asked, producing the cell phone again. The pissed-off look apparently had nothing to do with her.

She couldn't help but smile. "Oh, yes. Thanks."

He entered the number, listened for a moment, then shook his head. "Still no answer."

Now it was Karen's turn to be pissed off. She was not one to anger easily, and in the all the years she'd known Nancy she was sure she had felt only the brightest emotions toward her. But now *Why the hell can't she have an answering machine like everyone else?*

A little guilt came with this, but not much. Their home was a damn museum, two thousand square feet of the 1970s trapped in a vacuum. No answering machine, no computer, no cable TV, no cordless phone. It even *smelled* like the '70s. Nancy and Bud's refusal to join the rest of the world in the 21st century had caused a few minor problems before, but nothing serious. It was always something cute, something to be joked about. Karen and Mike even liked it in some ways—along with increased technology came increased negative influences. They didn't want the boys to have free access to cable TV or the Internet. Now Karen wondered if those sacrifices had been worth it.

"Okay, thanks. I'll keep trying on mine."

"Right."

He returned to his post, and she returned to her inching forward. Now she was sure—absolutely certain—he knew what she was up to. In another few moments she would reach the point where the shoulder ran out. She would have to make a decision then. Maybe the riskiest one of her life.

She tried Nancy's number again. A recorded voice told her for the hundredth time that all lines were busy. She wanted to smash the damn phone on the dashboard, slam it so hard that it shattered into a thousand pieces. She felt the knot in her stomach tighten, felt the overwhelming helplessness. And the rage— the rage at being forced to sit here and do nothing while her two children were somewhere on the other side of that bridge, perhaps scared out of their wits and wondering where their mommy was. The only thing she knew for certain was that she wasn't going to sit here for long. One way or the other, she was going to do something.

Soon.

*   *   *

Nancy kept the TV off as a matter of principle. Like Karen, Mike, her husband Bud, and about a zillion other people, she firmly believed television was bad for children. It had been bad enough in the '60s and '70s, but at least back then there were some good programs. Now it was almost all trash; mass-market brain candy. And not just incidental garbage, either—she and Bud had long ago decided there were certain media outlets that were purposely producing stuff that was bad for children. The drastic increase in sex and violence, for example, hadn't been some kind of cosmic accident—a group of people had decided to make that happen.

So when the boys were over, the TV stayed off. She knew Karen and Mike appreciated that; it was one of the things Nancy loved about them. They were trying to bring their boys up right, and it gave her hope; hope that the values of the '50s and '60s had not been completely obliterated. Besides, even if the world of television hadn't gone to the dogs, there was so much else to do. So many things that were more productive and educational.

A typical day for them began with breakfast at the small round table in the kitchen, which was covered with a vinyl tablecloth and always kept immaculately clean. Nancy prepared and served the meal while Bud and the boys handled the cleanup.

Then Nancy would take the boys into a spare room on the first floor that was once occupied by their daughter, Vicky, but had since been converted into a makeshift classroom with two small desks. Bud had attached a markerboard to one wall—one modernization Nancy had embraced rather than shunned. In all her years of teaching she always hated using chalk and was grateful that a better option had finally come along. Since neither Patrick nor Michael had seen the inside of a formal classroom yet, this playful facsimile thrilled them. Nancy had seen too many children begin their school years poisoned by parents who passed down their own bad memories. If nothing else, she was determined to fertilize a positive attitude and start them on the right foot. It wasn't so much the academic angle; that would come in its own time. She wanted to make sure they were comfortable in the classroom environment. And she had a selfish motive, too—she still loved the opportunity to dabble in the practice she held a great passion for.

After an hour or so of basic education, the boys were allowed to color or play in the basement while Nancy made lunch. Often Bud would be down there in his workroom, building or fixing something. Patrick and Michael would sit and watch him, awestruck by his vast collection of tools, nuts, nails, and bolts. He'd let them help if they could help, and these were the only times the brothers came close to fighting—one would get to turn a screwdriver or hammer a nail, and the other would become swollen with jealousy.

After lunch everyone went for a walk. Nancy and Bud needed the exercise at their age—especially Bud, who had a cholesterol problem and arthritis in his knees. They usually walked the few blocks to the corner of Joan Road and Bay Terrace, where there was a small playground. The boys would monkey about while their minders admired the view of Little Egg Harbor Bay and enjoyed the breezes rolling off the water. Then they'd go back to the house, and the boys would nap for an hour or so. Sometimes, if he'd been busy enough during the first half of the day, Bud would nap, too, affording Nancy some quiet reading time. Throughout the years she'd accumulated hundreds of paperbacks for what she called her "retirement collection." Now, at long last, she was getting the chance to knock them off one at a time. Most were classics, which she loved. Right now she was working her way through Mark Twain's *The Prince and the Pauper*.

Karen usually arrived between four-thirty and five, but sometimes she got caught at the office and Mike would pick up the boys instead. So far there had never been a need for Nancy and Bud to feed them dinner. In her heart Nancy knew Karen would die if it ever came to that, but she also silently wished it would happen just once. With both of her own children grown and gone, she missed the liveliness, and even the occasional craziness, of the family dinner table.

On this particular day, there had in fact been someone in the house each time the phone rang. Bud was in the basement, repairing a broken coffee table that he'd found on the side of the road. It wasn't that they didn't already have a coffee table, or that they were so poor they were forced to resort to picking through other people's trash. But there was a spare room down there that he planned to convert into a sitting area, a place where he could relax and do a little quiet reading of his own. He wasn't much for novels, but he did have a growing pile of handyman magazines that he wanted to absorb, some of which hadn't even been opened yet.

There was no phone in the basement, which meant he had to climb the stairs to answer the one in the living room. This was something of a challenge due to his achy knees, so, more often than not, he simply wouldn't bother.

That's what happened the first time Karen called. Bud figured it was probably a solicitor. Those sonsofbitches were terrorists in their own right, shattering the fragile privacy of a person's home. In spite of the FTC's efforts to keep them under control through the National Do-Not-Call List, certain groups—mostly charities and political candidates—still hammered away. Once they learned you had a little spare cash in your pocket, they were unable to control themselves.

So he heard Karen's first call—the one she'd made from the Tarrance-Smith office—and ignored it. When it kept ringing, he called up the steps, the bare bulb burning above him, to see if Nancy was there. When he received no answer, he put a foot on the first step, and the knee flared as if in admonishment for his foolishness. He groaned a little, let out a deep, why-do-I-have-to-be-getting-so-old kind of sigh, and stepped back. The knee immediately felt better, and he made a mental to note to—*maybe*—buy a cheapo phone and put it down here somewhere. He knew where the main line was, and splicing it would be no problem. Yeah, if he was going to spend more time down here, maybe that wasn't such a bad idea.

As the ringing continued he had grown so frustrated that he turned on the transistor radio over his workbench to drown out the sound. It'd been purchased at the PX in Fort Monmouth in 1977 and still worked like a charm. He rarely touched the tuning dial—it was usually set on whatever station broadcast the Phillies games. He twisted the knob until he found a muzak station. Music never really interested him one way or the other, but anything was better than the continual distraction of the damn phone.

The problem with the coffee table he'd found was that all four legs were wobbly due to severe wood rot where they were connected to the table surface. This was an easy fix—he simply removed the old, rusted screws, moved each leg to healthier wood, drilled fresh holes, and inserted shiny new screws. The end result was even more satisfying than he'd hoped—when he set the table on the floor and gave it a shake, it didn't even budge. And since the repair work had been done on the underside, it wouldn't be visible. *Good as new.*

With a groan and some more protest from both knees, he stood the table up on end and walked it into his future reading room. He placed it in front of a horrendously ugly plaid couch he'd bought at a yard sale down the street. The neighbor not only gave it to him for a bargain—ten bucks—he even carried it into the basement for him. (Bud was under the impression he was just happy to be rid of it, and from the look of it he understood why.)

There were three boxes of magazines in a dusty corner. Bud dragged one across the cement floor and set it next to the couch. Then, exhausted, he sat down, put his feet up, and took out the first issue. It featured a special NASCAR section and an article on how to build an eleven-foot rowboat.

Back in the workroom, the Muzak station, which broadcast from a tiny office in Philadelphia, interrupted its service to transmit an emergency message.

Bud Erickson didn't hear it.

* * *

Nancy and the boys were in the backyard, working in the small level patch of yard she'd cultivated for her garden. It had been a noisy morning. In her many years living on LBI she'd gotten used to the intermittent blare of sirens, but she thought they were worse than usual today. At one point she thought she heard the phone ring, but decided not to bother with it. She was having too much fun with Patrick and Michael.

Bud was inside. He could answer it.

EIGHT

*W*hen they were married, BethAnn and Kenny had two vehicles—her Toyota Celica and his Dodge Dakota.

The latter was Kenny's pride and joy. He was a truck man right down to the dust on his boots and the grease under his fingernails. His father had been a truck man, too, and his father before him. The Dakota was the first brand-spankin'-new vehicle anyone in his family had ever owned. He and BethAnn had lied in several places on the loan application and cut back on beer and pot for months to make the down payment, but it'd been well worth it. The obvious jealousy of their friends more than made up for the sacrifice.

Kenny took the truck when he left. BethAnn argued about it, but her soon-to-be-ex-husband didn't bother arguing back. He knew she didn't really want it, knew she was bitching purely for the sake of bitching. (Of course he knew—this tiresome habit was one of the reasons he was heading out in the first place.) She didn't really want it because it was a stick, and she had no clue how to drive a stick. He tried to show her a few

117

times but ran out of patience after the clutch screamed for mercy and the gears sounded like they were being tortured to death.

So she ended up with the Celica—a little putt-around junk heap he'd bought for a hundred bucks from a customer at the shop and fixed up in his spare time. It was primarily for her, but he sometimes used it on weekends because it turned out to be a zippy little thing that used virtually no gas. It required occasional attention due to its age and mileage, but since he was a mechanic it was hardly a burden.

In the years since Kenny had left, BethAnn had made no effort to keep up the maintenance. She followed an entirely different logic—drive it as little as possible and it won't need fixing. Her luck held for a while, but not forever. A few months earlier, in November, the car began coughing out puffs of sooty black smoke, and sometimes it would stall for no apparent reason while idling at red lights. The battery terminals were encrusted with dried-acid tumors, a sure sign the battery was on its way out. Since she didn't have the money to buy a new one, she occasionally scraped the crud with a toilet-bowl brush and hoped for the best.

She dumped the videotapes and the photographs into the trunk; the bags of junk food stayed up front with her. Wiggling her bulk behind the steering wheel was, as always, an effort. The part of her brain that was able to think sensibly once again suggested the idea of moving the seat back farther. The rest of her mind pounded the idea down—anyone who saw that would know she was grossly overweight, and she enjoyed laboring under the delusion that no one would notice otherwise. Also, the farther back the seat was set, the more effort was required to hold onto the steering wheel. As long as the seat was nice and close she could keep her arms in her lap and steer with a minimum of hand and wrist movement.

When she turned the key, nothing happened.

Nothing.

"What the—"

Tears filled the rims of her eyes. It wasn't so much the fear of not being able to escape in time, she was sure that if worse came to worst she'd be able to hitch a ride from someone (she'd heard on WNJN that this was one of the rules Harper had set— if you had room in your vehicle, you had to offer others a ride). It was the thought of having to ask for help in the first place, of having to rely on someone else, of losing control of the situation, that she didn't like.

Then she remembered: After the last time she'd used the car she had removed the positive battery cable to postpone the battery's imminent death by minimizing the drain on it. Kenny had taught her this trick ages ago.

She jumped out, unlocked the hood, and brought it up. She froze when she saw just how bad the acid leak had become— the stubby lead post wasn't even visible anymore. Acid had fluffed up around it like some psychedelic mushroom, all but consuming it within its speckly, greenish-white mass. It occurred to her at that moment that she'd been in the trailer, watching television, for four straight days.

She grabbed the toilet-bowl brush from under the driver's seat and hurried back. In spite of some vigorous scraping, the dried hunks of acid hung on tight. Something more severe would be required.

She flipped the brush around and tried whacking the tumors away with the plastic handle. Each strike was accented with an angry grunt, and each grunt was roughly one semitone higher than the last.

When this, too, proved futile, she dropped the brush and ran back into the house. A fine layer of sweat began to form on her brow. The drapes over the kitchen sink were looping and swirling gaily in the breeze, as if in celebration that she had left forever. Now, to complete the irony, they came to rest when she reappeared.

One of the drawers contained a handful of tools, but she couldn't remember which. As luck would have it, she had to yank all of them open before she found the right one (next to the stove). The tools were cheap; the kind you find at checkout lines, are meant to be used only a few times, and would never be found in the toolbox of any self-respecting professional. They were all in perfect condition, as Kenny had bought them for her but she never touched them. The hammer still had the Kmart price tag on the unstained wooden handle. She dug around until she found the flathead screwdriver, then raced back out.

The screwdriver produced the desired result—the acid broke away in dusty hunks. Once the bulk of it was gone, she used the bowl brush to take care of the finer work. Fresh acid seeped out from around the base of the terminal, but she didn't care about that. With any luck she might be able to wrangle a new car out of the insurance people, too. This could be a very profitable day indeed.

The cable hung nearby like a rearing cobra. When BethAnn touched the rounded clamp to the terminal, it threw a spark, causing her to jump. At least there was some charge left, she thought; hopefully enough. She placed the clamp over the post and raced back to the driver's seat.

There was life this time, but not much—the engine turned but didn't start. She looked at the dials and gauges in front of her, hoping beyond hope that she would somehow, suddenly and divinely, be given the knowledge to, One, identify which reading measured electrical power, and, Two, evaluate that measurement. She gave that up after about five seconds and tried the key again...and again...and again....

Then she stopped, knowing enough to realize she was pushing the battery closer to the end of its life with every attempt. Out of options and drained of patience, she lowered her head against the steering wheel and began crying. It was a high, squealing sound, broken by breathing hitches and so quiet it was almost imperceptible.

When she looked back up, her eyes were red and puffy, and they stared contemptuously at the battery through the narrow strip of visibility that ran underneath the open hood.

You piece of shit. You piece of no-good sh—

Then the answer came in a flash—the cable wasn't attached tightly enough to make the required connection.

She scrambled out and went inside again. This time she took a pair of vise grips from the drawer. Back in the driveway she removed the cable from the positive terminal, reapplied it, then tightened the nut until she couldn't tighten it anymore.

She was so excited—sure that it would work this time—that she literally flung herself behind the wheel. The car creaked and bounced like an old ship. She twisted the key, and when the engine roared into life she screamed, "Yeah! Take *that!*" and clapped like a delighted child.

She got out one last time to drop the hood. Then, returning to the driver's seat, she rolled all the windows down, trained her eyes on the rearview mirror, and set the transmission into reverse.

* * *

Brian Donahue knew he was in a no-win situation. He examined and re-examined all the possibilities and couldn't seem to arrive at any other conclusion.

If we find Mark, get on the road, and make it out alive, I'll be charged with endangerment....

He was sure of this, absolutely and unequivocally sure—Jennifer's mom would see to it. She was that type. Even if her daughter escaped unharmed, the scare alone would motivate her to get a lawyer and have him ripped apart; there wouldn't be enough meat left on his bones to fill a maggot's belly.

If I turn the car around right now...

...that might quell the storm brewing inside Mrs. King, but not her daughter. The seeds of hatred would be planted, and if Mark didn't make it...what then? Would *his* mom be after him, too? From what Jennifer had said in the past, the woman didn't seem to care much for her son; it sometimes seemed as though she regretted having a son at all. But would this still be her position if he were killed? Mothers have a way of protecting their children above all else. At the very least, the woman would have an easy lawsuit on her hands, so maybe the money would be her driving force—*Yes, your honor, Mr. Donahue had the chance to save young Mark's life, and yet he drove off in callous disregard....*

So he was screwed either way, and he damn well knew it. And the irony—once again—was that he got into this hopeless loop solely because he thought he was doing something decent. He remembered something one of his favorite teachers from high school used to say: "No good deed goes unpunished."

Jennifer hadn't said a word since the fight with her mother. She sat hunched forward, the phone limp in her hand, staring through the windshield without really seeing anything. She was trying to contain the tears, but the pain and the tangled confusion were overwhelming.

"Hey," Brian said softly.

For a moment it seemed as though she hadn't heard him. Then she turned to look at him—her eyes red and swollen—and said, "What?" Her throat was clogged with phlegm, temporarily reducing her normally pretty voice to a guttural growl.

He smiled, and for a flicker of an instant he looked like the Everyday Brian again, with his white short-sleeved shirt, his black tie, every hair combed into place, and that gleam of eternal positivism in his eye.

"We're going to find Mark, we're going to hit the road, and, as the shepherds say, we're going to 'get the flock out of here,' okay? *That's* the plan."

She returned the smile, but there was no sincerity in it. Her eyes left his, went down to the dead phone in her hand. He knew what she was thinking—turn it back on, talk to your mother, and get this thing cleared up. What was stopping her was equally clear—there wasn't any way to get it cleared up. The two women held sharply different viewpoints, and neither was willing to give an inch.

"We'll find him," he said, not fully believing it but acting the part to perfection. "Don't worry."

"I hope so."

They reached the entrance to the refuge and went in. They had passed the end of the traffic line a few miles back and hadn't seen a soul since. Brian said nothing but he was growing uneasier by the minute.

When Jennifer spotted Mark's car in an otherwise empty parking area, she came alive again. She sat up straight, put the window down, and began looking around.

"Mark!" she called, hands around her mouth. "*Mark!*"

Brian did likewise. As they pulled up next to his car, Jennifer opened the door and took off like a shot.

"Jen, wait!" he shouted, but she ignored him. She was gone in seconds.

He turned the motor off and got out. He checked his watch for the first time since they'd left the store—10:15. Less than ninety minutes to go.

"Shit," he muttered. Then he went down the trail after her.

* * *

It was only a turtle—a diamondback terrapin to be precise, which was fairly common to the area—but it was beautifully posed, the background perfect. It was resting atop a half-submerged log set in a tiny pool surrounded by a wall of young reeds. Mark couldn't have composed a better image if he'd designed it from scratch.

You don't create beautiful images like this one, you can only hope to find them.

He knew this was the bottom line when it came to photography, knew it to be the Big Secret. There were millions of amateur clickers out there who would never rise through the ranks simply because they didn't understand this. Striking images either existed or didn't, and that fact had absolutely nothing to do with the people or their equipment. The best photographers were the ones who recognized the brilliant shots when they encountered them. From there, the only real talent required was a level of technical skill with the camera.

There was an added challenge in this case—getting the perfect shot before the subject moved. Mark had photographed diamondbacks before, knew they were, like all aquatic turtles, skittish and untrusting. He had been following a sandy trail that brought him to a set of tidal pools scattered behind a rise about a hundred feet from the main beach. When he saw the animal, it saw him, too, and it leaned forward in a predive posture. So Mark froze. He froze to convey the message *I won't hurt you*, and the diamondback seemed to buy it. It took another few minutes for the turtle to relax again. Mark came forward so slowly that his movements were almost imperceptible.

He ended up in a crouch, one knee in the sugary sand, the other supporting an elbow to keep the camera steady. The animal seemed to understand what he was doing. It was no more than five feet away now. He'd never been this close to a diamondback; he was awed by its ornate carapace. He took a few landscape shots, then turned the camera sideways and took a few uprights. The composition was magical—the turtle at the bottom with the log underneath and the clear-as-glass pool of water all around it, the tan of the reed wall in the middle, and the cool blue sky above. He could see the image as a *SandPaper* cover, could see the headlines printed in the appropriate places and the *SandPaper* title running across the top. He took what he considered the best shot from the best angle, then varied the aperture setting and took some safety shots.

He took the last shot, brought the camera down, and admired his subject for a moment. The turtle appeared more relaxed now, as if it'd been photographed on prior occasions and was relieved to find that this was all the intruder wanted.

"Thanks for being so cooperative," he said with a smile. "Sorry I can't offer you a modeling fee." The diamondback didn't respond.

Slowly, Mark turned and moved down the trail. He looked back just before the pool was out of view and was struck by a momentary sense of sadness when he saw that the creature was gone. He was sorry he had disturbed it.

He went about rewinding the roll and removing it from the back of the camera. It was stored in its assigned compartment in the bag. His experienced hands loaded a fresh roll autonomously, permitting him the freedom to take stock of his surroundings. His first thought was that he had absolutely no idea where he was. He'd been to this refuge plenty of times, but never this far in. There was no sign of human interference, which was exactly why he came here.

He put his hands on his hips and absorbed everything, overcome by that familiar feeling of warmth and relaxation; pure happiness. He could definitely stay here forever, in a world that made considerably more sense to him than the other—the purity of the land, the benevolence of the creatures that dwelled in it. They all had natural enemies, of course; no world was totally without violence. But in this world violence was only a tool used to secure food or protect young. Animals didn't kill each other for their television sets or their leather jackets or for heroin. Funny, he thought, how humans often referred to other people as "animals" when they exhibited senselessly violent behavior. The analogy was fundamentally illogical.

He wondered what Jennifer would think of these musings. She came from a stable and loving household, and there certainly wasn't anything wrong with that. But he had a feeling her parents had furnished little space for such ideas. They were well-to-do, straight from the pages of the all-American handbook. They drove new vehicles, watched the evening news, put their money into safe stocks and IRAs, and wore their best clothes to church. They were cut from a very popular template, and within that design was virtually no room for one to wonder about things like nature and its many mysteries. So what did Jennifer really think when he talked about stuff like this? She always seemed receptive, sometimes even fascinated. But was it sincere, or was she merely intrigued because his ideas were so alien to any she'd encountered in her carefully controlled world?

He didn't know, but he would have to find out eventually. Meantime, he wished she were here to share this astonishing beauty, whether she truly appreciated it or not. He could teach her to appreciate it, to feel as he did. That would be one of the gifts he would give her, a positive piece of himself. He had little else to offer, he thought.

He checked his watch again. Still some time to go before she arrived. What was left to do? He'd taken all the shots he needed. He had plenty that were cover-worthy. Should he take more, just to be safe? Or maybe some shots for his portfolio. *Sure, why not—while I have the chance.*

Since this was a new area to him, he didn't know exactly which way to go. He felt like going to the right, so he went to the right. He followed the rise that separated the sea from the pools. He didn't know what treasures lay beyond, but he was excited to find out.

This was turning out to be one of the most enjoyable days in recent memory.

* * *

Carolyn King wasn't imposing in the physical sense. She stood five foot six—lithe, elegant, and quite beautiful for a woman of fifty-three. Boys who were young enough to be her sons still turned to look at her. She had her hair (which was naturally auburn) and her nails done once a week, and although she no longer worked out at a health club, she was disciplined with her diet and stretched in her bedroom every morning while watching the *Today* show with Matt Lauer and Katie Couric, neither of whom she liked.

No, it wasn't her aura of American elitism that struck fear in the heart of everyone she knew—it was her eyes. They were small, narrow, and steely, like those of a dangerous little animal. She looked angry even when she wasn't. Her normal, relaxed expression was one of bitter disappointment, the look of someone already stretched to the breaking point. One more annoyance, that look said, and I'm going to blow. Many people who knew her had never even seen her smile. If you told her something that would normally elicit a positive reaction—*My son just got accepted into Harvard* or *My husband made it through the operation*, she might nod and deliver a properly polite response, but there would be no enthusiasm, no *Hey, that's terrific!* Some people thought of her as "unimpressable." Others felt she was just plain cold, emotionally unplugged. The general consensus of all outside her immediate family was that this was one scary bitch.

Now, making no effort to soften her reputation, she burst through the front door of the Harvey Cedars Police Department, steely eyes blazing. With her fingernails manicured to perfection and a pair of diamond earrings dangling obtrusively from narrow lobes, she looked like a character from a soap opera. The only other person around at that moment was Terri Houghton, HCPD's dispatcher. She was behind an inch-thick pane of smoked glass, in a tiny room and surrounded by a bank of blinking and beeping electronic equipment. The microphone in front of her looked like something from the J. Edgar Hoover era. It was in fact a vintage RCA Ribbon Velocity Type BK-11A from 1960, discovered by Chief Tanner at a flea market a year earlier and installed as a novelty.

Houghton, a small, plump young woman of Polynesian descent who was in fact born in Hawaii, recognized Carolyn King at once and was instantly terrified. She'd had very little interaction with Mrs. King through the years but knew the woman's reputation well. She also knew that her husband, Burton King, was one of the wealthiest men on the island and a close personal friend of Chief Tanner's as well. They played cards together at the Surf City Yacht Club on Friday nights.

King zeroed in on her like a Stinger missile. She moved to the glass that separated them and, without any preamble, said, "Where's Chief Tanner? I need to speak to him right away."

"He's not here at the moment, Mrs. King. He's at—"

"Is there any other officer available?"

"Well...yes, Officer Mitchell is here, but he's about to—"

"Have him come up here, please."

Houghton paused. Jeff Mitchell was not only the youngest and cutest guy on the force (wife and family notwithstanding), but he was also on his way back out to direct traffic by the Eckerd Drug Store on the island side of the Causeway. This was a particularly sticky area, with a confusing array of little side streets and one-way turns. Two men were already there, but a third was badly needed. The last thing Houghton wanted to do was feed poor Jeff to this carnivore.

"Mrs. King, he has to go to—"

Her hand struck the counter with such force that Houghton jumped.

"Listen, young lady—my daughter has vanished. She's gone off to find her goddamn boyfriend, she won't answer her phone, and I don't know where she is. But I do know this—if someone here doesn't help me find her *right now*, you're going to have a lot more trouble on your hands than a tidal wave!"

Their eyes were locked together, King's wild with rage, Houghton's wide with fear and a long measure of morbid fascination. She had always been intrigued by forceful, gutsy people, the way they didn't seem to care what anyone thought about them, how they tore through the usual barriers in life like tissue paper. For a moment she was unable to pull away, mesmerized in the same way one was when passing the scene of a car accident.

"I'll...I'll get him right now."

"Hurry!"

She scrambled out of her seat, King watching her every step of the way. When she returned, she was scurrying behind Officer Mitchell, who was considerably taller. A human shield.

There was a buzzing sound, and Mitchell opened the door that separated the lobby from the hallway. He was slender and lean, with wispy brown hair combed in a one-stroke sweep across the top. Although he was born and raised in Forked

River, he had an easy, midwestern look about him. His mother was, in fact, from Cheyenne, Wyoming, where her family had lived since 1824.

"Can I help you, ma'am?" he said with a smile. His voice was deep and manly, resonating like a cello note. No doubt Houghton had warned him that crazy Mrs. King was out there and in a ripe mood.

"Yes, officer, you can. My daughter, Jennifer, is missing." She took her cell phone from her pocketbook and shook it in the air. "I've tried to reach her on this thing for the last half hour, but there's no answer."

"Do you know where she might be?"

"The last time I talked to her, she said she was in her boss's car on her way to find her boyfriend."

"May I ask where she works?"

"She works at the Acme on the Boulevard."

"Terri? Would you kindly call the Acme and see—"

"I've already done that," King said impatiently. The words that were left out at the end but were there nonetheless were, "you idiot."

"And?"

"And there was no answer."

Terri watched this exchange from the safety of her little booth, and marveled at Jeff's calm. It wasn't an act, either—she hadn't seen him lose his temper once in the four years he'd been here.

"Okay, where do you suppose they were going?"

"I told you, to find her boyfriend."

"I know, but where?"

King paused, studying the man carefully, probing for a sign of weakness. She didn't like having questions put to her that she couldn't answer. She'd been on a roll, and now she'd hit a bump in the road. Usually when she found herself in this situation all she had to do was bear into someone with those piercing gray eyes (she knew as well as anyone else how unnerving they could be; she had fully assessed her own strengths and weaknesses before she was out of her teens), and they'd back down. But that approach didn't seem to have any effect on this man, and it irked her.

"I don't know."

"She didn't say anything to you about seeing him earlier today? Yesterday?"

"No."

"What can you tell me about him? Do you know his name?"

"Mark, Mark White."

Mitchell knew the name from somewhere, he was instantly sure of that. But where?

"Do you know where he lives?"

"On the island."

"Do you know the town? The street?"

"No...not really."

Now Mitchell paused to evaluate her. King had some idea what was going through his mind: What a great mother—her daughter has a boyfriend and she doesn't know the first thing about him. Just one more ignorant bitch with too much money that the rest of us have to put up with.

"He's a photographer," she added quickly. "I know because he—"

Mitchell snapped his fingers and pointed. "The *SandPaper*. That's where I've seen his name."

"What?"

"The local free paper. Here, I'll show you."

Terri buzzed them back in and he escorted Carolyn King down the hall to his office—a tiny, brightly lit space with an old wooden desk that had been donated to the department by the elementary school during a major renovation almost ten years ago. There was a tall filing cabinet in one corner, and a modest array of framed citations on the walls. Everything was neat and orderly, but not to the point where Mitchell seemed anal.

He took a folded newspaper from his desk and held it up.

"This thing," he said.

King nodded. "I've seen it around."

He laid it flat and started paging through it.

"Officer, we don't have—"

"Here, right here."

He held it up again, folded awkwardly so only one photograph was showing. It was a shot of two children, one boy and one girl, standing on the beach with an older man—possibly their father. A group of sea gulls had gathered nearby, and the father was helping the kids feed them something from a paper bag. Underneath the photo at the lower right, in italics, was the line *Photograph by Mark White.*

"Is this her Mark White, Mrs. King?"

"Jennifer has talked about him taking pictures for a newspaper, so I suppose it is."

Mitchell took the paper back and turned to the inside front page. He found the masthead, saw Mark's name listed as a staff member, and called the main number. Someone picked up on the first ring.

"SandPaper," came a woman's voice.

"Hi, this is Officer Jeff Mitchell of the Harvey Cedars Police Department. Very quick question for you—would you happen to know where Mark White is today?"

"That's the sixty-four-thousand-dollar question, Officer Mitchell," the woman said. He quickly gauged her as late twenties, early thirties. "He was supposed to be taking pictures over at the Forsythe Wildlife Refuge, but he hasn't answered his cell phone. We've called a number of times."

"Could I have that number, please?"

"Sure, it's 609-555-6771."

Mitchell was sitting now. He scribbled the number on a little pad that had his name printed in tiny type at the top, underneath a watermark of the department's logo.

"And would you happen to know his home number as well?"

"Yes, it's 555-4309."

"Brant Beach?"

"Yes, but he's rarely there."

"Really? Why's that?"

"He and his stepfather don't get along. He doesn't get along too well with his mother, for that matter. He's here all the time."

"I see. Okay, thank you. Look, I'm sure you're busy over there—"

"We'll all be out of here in about fifteen minutes."

"I don't blame you. But please, take down this number—it's my cell phone, which may or may not work, but it's worth trying—and let me know if you connect with Mark. His girlfriend's mother is here with me, and we can't seem to find either one of them."

"Sure, go ahead."

"609-555-2177."

"Okay, officer, I will."

Mitchell thanked the woman and ended the call.

"Well?" Carolyn King demanded.

"They think he's at the Forsythe Wildlife Refuge. That's where they sent him on assignment today. I'll radio one of the officers in the area and—"

"No, I'm not leaving this in the hands of someone else. I'll go there myself."

"Mrs. King, there'll be so much congestion by the bridge it'll be impossible to cut through it."

"I don't care. I'm not going to stand around here waiting."

They watched each other for a few seconds. King had no intention of negotiating this point, and Mitchell had no doubts about that. He also had no doubts that this woman not only would indeed try to cut through the traffic that was most assuredly thickening at the base of the Causeway right now, she might even find a way to do it. Whether she did or not, one thing was certain—it wouldn't be a pretty sight.

He sighed, got up, and took his jacket from the back of the chair.

"I'll take you, Mrs. King. It'll be a lot easier to get through in my squad car."

"That's fine," she replied, victorious yet again.

"And I'm radioing ahead in case someone's already there."

"That's fine, too."

Oooh, thank God I have your approval, Mitchell thought.

He set his hat in place and gestured toward the door.

"Let's go," he said. "We probably don't have much more than an hour."

Just before exiting, he yelled to the back—"Terri, if I'm not back in time...."

Terri stuck her head out the door of the dispatcher's room. She didn't speak, but then she didn't have to—her pained expression said it all.

"You and the others get the hell out of here," Mitchell completed the sentence flatly.

* * *

"What we need to do is get you in the action," Wilson was saying, rummaging through the closet. He'd occupied this office for almost six months now, yet the smell of new carpet was still prominent. "I know there's a sweater in here somewhere. That blazer makes you look too much like a banker. You've got to go

134

for a more casual look. Try mussing your hair up just a little bit. Not too much."

Davis, sitting in one of the two chairs that faced Wilson's desk, was nodding and grunting without digesting a single word. He checked his watch, then the clock on the wall, then looked out the window. Above a row of houses he could see the Atlantic, blue and beautiful beneath the clear spring sky. And so peaceful at the moment. Downright picturesque. Yet somewhere out there, hundreds of miles away, death was rolling toward them. What would it look like when it appeared on the horizon? Would the waves be curled over like the one that opens and closes every episode of *Hawaii Five-O*? He didn't know, and he wasn't eager to find out.

"Ah, here it is."

Wilson came back with an over-sized maroon V-neck that was obviously the property—or at least the prop—of his former employer. In fact, Davis thought he recognized it from one or two of Harper's public appearances. *How symbolic is this?*

"Try it on," Wilson said, tossing it to him. He picked up the remote and turned on the TV set in the far corner. NJN's Debbie Phillips was reporting from the western base of the Causeway, a line of traffic moving slowly but steadily behind her. In the background, unnoticed by most viewers, Karen Thompson sat in her car on the side of the road.

Wilson switched around, starting with the major networks. All commercials. Then he went to cable. CNN was on a break and FOX was giving an update on a bank-robbery-turned-deadly-shooting in North Carolina.

When he landed on MSNBC, his heart stopped. The screen was divided into three sections—a thin strip along the bottom, a slightly wider strip running up the left side, and then the largest part in the remaining area. The headline on the bottom read, BREAKING NEWS and, underneath it, "Major Tidal Wave

Expected To Strike Southern New Jersey Coast." In the left sector, near the top, was a small, smiling photo of Donald Harper. Underneath it were the words, "On The Phone With: Donald Harper, Mayor Of Long Beach Township, New Jersey." Adela Callendar occupied the rest of the screen.

"What...the hell is this?" Wilson said, mostly to himself. Davis, who had gotten the sweater over his head but was still struggling with it, stopped to look, too.

" ...and do you think you'll be able to evacuate the island completely, Mr. Mayor?" Callendar asked.

"Well, we're doing our best, Adela, that's all I can tell you at this point." Harper's voice was distorted by static and other interference. "We have over ten thousand residents, and we estimate that at least half of them are on the island at the moment, along with an unknown number of tourists. We've got all lanes on the Causeway going out except one, reserved for large military transports, buses, and other vehicles coming in to evacuate large groups of people. We've got several helicopters on the way, and every boat on Barnegat Bay has been deputized with orders to go back and forth between the island and the mainland."

"It sounds like the island is in good hands," Callendar said.

Wilson's blood boiled.

"Well, we're trying. Just say a prayer for us, please."

"We certainly will, Mr. Mayor. Thank you for your time."

"Thank you, Adela."

The lefthand sidebar slid away, returning the screen exclusively to Callendar.

"We'll go to a commercial break right now, and will be right back with Dr. Daniel Kennard, a tsunami expert who is Director of the Pacific Marine Environmental Laboratory in Seattle. We'll check back again with Mayor Donald Harper, in charge of the evacuation effort on Long Beach Island, New Jersey. Again, if you're just joining us, the headline today—a massive tidal wave, more accurately known as a tsunami, believed to be the result of a terrorist bomb plot gone awry, has formed in the Atlantic Ocean and is at this hour moving on a direct course..."

"This is bullshit," Wilson said, his eyes glazing over. "Harper shouldn't be talking to anybody. He effectively resigned this morning." He turned to Davis. "That should be you on MSNBC."

Davis's jaw pumped a few times, but nothing came out.

"I'll be damned if the media lets him come out of this looking like a savior," Wilson said. He grabbed his jacket from the back of his chair. "Come on," he said to Davis.

*   *   *

Karen wanted to jam the pedal to the floor and roar up the bridge. She wanted to, but she wouldn't. The risk would be tremendous—the very efficient and disciplined Corporal Moreland undoubtedly knew how to shoot out a car tire. And Karen had a feeling that a few of his friends were on the other side. It would only take a few words into the walkie-talkie to alert them. What was that saying she'd heard on one of those police shows? Something like, "You can outrun a car, but you can't outrun a radio."

She waited until he looked in her direction again; she knew he would. When he did, she held up a hand to her ear as if she was holding her cell phone, and shrugged as if to say, I still can't get through.

When he came over she said, "I'm sorry, Corporal, but could you try on your phone again?"

"Yes, ma'am."

He entered the number and waited. As she fully expected, no one answered.

"Sorry, ma'am, there's no response."

She gripped the wheel and gazed angrily forward. "Well, what am I supposed to do?!" she snapped, using her hand for emphasis. "Do you really think I should just sit here and wait while—"

"Actually, I have an idea," Moreland said. "I've just been told that the local police are sweeping the area, looking for people who haven't gotten out yet. I can tell them what's going on with your boys and ask them to send someone to the house."

"I can't just go over there and get them myself?"

"No, ma'am, I'm sorry."

A tear broke from her eye and ran down her cheek. She wiped it away quickly. "All right, fine."

Moreland replied with a single nod—the same gesture he undoubtedly used with his superiors—and produced the cell phone again.

Her eyes still on that rising stretch of white road with the broken yellow lines running up the middle, Karen whispered another prayer to the God she'd worshipped her entire life.

* * *

A dispatcher received Moreland's call and consulted a hastily written list she'd made of which officers were in which areas. The Ericksons lived on the secluded corner of Julia Avenue and Julia Lane in Holgate. Ted Ramsey was over there. The dispatcher was a thirteen-year veteran and processed the information in a heartbeat—Ramsey was in car twenty-two, a navy-blue '97 Chevy sedan with a burned-out right taillight. She got behind the microphone and made the call.

A few streets over from the Erickson's home, Ramsey was cruising along with the windows open, one big hairy arm hanging out as he looked for any coat-hangerless doors. He hadn't seen any yet and was frankly hoping he wouldn't. He had been born and raised here and was wholly devoted to his job and to the people of this community; he knew them all and cared a great deal for some of them, but he also had a family—a wife and three little girls—and, like many others this day, he didn't want to be on the wrong side of the Causeway when that wall of water came over the horizon.

Then he saw a door conspicuous for its lack of a hanger. Sonofabitch, he swore under his breath as he realized whose house it was. He knew the family better than he cared to—the Connallys. LBI's resident poster family for dysfunctionality. They'd had it all—drinking, drugs, petty theft, violence. Sometimes the two sons lived at home, sometimes they didn't. The daughter had left years ago, dropping out of high school and moving out west somewhere. She'd been the smart one, Ramsey thought. What chance do you have of putting a life together for yourself in that kind of environment?

For all he knew they had left and, just to be defiant, one of the boys purposely left the hanger off the knob. Wouldn't be the first time one of them went out of the way to defy authority.

He parked in the street with the motor running and his temperature rising. He decided to go around the side instead of the front. As he reached the driveway, he noticed there were no cars; the family had three. Another good sign they had in fact left. He tried the door, but it was locked. He pounded on it and rang the bell. He would wait exactly thirty seconds, he told himself. When the deadline passed, he hammered one more time, then turned sideways and rammed it with his shoulder. The cheap deadbolt ripped from the aged molding without resistance.

"Anybody home? Hello?"

There was a strong food smell, which undoubtedly had seeped into the walls and the carpeting and was now a permanent part of the house's personality. He moved quickly from room to room, following a floor plan that matched a hundred other postwar homes in the area. He started in the kitchen, then went into the living room. To the left was a hallway with doors on either side and one at the end. He pushed each one back just far enough to look in. It took no more than a minute to sweep the entire first floor.

Next was the adjoining garage. Entering, he saw cardboard boxes everywhere, some split at the corners with their contents pouring out like entrails. Newspapers were piled dangerously next to the furnace and the water heater. *No risk of a fire after today*, he thought darkly.

As he turned to go back inside the house, a garbled voice cut into the stillness—"Twenty-seven report, twenty-seven report."

He took the walkie-talkie from his belt. "This is twenty-seven. Go ahead."

"Ted, I just got a call from one of the National Guardsmen. He's got Karen Thompson with him. You know the Ericksons, over on Julia and Julia?"

"Sure, Bud and Nancy. Why?"

"Apparently they watch the Thompsons' two boys, and they haven't been answering their phone. Karen works on the mainland and wants to be sure they got off the island. Can you check it out?"

"Soon as I get out of here. I'm in the Connally's house."

"What are you doing there?"

He started down the hallway, his mirror-polished boots clomping on the worn linoleum.

"No hanger on the door. No cars in the driveway, either, so my sense is they left and didn't put one out."

"Big surprise."

"With a little luck they'll take the insurance money and move south."

"That'd be nice."

"Anyway, I'll check out the Erickson place. I'm only two blocks away."

"Right. Over and out."

"Out."

He replaced the unit and went through the living room to the carpeted staircase.

"Hey! Anyone up there?"

He paused, listening, and debated whether or not he should even bother going up. Again, procedure demanded it, but with every second making a difference, was it worth it? What was the logic he was working against? The idea that someone would knowingly stay here? Ramsey was born and raised Catholic and cherished the gift of life as much as anyone, but one amendment to those beliefs was the strong opinion that people could do with their life as they chose, and if someone wanted to sit around waiting for a tsunami to come and subtract them from the population so be it. He knew this was not in step with the dogma of his profession, but that didn't stop him from thinking it.

"Hey, I said is anyone up there?"

Again he paused, and again he heard nothing.

He decided to abandon procedure and get moving to the Erickson's place. They were nice people, good people, people worth being concerned about. These idiots couldn't even spare five seconds to put a goddamn coat hanger on the front door.

Then he heard the groan. It was weak, but it was definitely human.

He bounded up the steps three at a time and came to a short hallway that connected two rooms. Both doors were closed. He tried the right one first and was hit with another vicious stench—unwashed clothes intermingled with the unmistakable aroma of marijuana smoke. The slanted ceiling that followed the angle of the roof were covered with posters of rock bands from all eras—Jimi Hendrix and Led Zeppelin, Judas Priest and Def Leppard, Phish and Dave Matthews. There were empty plastic soda bottles (Dr. Pepper, mostly) and paper plates with dried food pasted on them. But no people. He closed the door before nausea set it.

Opening the second one revealed the source of the groan— sprawled on the bed was Kevin Connally. Early twenties, acne, crew cut, bad teeth, all bones and elbows. His room didn't smell much better than his brother's. His eyes were closed but he was smiling, head arched back slightly, hands on his stomach. On the nightstand beside him was a hypodermic needle. Somehow Ramsey doubted it was for insulin injections.

"Oh, shit...."

He moved in and shook Connally by his knobby shoulders. "Come on, wake up. Snap out of it!"

He slapped him lightly on the cheek (inwardly he wanted to slap him so hard his head spun around like a top, making that *whupwhupwhup!* cartoon sound). Connally just groaned some more.

Ramsey slid his hands under the kid and lifted him. There was virtually no effort required; he couldn't weigh more than a hundred and twenty pounds. It seemed obvious that the drugs were slowly but surely eating him away. How bad was the addiction, he wondered. Was the kid taking in food at all? And where was he getting the cash? Ramsey was pretty sure he didn't have a job. Was he selling to support his habit? And did that mean there was a flow of the stuff on the island? He knew LBI wasn't clean—what town was anymore?—but he was pretty sure it wasn't a major problem. And what about the kid's parents? Did they know what was going on? Even if they didn't, this would mean trouble for them—big trouble. Huge fines, maybe even jail time. Kevin wasn't a minor, but he was still under their roof. Was he one of these kids who forbade their parents from entering his room, and were they stupid enough to obey? *What a friggin' mess*, Ramsey thought. Under different circumstances....

Hoisting Connally over one shoulder, Ramsey turned sideways to get him through the bedroom doorway. He had to exercise some peculiar geometry to turn him again so they could go down the staircase.

A few steps down, Connally began to convulse. It wasn't an unusual response to filling one's system with foreign chemicals, but, in his haste, Ramsey hadn't anticipated the possibility. He released the boy on reflex, then tried to grab him again. It was this second motion that caused him to lose his balance and fall forward. The two of them moved through space in slow motion, time stretching into infinity in every direction. They rejoined at the bottom, Connally bouncing and rolling down the carpeted steps while Ramsey sailed over him. Ramsey's head struck the wall above the landing, knocking him unconscious. Connally continued convulsing for a few minutes, then came to rest. He was not unconscious, per se—he had simply slipped back into his crack-induced state of ephemeral nothingness.

They lay together like lovers as sunlight reached through the vertical blinds and drew long shapes on the carpeting.

* * *

BethAnn had just about reached the entrance/exit to the trailer park when Mrs. Foster popped into her head.

She would be eighty-nine this year. Eighty-nine and still kicking, as she liked to say. *Kicking is hardly the word I would use*, BethAnn thought. The woman moved at about the speed of evolution. She had more wrinkles than a dried apple. And she wore a wig that was so phony it should've had a chin strap.

But what really irked BethAnn about her, although for the life of her she couldn't understand why, was the way she shuffled her feet—*shh-shh-shh-shh*—like pieces of sandpaper being rubbed together. She could hear the woman outside her window in the mornings, putting out the garbage, then shuffling back into her Fleetwood doublewide—*shh-shh-shh-shh*. How long had she been doing that? BethAnn often wondered. Did she do it when she was younger, back in the early Jurassic?

Mrs. Foster also wore the same thing every damn day—that white-and-light-blue floral sundress, the one with the food stains and the frayed hemline. Easy on, easy off. You could even sleep in it. The irony of being critical of someone else's hygiene never occurred to BethAnn. Her own considerable odors were acceptable, but she found those of others revolting beyond description.

Everyone else in the LBI Trailer Park loved Mrs. Foster. She was small and sweet, quick with a smile and a reassuring, grandmotherly sentiment. She seemed to have an interminable supply of warm wishes and positive thoughts. She would apologize profusely if you needed help with something and she couldn't give it. She would first apologize, then explain in detail how she once was able to do so much, back in the days when Ike was President and you could walk the streets of Manhattan at night with no worries.

BethAnn was certain she would not have heard about the wave; the woman did not own a television set. (For the life of her, BethAnn simply could not understand this—she had no problem watching TV all day long now. It would be nearly impossible not to when you were old and infirm and there was very little else you could do.) When she walked to her car on workdays, she would see Mrs. Foster's smiling face by the window near her door. She'd been in Mrs. Foster's trailer just once and remembered there was an easy chair over there. Alongside it was one of those lamp/magazine rack combos, and it was stuffed to the gills. She didn't notice what magazines they were, but she made an educated guess that they were typical "old-woman stuff"—*Reader's Digest* and all that AARP crap. Whatever the case, she had not seen a TV set anywhere.

So now, BethAnn suddenly found herself in conflict. First of all, she knew—knew—what the correct moral choice was. She knew damn well what she should do—she should make the effort. Regardless of what comes from it, she'd have done the Right Thing.

But there were problems with this, and they zoomed through her frantic mind in a blur. For one, their trailers were deep in the park—almost in the farthest corner, in fact. Furthermore, getting Mrs. Foster into the car might not be so easy. She probably had dozens of sentimental items she'd want to drag along. It would be bad enough losing time having to explain the situation to her—and there was no guarantee she'd even believe it—and then to have to lug boxes of carnival glass and tarnished silver jewelry, or whatever.... There was also the possibility she wouldn't even want to go—she might adopt that dramatic "I'm too old, it's time for me to die anyhow" attitude. Was risking your life just to hear that crap really worth it?

Something else occurred to her—she wasn't the only god-damn person who lived over here. There were dozens of others. Surely someone else would check on her....

Of course someone will, she told herself. She'll be fine.

The final factor was this—she'd heard that the police were making a sweep of the area for anyone who hadn't gotten the word. *That's it,* BethAnn's mind-voice said sharply. *One of LBI's finest will throw her in the back seat whether she wants to go or not.*

And the best part of all is that nobody will ever know you had any of these thoughts in the first place.

A chill came over her like a winter breeze, and she got the car moving again. She felt another layer of self-hate settle over the existing quantity like a fresh bedsheet settles over a mattress. Then she gathered all the evidence of this peculiar self-conversation and buried it 4,000 leagues down in her mind, in a holding area that was growing ever closer to full capacity.

*   *   *

Sarah Collins and Dave Dolan had managed to record every notable reading from every instrument even though the damn phone had been ringing almost nonstop for the last hour.

One of the callers had been the public relations director from Rutgers, who instructed them not to speak to members of the media. Collins couldn't imagine that they'd even know where to call but, sure enough, not more than ten minutes later someone from NBC was on the line asking for an update. She told the reporter he had the wrong number because she couldn't think of anything better to say. She was amazed the reporter had managed to zero in on her so quickly.

As she set the phone back into its cradle, she pondered the career possibilities this experience might bring. She certainly would become something of a minor celebrity in the oceanographic community, as the person who spotted and then charted the first North Atlantic tsunami in decades. Would it help her take the next step, whatever that was? Maybe. Then again, maybe not. It might be considered little more than a novelty. Perhaps she could write a book about it.

She got back into her chair. Dolan lingered nearby with his clipboard as Collins trained her eyes on the main monitor. She sipped a Diet Coke and waited. When the numbers hiccupped again, she almost choked.

"Christ!"

Dolan turned and saw the numbers briefly before they switched back to a more normal reading.

"That wasn't what I thought it was," he said dully.

"Let me make sure," Collins said, leaning forward and running a quick diagnostic. As she feared, the instruments were fine—the tide gauge really had picked up an open-sea rise of almost six feet.

And that was just the first wave in the group.

"My God," she said. "This thing's a monster. Oh...my...God!"

"Holy shit," was all Dolan could add.

"I've got to call Trenton," she said, getting back up. There was the slightest quaver in her voice. "This is unbelievable."

NINE

*T*he President of the United States sat with his National Security Advisor, Kathryn Moore, and followed the story on FOX News. The Vice President had been with them briefly, then left for a meeting at the Pentagon. The Secretary of State was currently in New York, at the UN.

On the left half of the TV screen, field reporter Rob Little, on only his fourth assignment for the network, stood on the shoulder of Route 72, on the eastbound side. Behind him were three long lines of traffic, heading out. They were moving, but not at any great speed. Red and blue police lights swirled at various points in the distance. On the other half of the screen, anchor Steve Shephard sat behind the news desk in the FOX offices in New York, dealing questions and nodding at the answers. And in the lower left corner, perhaps in bad taste but there nevertheless, was a digital clock with "Time Until Tsunami Strikes" printed underneath it. Minutes, seconds, and tenths of a second were represented, the latter a decision by the producer to heighten the tension. The two digits were moving so swiftly they were indistinguishable, the last one little more than a blur.

"I would have expected FOX to show more class," the President said, nodding toward it.

"They all have one now," Moore said. The President shook his head.

"With less than an hour to go," Shephard was saying, "do the authorities in the area now believe they'll be able to get everyone off the island?"

"They aren't saying, Steve," Little replied. "We've learned that Long Beach Island, or 'LBI,' as the locals call it, is home to approximately 11,000 people. One of our math wizards worked up some numbers for us—" he consulted a handful of papers that had previously been out of view, "and we determined that roughly fifty people would have to pass this spot where I'm standing every minute in order for 6,000 to go by and still maintain a reasonable safety margin. In the half hour since we got here, with the crew helping to count, we have yet to see more than forty in any given minute."

The President shook his head again. "My God. Are the choppers and boats on their way?"

"Yes, Mr. President."

"How many?"

Moore consulted her own paperwork. "There are sixty-four helicopters and twenty-seven speedboats within range that can reach the island before the deadline. Coast Guard, National Guard, Army, Navy...everything."

"What about private craft? Have they been deputized?"

"Yes. We don't have exact numbers on those, though. It's a catch-as-catch-can situation. We simply don't know who has what, or where the owners are."

"And no chance of landing a big plane on the island's main road? We could get a hundred or so people out in one go."

"No, sir. There would barely be enough room to land, let alone take off again. And that would presume the roads were clear, which they won't be." She paused, frowned, then added the caveat that couldn't be avoided. "Even at the end."

The leader of the free world leaned forward, elbows on his knees, and put his hands together as if in prayer. He raised them until the tips of his fingers were touching his lips.

"My God, Kathryn, there must be something more we can do."

Moore wanted to wave a magic wand and come up with the perfect answer. But she didn't have a magic wand, and, as with so many other problems of this magnitude, there was no perfect answer.

Elsewhere around the nation, interest in the crisis was continuing to grow. In Manhattan, a bar called Lenny's put a handwritten sign in the window notifying passersby that they could come in and try a new drink called the "Long Beach Wave Rider" for only one dollar while following the story's latest developments on five screens, each featuring a different news channel.

In Grand Bank, Newfoundland, where the last tidal wave had struck the Eastern Seaboard in 1929, the Methodist Church held an impromptu prayer service. Forty-three people attended, including two survivors of the '29 strike. The minister based his sermon on Exodus 14:21–22, where Moses and his followers escaped Egypt by parting the Red Sea.

Back at the Rutgers Marine Field Station in Tuckerton, the two scientists who first detected the tsunami had began loading their personal items into their respective vehicles. Dr. Sarah Collins, who drove an old Chevy pickup, also loaded as much of the Rutgers equipment as possible. She knew the big wheels over there would appreciate it, and brownie points were brownie points, after all. Dave Dolan, her assistant, continued to monitor the wave between trips to his car, scribbling as many notes as his aching hand would permit, hoping to record as much data on this once-in-a-lifetime event as possible.

Regina Thomas, New Jersey's Secretary of the Department of State, had called Tuckerton twice for updates and would certainly call again. Like her boss, she was fishing around for something positive, something encouraging. Perhaps the tsunami would somehow die down, lose steam—at least one expert had scoffed at the notion of a tidal wave reaching the Jersey shore given the relatively shallow depth of the water over the continental shelf. Collins said that was not a theory she could support given the readings. The secretary asked if it might "change course." Collins patiently explained that a tsunami wasn't like a hurricane, one force traveling in one direction. In simplest terms, it was a series of concentric, expanding circles, like those that radiate outward after you throw a rock into a pond. As far as their instruments could tell, several waves were on course and on schedule.

Thomas also asked if radiation from the dirty bomb posed a threat to the health of coastal residents, or the local fishing industry. Collins said she doubted it, as it would be so widely-dispersed, but hurried to add that this wasn't her area of expertise. She urged the Secretary to pursue the issue with the EPA.

On LBI, at the Undertoe Service Center in Beach Haven, twenty-three cars formed a line down the shoulder of Long Beach Boulevard. The drivers honked incessantly, shouting that no more than a buck or two for gas was necessary. But there was always some idiot who wanted just a bit more or didn't have cash and had to pay by credit card. At one point a guy in a light blue minivan asked for a full tank, and when the attendant—a tall, sleepy-looking Middle Eastern kid—refused, a heated argument ensued. That prompted another man to get out of his car and tell the van driver the kid was right. That descended into a fistfight, the van driver's horrified wife and kids watching through the windows as their father rolled around on the gum-spotted cement with some bulky stranger. A cop who had been directing traffic nearby came over and issued a general order on the spot (which he was not technically allowed to do, but he doubted anyone would bother to stop by town hall and check the books at the moment)—each vehicle would be allowed three dollars' worth of gas. No one had to pay, but the attendants would keep a running tab and the station would be later reimbursed by the town. The idea was received so well that the officer reported it to his chief, and within minutes it became an islandwide decree. He returned to his post half proud of himself and half begging God that three bucks would be enough and that no one would run dry halfway over the bridge.

In Loveladies a kid named Freddie Palmer was having a field day. Palmer was a high school dropout who had learned the art of theft before he reached his teens, and had a police record a mile long by the time he was twenty-one. He'd been in and out of a handful of juvenile detention centers and once spent two months in the county slammer for stealing a car, driving it into the middle of the Pine Barrens, putting a cinder block on the gas pedal, and ramming it into a tree. He walked around in filthy clothes with his hair unkempt and a crooked smile on his face, purposely making eye contact with people just to make them uncomfortable. The cops hated his guts and fantasized about the day when they could nail him doing something really hefty and put him away for good. Since so many homes had been abandoned in haste, many of them were unlocked, so he decided to try every door on every house. He had no intention of sticking around any longer than necessary; he just wanted to gather up a little booty before he made his escape. It would be all but impossible for anyone to prove his guilt, and opportunities like this didn't come along that often.

Back in Brighton Beach, sixty-four-year-old Alma Wattley wanted desperately to jump into her '98 Ford Crown Victoria and get the hell out of town, but she couldn't quite bring herself to do it. Known affectionately among her neighbors as "The Cat Lady," she had taken in hundreds of strays over the years, had cared for and loved each and every one of them. At this point in her life she had only twelve, and at this particular moment, just eleven of them had been located.

*　　*　　*

Brian was calling both of them now, raising his voice in an angry way Jennifer had never heard before and didn't even know he was capable of.

She could hear him loud and clear, knew he was no more than maybe a hundred yards away. But she had made the decision not to answer. If she answered, he would insist they leave. She looked at her watch, knew how much time was left. Brian would make her go, would physically force her if necessary. He was being the responsible adult; she knew that. But she still had to find Mark. She couldn't just leave him here. Brian didn't understand that, didn't care about him the way she did. No one cared about him the way she did—not Brian, her mother, Mark's mother, or Mark's pathetic stepfather.... He was all alone in the world, this sweet, wonderful person who wouldn't harm a fly, who took pictures of animals and wrote poems and bought ice-cream cones for children with money he barely had. And no one cared about him one goddamn bit.

She sat down, brought her knees up, and cried. She made sure to keep it quiet so Brian wouldn't hear. He kept calling, and at one point he must've come within twenty feet. She was scared then, scared and unsure what she would do if he discovered her. But it never came to that—he turned and went the

154

other way. His voice faded, and then disappeared entirely. She was alone, alone and able to do whatever she wanted.

She stood up, tears still running down her cheeks, and headed in the opposite direction. Through her phlegm-clogged throat she yelled for him. She ran in whatever direction the sandy path took her, knowing she had no idea where she was going, and only the faintest notion of how to get back.

*   *   *

Brian returned to the car to get his cell phone out of the glove compartment. He rarely used it, couldn't even remember the last time. He was at the store 24/7 and had almost no social life, so no one ever called him. The store was his mistress. How sad is that?

He shook off this familiar question and, standing there with the passenger-side door open and one foot on the jamb like some highway trooper, turned the phone on. It beeped once and lit up, then went dead again. He repeated the action and the same thing happened.

"Shit."

Of course the battery was dead—why wouldn't it be?

He leaned into the car and went back into the glove compartment. There was a charger in there somewhere, he recalled. Came with the phone. He'd never used it, but now was as good a time as any to learn. As soon as he found it he realized it had to be plugged into the cigarette lighter. He wasn't even sure where that was, as he didn't smoke and never had. It wasn't anywhere in plain view, for instance under the stereo like it was in Jennifer's car.

After some frantic searching he found it inside the ashtray and mumbled something about what a stupid place that was to put it. His annoyance upgraded to near-rage when everything

155

was finally hooked up and the phone still wasn't charging. Two more precious minutes were blown consulting the owner's manual, which had a too-general-to-be-useful table of contents and no index. He finally found a reference to the fact that the car needed to be running for the charger to function, and cursed himself because this was something he already knew. From the passenger seat he fumbled the key from his pocket and stuck it in the ignition. The phone beeped the moment he turned it on, this time in a gleeful sign of life.

He took a deep breath and dialed 911. The thought that damn-near every cell phone in the area might be in use and that he'd have trouble acquiring a signal was set aside for the moment. Miraculously, someone picked up on the first ring.

"Emergency services, how can I help you?"

"Please put me through to the Long Beach Township Police Department right away. This is an emergency."

He sounded like he'd just finished the Boston Marathon. He put a hand to his chest to calm himself down.

"What is the nature of the emergency?"

"I'm at the Forsythe Wildlife Refuge looking for two missing people. Please put me through to the Long Beach police."

"Hold please."

The line went quiet, and for a terrifying moment he thought he'd lost the connection.

"God, no...."

He knew how lucky he'd been to get through in the first place, knew it was the same kind of luck that enabled some people to call Ticketmaster during the first five minutes Bruce Springsteen tickets went on sale and get floor seats at face value. What were the odds he could do it again? A hundred to one? A thousand?

Then, mercifully, another person—the same woman, as it turned out, who had asked Officer Ramsey to see what was going on at the Erickson house—said, "Long Beach Police Department, how can I help you?"

"My name is Brian Donahue, and I'm sitting in my car in the Forsythe Wildlife Refuge, at the southernmost end of the island. There are two people missing here, and I need help fast. Can you send an officer? Preferably someone with a bullhorn?"

"I'll try to get someone over there, but all of our officers are tied up right now, as you might expect. There's only about an hour left. If you can't find these missing folks soon and an officer doesn't arrive...."

There was a brief pause, and then Brian said, "I understand."

*　*　*

Mark was down to two rolls. He'd shot more than fifteen. There were plenty of great pictures captured in those long brown strips of celluloid. He had a gut feeling the terrapin shots would be the big winners. Those were his "definites"—the type that motivated his editor to give him future assignments. Others were certainly usable, too, maybe not as covers, but as interiors. He felt proud and satisfied. The latter was a rare and precious sensation that only came at the end of a long shoot. The job was done, the objective achieved. It was all downhill from here.

He sat in the sand, hung his arms loosely around his half-raised knees, and watched the surf. He was tired, he realized. Tired right down to his bones. When it came to photography, it wasn't the duration that drained you, it was the intensity. A sprint, not a marathon. He was so hyperfocused that he found himself shaking at times. The anxiety, the eagerness to get those shots was almost overwhelming. If nothing else it certainly made great demands on your energy. He had learned this long ago, planned for it by taking in a lot of carbs and sugars before every assignment. But even that didn't help much. It was as if every muscle, every nerve, every thought came together in one ultraconcentrated effort. Perhaps the results were fulfilling, but the expense to the system was brutal. It was a hangover of sorts, he thought as he sat there with the acrid scent of sand and salty sea air drifting through his nostrils.

His thoughts turned to Jennifer. He could picture her sitting in the back of that ancient warehouse, under the glow of that ancient desk lamp, pecking away on that ancient keyboard, her retinas slowly degenerating from that ancient monitor. She was a trooper, that one. The all-American Good Girl. She complained a little when she found out she had to go in, but not much. He had a feeling he knew why she'd drawn the low card. He knew what BethAnn Mosley was all about two minutes after he'd met her. He'd always been able to see into people. He could detect the bad as well as the good and he knew she was wicked. His gifted insight was what fed his ever-growing love for the girl he hoped to marry someday—he saw the good, knew it was pure and whole, and that she was the real thing. He was lucky to have her. He would do whatever it took to hold onto her. She was the future.

He got out the cell phone again. He figured he'd give her a call, just to say hi and see how things were going. He held the phone up and stared at it, his thumb on the "ON" button. Then he wondered, *Should I really do this? I don't want to come across any needier than I already do.*

This worried him constantly. He wanted her to know that he needed her, but he didn't want her to start thinking he was desperate. He didn't want her to feel he was a burden, a weight around her neck. Whenever he thought of this, he thought about a kid in high school named Doug Troost whose father had been dying of gradual heart failure. The family was not able to afford nursing care at home, so Doug's mom watched him during the day and worked evenings, with Doug taking the night shift. Mark never forgot the put-upon expression Doug always wore. It was as if there were an invisible 5,000-pound slab resting on his back every minute of every day. When his father finally passed away during their senior year, Doug cried for weeks, Mark remembered, but there was also a palpable sense of relief, a freshness and a light in his eyes that had not been there before. It couldn't be suppressed.

He feared becoming like Doug Troost's father to Jennifer—not a physical dependent, but an emotional one. He feared the day when he picked her up from work or from her house and sensed—even just a little—that same put-upon air that had given Doug Troost's spirit such a beating all those years ago. She'd stop thinking of him as her great love and start thinking of him as a chore. They'd still spend time together, but she'd dread rather than relish it. The enthusiasm would be gone, replaced by habit and discipline. And then, ultimately, she'd wake one morning gasping for breath and realize she had to put an end to it.

This thought literally terrified him. Sometimes he got stuck thinking about it late at night and couldn't fall asleep. Sometimes he dreamed about it and was jolted awake. And every time he found the reassurance he needed in only one thought—*I will not do anything to cause it.*

He put the phone back in the bag, then lay back and laced his hands together behind his head. It was cloud-watching time. He felt particularly good all of a sudden—tired, but content. He was proud of his self-discipline, and the thought crossed his mind: *I might just be able to swing this relationship after all.* And someday, he decided, he'd tell her about all this; after they were married, in their own home, and had a flock of kids. He'd tell her about all his insecurities, all the demons he kept at bay while they were dating. Maybe it would make him seem heroic, privately suffering to maintain their love. He could deal with that. There were worse things in life than having the girl you love think of you as a hero.

What made him take the phone back out of the bag and finally turn it on was the unnamed restlessness that had driven him throughout most of his life—that undying desire to do something useful with his time. He enjoyed watching the clouds pass for a few minutes, but couldn't lie here all day long.

A quick calculation told him he could, if necessary, get back to the car, take a quick trip over to the Acme, get a few more rolls of film, and get back before Jennifer arrived. What he needed to know before even bothering to go was whether his photo editor wanted any subjects in particular. He'd say he was finished with the potential cover shots, maybe fill him in briefly about the diamondback pictures, then say he had time for more—was there anything else they needed?

He returned to a sitting position and turned the phone on. Immediately upon acquiring a signal the message appeared on the little screen, "You have voice mail."

He smiled, thinking—hoping—Jennifer had left him a little love message. She often did that—"Just calling to see how you're doing and to let you know I'm thinking about you," or, "Just called to say I love you. Call me back when you get a chance."

He dialed into his mail and waited. It took longer than usual for the call to go through, which he found peculiar—he was in the middle of nowhere and couldn't imagine how much interference there'd be. He checked the screen to see if the signal was flat. It wasn't. In fact it was reading full strength. He shrugged and brought the phone back to his head.

"Your voice mail is full, please check your messages."

"That's ridiculous," he said aloud, annoyed. Hardly a week seemed to pass without some technical problem affecting his life.

He hit "1" and "enter," then heard, "You have twenty unplayed messages. Press the star key to hear new messages."

He gave a quick snort and shook his head. "Pathetic."

Then he hit the star key and listened.

*   *   *

Sarah Collins called her former professor again. Dr. Kennard answered on the first ring.

"Sarah?"

"Daniel, I'm going to read some numbers to you." She had a pile of papers in her hand, all fresh printouts. In the background, Dolan was starting to load things into boxes.

When she was finished, Kennard said, "Are you certain those readings are correct? Are you absolutely sure?"

"Yes. I did them all twice, and I ran a systems diag, too. Everything's working fine."

There was a pause, and then, "Listen, Sarah, as soon as you've sent out the necessary alerts, get the hell out of there. If those readings are right, you're in the path of one of the biggest tsunamis in recorded history."

*   *   *

Officer Jeff Mitchell, in his Harvey Cedars squad car with the lights swirling but without the siren on, worked his way down to the Causeway, riding mostly along the northbound shoulder, which, by order of Mayor Harper, had been left clear for emergency vehicles. All other lanes, including the shoulder on the southbound side, were open for general use and now flowed toward the bridge. Harper had also ordered that all cars parked on either shoulder be removed. Regardless, Mitchell encountered two, which he circumvented simply by deviating onto the sidewalk. As the vehicle bounced and scraped along the cement, Carolyn King remained silent and stone-faced in the passenger seat.

He was forced to use the siren when he reached the bridge, where traffic wasn't moving as fast as it should've been. He felt a twinge of guilt as he broke the flow to get through. *It's only a few seconds, but will they count later on? Did I just sign the death warrant of someone at the end of the line?*

He peered over at his passenger, the reason he had to stall the traffic in the first place. She was staring straight ahead through the window, expressionless and apparently not the least bit concerned. Why was that so surprising?

He tried to be empathetic, tried to put himself behind her eyes. As a father of two, it really wasn't all that tough. There was a part of him that admired her ruthlessness, her extreme focus. He'd had good parents and a good, solid childhood. Had they made similar decisions for him, decisions they never told him about, that he'd never know about? And would he do the same in a similar situation?

Of course you would. How could you not?

He guessed, accurately, that Mrs. King was under severe emotional strain. In fact, it was agonizing for her, pure torture. He felt this instinctively, as only a good cop can, and his attitude toward her softened. He wished he could do more, do something to soothe her soul. But he'd seen people like her all his life, knew the personality well. She was practical and pragmatic to a fault. Words were no substitute for action—she wanted results. The only way she'd feel better about her missing daughter was by rescuing her. Period.

He took the cell phone from his belt and flipped it open.

"I'm going to try calling Mark's home. Maybe he's there."

"Didn't the newspaper say he hardly ever was?"

"Yes, but it won't hurt to try."

He had to redial the number sixteen times before it worked. As soon as the call went through, he switched to the speaker.

"Hello?"

It was a male voice, low and gruff, and with the slightest hint of an accent—Southern or Midwestern, Mitchell thought.

"Is this the home of Mark White?"

"Yeah, who's this?"

Mitchell's spine tingled—not from joy, but from wariness. He'd heard voices like this before and it was that of a suspicious, unsympathetic man. He didn't like to profile, but wasn't it part of a cop's job, at least sometimes, to do just that? Wasn't it a resource like any other that, when used responsibly, held genuine value?

"Officer Jeff Mitchell, Harvey Cedars Police."

"Police, huh?" There was a pause. "Do you know where Mark is?"

"That's why I'm calling. I was hoping maybe you did." Mitchell remembered the girl at the *SandPaper* saying something about Mark having a mother and stepfather. "Is his mom there?"

"Yeah, but she's pretty upset right now. She doesn't know where he is, either, and we're trying to get packed up and out of here."

"May I speak with her, please? It's important."

There were some indefinable noises, then Mitchell heard the stepfather say, "Angie?" faintly. He glanced at King from the corner of his eye. She looked thoroughly disgusted. He could almost read her thoughts—*She's never going to see that boy again. I'm not getting mixed up with a family like that. I wouldn't dirty my hands with—*

"Hello?" It was a woman's voice, light and airy. She didn't sound particularly upset, Mitchell noted, but she did sound thoroughly confused.

"Mrs. White?"

"Yes?"

"This is Officer Jeff Mitchell, Harvey Cedars Police Department."

"Who?"

King rolled her eyes.

"Jeff Mitchell. Harvey Cedars Police."

"He's a cop," the stepfather said impatiently in the background.

"Yes, officer? What's the trouble?"

"I'm in a squad car heading toward the Forsythe Wildlife Refuge."

"The Forsythe...Wildlife...Refuge?" She said it with the halting uncertainty of a child just learning the words.

"Yes, ma'am. I believe your son, Mark, may be there. At least that's what they told me at the *SandPaper* office."

"Oh."

Silence. Mitchell waited for more. He and Carolyn King locked eyes for a moment.

"Ms. White?"

"Yes?"

"Can you confirm that Mark's there?"

More silence. Mitchell wondered if perhaps the word "confirmed" threw her off.

He was just about to rephrase the question when she said, "Uh, no, I can't. I...I'm not sure where he is."

King shook her head.

"Do you know about the tidal wave?" Mitchell asked.

"Uh, yes. Yes I do. We were just about to leave when you called."

"Aren't you worried about your son, not knowing where he is?"

"My son is quite capable of taking care of himself," she said with as much force as her butterfly's voice would permit. *Was*

that pride or anger? Mitchell wondered. Probably the latter. He
sensed there was a lot more brewing beneath the surface in the
White household than he'd figured on, but frankly he didn't
want to get into it right now.

"Well, ma'am, I understand he may be with his girlfriend and
that they may not be aware of the danger."

"You could try his cell phone," she said helpfully.

"Have you?"

"Yes...a little earlier."

You didn't even need to be a seasoned cop to know this was
a lie. Mitchell's stomach knotted. He was a fair and objective
man, but people like this made him wonder if human beings
really were the superior race on the planet.

"And...?"

"I couldn't get through."

The stepfather piped up in the background, "What the hell's
he grillin' you for?" Jeff heard the voice of someone who had
had his fair share of encounters with the authorities. "We gotta
get the hell outta here."

"Well, please keep trying. If you reach him, let him know
that a police car will be arriving soon."

"Oh, thank you, officer," she said magnanimously. "Thank
you so much."

Mitchell could tell she was genuinely grateful—not because
someone was going to try to find her son, but because she felt
the burden had been lifted from her shoulders. He also fully
understood in that moment why Mark didn't spend much time
at home. He applauded the kid for having the guts to get out of
there, away from those two, and to try making something of
himself.

He terminated the call without another word, thinking, *If we
all survive this, I'm going to find out just what goes on in that house.*
He wasn't even sure if he could, legally—Mark was obviously over

eighteen, so what responsibilities did his mother have to him? She still had a moral responsibility, yes, but he didn't get the impression morality was something that kept her awake at night. Legally, on the other hand....

"How the hell can anyone be so—" he grumbled angrily to himself, then, startled, he remembered he had a passenger.

"Sorry about that, Mrs. King."

He looked over at her, waiting for an admonishment.

Instead, without even the subtlest change in demeanor, she said, "That's all right, I was just thinking the same thing."

He allowed himself a smile and a little laugh.

"We're going to find your daughter, you know. Don't worry."

From the corner of his eye he saw something that blew him away—a small tear rolling down Carolyn King's cheek. Thinking she'd be embarrassed if she knew he'd noticed, he kept his eyes squarely on the road and said nothing.

To his surprise, she made no attempt to wipe the tear away. "I believe that," she said in a near-whisper.

*　　*　　*

Marie was at the window, peering through the blinds. All of her personal items had been removed from her desk and placed in a brown paper shopping bag. The bag and her pocketbook sat on her desk chair, standing primly upright, waiting for her.

"He's here," she said, and turned back. She almost jogged to the chair to retrieve the stuff—Harper couldn't remember the last time he even saw her walk fast.

"Good luck, Marie," he said.

"Thanks, Donald."

She turned to go, then stopped and turned back. "When are you leaving?"

Her husband, Art, began honking wildly outside.

"Soon. Very soon."

"Don't wait too long," she said, sounding motherly again.

"I won't."

She reached for the knob, then paused and looked back one last time. Her eyes became glassy and red-rimmed. Her lower lip quivered just slightly.

"It's been an honor working with you," she said, her voice weakened by despair but steady. "You're a good man, Don."

Harper smiled. "Thanks, Marie. You've been great, too. I wouldn't have wanted anyone else in the world as my secretary."

She smiled back. "God bless," she said hoarsely, and went out. Art was honking more frantically now, yet Harper barely heard it. It was somehow detached from his own reality, soft and distant, like a radio playing in another room. He heard the car door slam, then the squeal of tires as if the driver was an insolent teenager.

He wandered over to Marie's desk, to the pile of messages she'd organized so he'd have no trouble finding them once she was gone. He picked them up, shuffled through them. All unimportant, insignificant. More media outlets, well-wishers, locals sniffing around for brownie points by asking what they could do.

He did need to make a call to Chief Garrett to see what was going on. This led him back into his office, where he picked up the phone and began dialing. Then he heard the front door open again. His first thought was that Marie had forgotten something, some personal item. Art would be pissed. Harper didn't know him that well, but he knew the man had a short fuse. He was one of those bulky waterfront guys with the broad, three-step nose and sweaty crew cut.

He put the phone back in its cradle and went out. If he listed the one hundred people he thought were most likely to show up at this moment, Tom Wilson wouldn't be on it. He wouldn't be on any list of people Harper thought he was likely to see, except perhaps in court. Elliot Davis was trailing close behind him, looking sheepish and uncomfortable.

"What are you doing here, Tom?" Harper asked. It came out quite pleasantly considering the emotions behind it. It was the political training, he thought.

Wilson, as nervous as a fifth-grader giving an oral report, said, "We saw you on MSNBC."

"How'd I do?"

Wilson jabbed his forefinger at him like a parent scolding a naughty child. "What I want to know is what the hell you think you're doing."

Harper acknowledged the finger and Wilson's reddening face and couldn't help but smile.

"The finger, Tom—what bad form."

"This man right here," Wilson went on, now pointing the finger at Davis, who jerked back as though it was a loaded handgun, "should have been there. He's the one who should be speaking for LBI, not you. Your time is up."

Harper put his hands in his pockets and began rocking back and forth on the balls of his feet. "Oh, really? Well, that's fine with me. In fact I have to call MSNBC's Adela Callendar back in a little bit. Would you like to do it instead, Elliot? There shouldn't be any more than, oh, two or three million people watching the broadcast. You're more than welcome. How about it?"

"Well, I...I guess I could."

"In fact, someone needs to call Chief Garrett, too. Would you care to do it?" He walked back to his desk, picked up the phone, and tapped in the number. In the meantime Davis checked his watch and glanced out the window.

"Len? It's Don. Hi, hi. So what's going on? Oh, okay...I see. Well, hang on a sec."

He covered the mouthpiece and said, "Elliot, there's a school bus broken down on Ocean Boulevard between Lillie and

Texas. Twenty-nine kids on board. What do you suggest they do?"

Davis's eyes moved around crazily as he searched for an answer. "Well, you could...I mean, I suppose what you could do is, um...."

"You can't suppose at a time like this, Elliot. They need a decision."

"Well...."

Harper leaned forward slightly, eyebrows raised, "Yes?"

Davis threw his hands up. "Christ, I have no idea. How the hell should I know?"

Harper brought the phone back to his ear. "Len, a group of military helicopters are due to land at one of the pickup points on the beach a few blocks down from there, by Louisiana Avenue. Have them begin taking those children out as soon as they get there. The kids get priority over the adults, on my order. If anyone tries to weasel their way ahead of them, forcibly remove them."

He put the phone back in its cradle and slowly came forward. The smile was suddenly gone.

"This isn't a game, Elliot. There are real people out there, trying to get off this island before a wall of water like nothing we've ever seen comes and wipes it clean. Some of them won't make it, no matter how hard we try or how fast we move. People are going to die before the day is over. This isn't a figure written into one of your bank ledgers that you can erase. This is real. If you can't handle it—if you can't handle that kind of pressure—then you're the one who shouldn't be here. You're the one who shouldn't be trying to get into this job, because it's times like this when leadership matters the most. The phone call I just made was part of the routine. It wasn't a big deal, just routine. Finding solutions, making decisions—that's what it's all about. It's not about making speeches and shaking hands and getting the best tables in restaurants. It's about rising to the occasion when things aren't going well."

He was no more than two feet from Davis, and the latter was flushed and sweaty, regarding Harper nervously.

"Now, do you want the job? If so, it's all yours. This is your big chance." He picked up the phone on Marie's desk and held it out. "MSNBC is waiting for a call. They'll want an update on what's going on. After that you'll need to talk to Garrett again, then the National Guard, the governor, and maybe the White House. How about it? Can you handle it?"

Wilson watched the exchange with wide-eyed fascination.

"I...I...."

"Come on, Elliot. You want to talk the talk, you gotta walk the walk." Suddenly, Harper smiled again. "Oh, and did I mention that a good captain always goes down with his ship?"

At first it looked like Davis had fallen off the edge of Marie's desk because he was leaning back so far. But then he scrambled to his feet and rushed out without another word, pushing the glass door out of his way while his tie flapped crazily over his shoulder.

Harper straightened his posture, put his hands on his hips, and said, "That was the best guy you could find, Tom?" He shook his head. "Unbelievable."

Wilson, who looked like his dog had just been run over, turned without a word and headed toward the same doors through which his protégé had just escaped. Before he reached them, however, Harper said, "Where do you think you're going?"

"What?"

"I've got no secretary, and I can't do all this by myself. Get on a telephone."

Wilson paused, looked away, then looked back. "Are you serious?"

"Yes, I'm goddamned serious!" He snapped his fingers and pointed to the phone. "I need you to get Governor Mayfield on the line for me."

"But I...I was going to—"

"I forgive you, okay? Now get to it!"

Harper unleashed that smile again—the smile that could charm a dying man out of his last heartbeat, the smile that could stop a child from crying. And, perhaps most importantly, the smile that had inspired thousands of voters to leave their homes, drive to the polls, and give this man their unswerving support. The last of Wilson's defenses fell away.

"Anything I can do, Don."

＊　　＊　　＊

Karen was outside her car now, leaning against the door with her arms crossed.

Her neck was sore—sore from looking down at her watch. It was a cheap job she'd bought from a street vendor during her last jaunt to Manhattan. The "gold" would surely fade over time. She got it to wear at the office, nowhere else. Clothes, accessories, anything that went to work fell into the category of "good looking but cheap." You didn't go crazy spending money on work stuff because you weren't being judged on your appearance. You didn't get a raise or a promotion based on the manufacturer of your handbag or how much money was spent on your last haircut. At least not with her job. She was frankly surprised the watch still worked and even looked pretty decent. It couldn't have been more than ten bucks.

She knew how much time was left. She probably knew better than anyone. The radio was on, tuned to NJN. They were giving the most sensible, most useful updates. They were in direct contact with the Rutgers people at the Tuckerton marine station and were getting up-to-the-minute reports on the tsunami's progress.

She also knew exactly how much time had passed since Corporal Moreland had spoken to the Long Beach police dispatcher—twenty-four minutes. Almost a half hour. Time was being wasted here. There was only about an hour left, so why hadn't they heard anything? *What the hell is going on?*

She made a decision at that moment that she would stick to more firmly and with greater conviction than any other in her life—the time for bullshitting was over. She'd been more than patient. Much more. It was time to take the matter into her own hands.

It was time to go get her boys.

She marched over to where Moreland was standing, his back turned as he watched his sergeant continue his traffic-flow duties. By the order of Mayor Harper, every "traffic director" along the evac route held up a large sign that said, "DO NOT STOP FOR ANY REASON. VIOLATORS WILL BE PROSECUTED." Moreland's sergeant actually smiled when the order came over the radio. His nerves were as brittle as kindling, and he was sure he was going to shoot someone sooner or later. The combination of the sign and his naturally intimidating appearance—further enhanced by the addition of mirror sunglasses that looked like a prop from a Sylvester Stallone movie—seemed to be working. The traffic was moving more briskly than it had all day.

Karen tapped Moreland on the shoulder. He spun around instantly, as if spring-loaded.

"Yes?"

"It's been almost a half hour," she said, tapping her watch. "I need to know what's happening."

"Ma'am, I—"

"No more of that 'ma'am' shit, Corporal. Are you going to call again? Right now?"

Moreland glanced back at his sergeant briefly, hoping he might get involved and throw him a lifeline. No such luck.

He took the phone from his belt and said, "Yes, I'll call them right now."

He hit "REDIAL" and brought the phone to his head.

"Yes, is this the dispatcher? This is Corporal Moreland again, on the western side of the Causeway. I called about twenty-five minutes ago concer—what? Can you repeat that? Okay, I see. Thank you." He returned the phone to his belt.

"Well?"

"They haven't heard from the officer who was sent over there. They've tried his radio multiple times but received no res—"

Karen walked away from him, toward the car. Then she stopped, turned, and came back.

"I'm getting in my car and going over that bridge. I'm not wasting another second while my kids are over there."

Moreland started to say something, but Karen cut him off before the first syllable by putting a hand up. "You want to try to stop me? Go ahead. But you'll have to use force, because nothing short of that is going to stop me from finding my boys."

She started to walk away again, then turned back one more time and looked him square in the eyes. "If you have any balls at all, you'll radio your friends on the other side and tell them to let me pass."

She pivoted for the last time, got into the car, and gunned the engine, spraying dirt and gravel into the nodding weeds. The tires hit the pavement with a squeal.

Moreland never took his eyes off her. He didn't reach for his rifle, he didn't call for his sergeant. He just watched her. And when she was just about to the top of the bridge, he got out his walkie-talkie and told his counterpart on the other side that a woman in a gray Maxima was headed his way, and that he should only stop her if he didn't have enough trouble already.

TEN

*F*or a while BethAnn thought Lady Luck was—for once—on her side. Was it possible, on this day of all days, that there was no traffic? Had they actually managed to get everyone off the island already? It was eerie, like a post-apocalyptic scenario—the clear blue sky, the wind blowing sand and bits of trash around the streets, but no signs of life. A few cars here and there, doors and windows left open, but no people. Not even a lone dog or cat. Very creepy.

Then, toward the northern end of Beach Haven where Bay Avenue becomes Long Beach Boulevard, the rear of the traffic line came into view. The brake lights of the very last car, a powder-blue Dodge Dart that was new when Nixon was President, were glowing like rubies.

She came up to it fast and stopped about three inches from the bumper. The driver was barely visible—just a cloud of hair and two sets of knobby knuckles on the steering wheel.

Another grandma.

She wondered briefly if this was God's way of paying her back for leaving Ms. Foster behind.

"Come on. Come ON!"

She honked, mostly out of frustration, and wasn't surprised when the old woman didn't react. Probably used to being honked at. Probably been honked at every day for the last two decades.

She let a little space grow between them, then swerved out of the lane to get a look at what was ahead. Just a long line of cars and a few cops on the shoulder, waving them on. They were holding signs that she couldn't read from this distance. "Will Work for Food," maybe? Or how about "Contributions Welcome"? Good a time as any to be running the coin toss, where they set an empty recycling bucket on the side of the road so passing motorists could throw out their loose change. BethAnn never, ever contributed to the coin toss campaigns. The cops or the firemen would occasionally give her withering looks, but she pretended not to see them. She didn't contribute to anything. No charities, no solicitors, not even a solitary dollar folded twice and slipped into the donation can of a Boy Scout standing outside the post office. She didn't leave tips in restaurants, either. She thought people should contribute to her. Who did they think she was? Bill goddamn Gates?

They'll all be out of work in a few hours anyway, she thought with a nasty smile. Then it occurred to her that she'd very likely be out of work, too, and the smile vanished. Everyone would be looking for work. She shivered at the thought of having to go on interviews—dressing up, kissing ass, pretending you really wanted the job.

When the smoke first appeared, creeping over the hood like a ghost, she thought it was exhaust from the Dodge Dart's tailpipe. She perked her head up like a little kid trying to see what was on a tabletop. Her first impulse was to roll down the window and squawk something about the car being a pile of crap, though she was fully aware that she wasn't exactly driving a Rolls Royce herself.

Then a red light flashed on the dashboard. She didn't know one indicator light from the other, but she figured out the meaning of this one quickly enough—it had a little thermometer graphic on it. That could only mean one thing....

"You're kidding me!"

She pulled violently to the shoulder and got out, slamming the door ferociously. Her face was as pink as a boiled ham, her jaw tight like a fist. She didn't notice the other cars that had joined the line on the road. People watched her from behind their closed windows, the screens that shielded them from the increasingly surreal day that was unfolding outside.

Amid the smoke and the snake-like hissing, she found the safety catch with her trembling hands and pulled the hood up, releasing a giant ball of steam. It reeked of antifreeze and whatever industrial coating had been slow-cooking on the inside of the radiator for the last half hour. She gagged and waved it away.

When the air cleared, she took one long, labored look at the smorgasbord of wires, tubes, cables, plugs, cylinders, caps, rotors, and other alien shapes, and wanted to scream. She knew enough about car basics to realize the problem in this case was the radiator, that it probably didn't have enough water or whatever. But she had never actually done any work on a car, so she wasn't even sure where to begin.

She followed the trail of smoke—she still thought of it as smoke rather than steam—and located the radiator. Right smack in the center, inches below her sizeable gut, was an aluminum cap with the legend "REMOVE TO ADD FLUID."

I can do that.

If she'd possessed the patience to read on, what followed would never have happened. In her I-just-learned-something-new enthusiasm, she pressed the flat of her palm on the cap to turn it, and blades of pain shot through her like lightning bolts.

She pulled away with a shriek. A red circle about the size of an Eisenhower dollar formed in seconds, and she knew from past stove accidents that it would transform into a giant blister before the end of the day.

She looked at the car angrily and gave it a kick in the fender. That hurt—her, not the car—but she went out of her way not to show it so as not to give the vehicle any further satisfaction.

When the pain subsided she tried again. This time she covered the cap with the end of her shirt and used the other hand. As soon as it came free, a groan emanated from the radiator. It sounded like an old man on his deathbed. She leaned down for a look inside—the radiator was bone dry. She knew it needed one of two things—antifreeze or water; either would suffice. This was something she'd learned from her ex-husband, though she told herself she'd picked it up somewhere else.

She knew she didn't have either fluid, but she went through the act anyway, opening the trunk and looking under the large vinyl flap that covered the spare tire (which had lost so much air it was useless). Then she felt around under the seats. For a moment she considered asking someone who was driving by if they could help, but this violated a rule she had followed all her life: Don't ask anyone for anything.

She quickly evaluated her surroundings. No convenience stores, no nearby gas stations. No place she could get a quick gallon of water.

Then she realized every home had water, including those that surrounded her right now. There were literally hundreds of them, and that meant all the goddamn water she needed was readily available.

Just to her right was a two-story Cape, white with maroon shutters. A coat hanger was on the front door, an indication that everyone was out (a quick appraisal down the row of neighboring homes told her pretty much everyone had left, and a voice in her mind said, *Better get your butt moving, girl*). She hurried up the steps, hoping beyond hope the door wasn't locked.

It was.

"Why lock the door? What's the fucking point?" She gave it a sharp kick, marking it with a small black smear.

She hustled back down the steps and went to the next house. It, too, was locked tight. So was the next, and the next. She had to try nine houses before she found one that permitted entry—a one-time beach shack that had been glorified by aluminum siding, a large bay window that would allow passersby to see pretty much everything in the front room, and a colorful bed of geraniums. She would've bet her life it was owned by retirees on a fixed income.

Opening the door, she was almost knocked over by the acrid stench of pipe tobacco. The smell had seeped into the '70s-style shag carpeting, the tweed furniture, the paneled walls...it would be impossible to remove. Impossible. The only way to—

Better get your butt moving, girl.

She passed through the living room and found the kitchen easily enough. There was an intersecting area not much bigger than a phone booth to which all four rooms connected—living room, kitchen, bathroom, and bedroom.

The kitchen, like the living room, was a journey back in time—the linoleum floor, the floral wallpaper, the porcelain sink. It was all in remarkably good condition, a flashback to the '70s.

She tried the faucet, half-expecting nothing to happen the way things were going, and was genuinely surprised when cold water streamed out without complaint.

She needed a container and found one in the ancient but immaculate fridge—a gallon of nonfat milk, nearly full. She poured it down the drain—*blurpblurpblurp*—and filled it from the faucet. On her way back out, she noticed a jewelry box in the center of the bedroom dresser. It was covered with black felt, torn and dusty. She went through it quickly, disappointed to find only cheap costume stuff, all of it reeking of mothballs. She took nothing and didn't bother closing the lid.

Back at the car, she poured the water into the radiator carefully. It sizzled like a hot fry pan dunked in a wash basin. When the container was empty, she realized she'd need more, so she went back. She considered investing another minute or two in search of something worth taking, but dismissed the idea. This wasn't a good time to screw around. Besides, people who lived in houses like this didn't have anything of value.

She made four trips before the radiator was filled to the top and began to overflow. She tossed the plastic container aside and pressed/turned the cap into place. Then she slammed the hood and squirmed back behind the wheel. The stress of the situation had made her hungry, so she ripped open a bag of Doritos. (When she realized she'd forgotten cheese sauce, all thoughts of the oncoming tidal wave left her in a momentary flash of irritation.) The car started on the first try, and she inched her way back into the crawl. She checked her watch and was satisfied she'd be okay. She smiled broadly, proud of her automotive skills.

It never occurred to her that the reason the radiator had gone empty in the first place was because it had a leak.

* * *

Brian waited by the cars—waited for Jennifer and Mark to appear over one of the sandy rises, running hand-in-hand and ready to get the hell out of there; waited for a cop to show up with a bullhorn. His nerves were dissolving like sugar cubes. He paced; he chewed his fingernails. He wondered if he'd made a mistake by offering to help in the first place. It had seemed like such a noble idea at the time, but he'd been punished for doing the "right thing" before, plenty of times, in fact. So why did he keep doing it? Why did he bother?

He realized it was in fact one of two major mistakes he'd made that day—the other was calling for the cop in the first place. Of course he had to—but now he was glued to this spot, forced to remain here until someone finally came. If he left, the cop might get the wrong idea—he might think they'd already gone. He also wouldn't know what was going on; Brian had to be there to explain the situation. So basically he had trapped himself.

He checked his watch. Not so much because he wanted to know the time, but because he always checked his watch when he felt disoriented and disorganized. It was a way of getting everything back to square one—he'd run his fingers through his hair to straighten it, adjust his shirt and pants until he found that perfect "comfort zone," then check his watch. He'd been practicing this sequence for so long that he could do it in one smooth, fluid motion, and it took all of about five seconds. The hair always came first, then the clothes, then the watch. When he saw the latter this time, his heart stopped.

"Oh Christ...."

Less than an hour left. Maybe fifty minutes....He did a quick estimation—If I took off right now, right this minute, I'd have to cover about eight miles to get to the bridge. There'll be a million cars, and they'll be crawling like snails.

It was the first thought of self-preservation he'd had since leaving the supermarket. And with it came the desperate question: *Have I already passed the point of no return?*

Brian was a decent human being, but even that only went so far. He was scared now—truly and honestly terrified. For the first time in his life, he had to consider his own fragile mortality.

A string of peculiar thoughts came from some unknown place in his mind.

I am standing here now, feeling the wind on my face and the solid ground beneath my feet. But later I may not be here at all. There may be nothing left of me but a bloated body with water-clogged lungs. I will be floating in space, in a dark and starless chasm with no beginning and no end. I will drift, on and on, forever and ever....

His stomach tightened. This wasn't time for damn poetry. The first half of the bizarre ramble was true enough—he was alive right now, taking in oxygen as blood surged through his veins. He had to keep it that way. No one would fault him for that. (Well, maybe Mrs. King would, but there wasn't time to worry about her.) The correct thing to do at this point would be to make one last-ditch attempt to track them down, then start making his way to safety. *Surely the local government has set up some contingencies. We haven't simply been left here to die. The Feds are probably involved by now. The National Guard at least.*

He climbed onto the roof of his car and surveyed the area, holding his hand up to his shade his eyes.

"JENNIFER! MARK!"

He screamed it so loud that his throat burned.

"JEN-NI-FERRRRRR!"

He waited. Precious seconds slipped away. He could almost hear the ticks of a giant clock—a clock that was getting louder all the time.

Back in the real world, he heard nothing—no response from either of them. Some birds twittered in the shrubbery (they'd probably survive, he thought bitterly), and the ocean made its usual calm-but-powerful sound somewhere in the distance.

"MARK! JENNIFER! WE HAVE TO LEAVE RIGHT NOW!"

He tried to emphasize the last two words with increased pitch and volume, but it didn't really work. His voice, not particularly strong to begin with, was almost shot now.

He scanned the area one last time, and when he received no evidence of them, he began crying.

"Aw, come on you two," he said to himself, the words breaking up.

He got down slowly, climbed behind the wheel of his tired little car, and started the engine.

A note. Leave a note.

"Good idea," he said out loud. He dug through the glove compartment and found an old Chinese-food menu that had been left under his windshield wiper. It was printed on pink paper, crudely designed and with loaded with typos. But the back was blank, so it was perfect. He took his trusty silver pen from his shirt pocket, held the paper against the dashboard, and wrote:

> *Jennifer and Mark,*
> *I waited as long as I could. I hope you are both able to get out of here in time. I called the LBI Police and asked them to send someone.*
> *I really did wait as long as I could.*
> *Good luck.*
> *Brian*

It wasn't enough, obviously. It didn't say anything close to what he really wanted to say. But then how could it? He'd have to be here for hours to say it all; even then it wouldn't be enough. This was like breaking up with someone who still liked you; there simply wasn't a right way to do it.

He got out, barely able to keep the tears under control, and put the note under Mark's windshield wiper. He tried to imagine the two of them out there, young and scared and together. He identified his third major error of the day: letting Jennifer take off like she did. He should have known, should have realized she'd do that. She was normally such a calm and level-headed girl, but she wasn't in her right mind. And her parents had shielded her too much, shielded her from all of life's ugliness, so much so that she had no idea how to deal with a crisis. In her perfect little world the greatest crisis involved something that went wrong at the store. Brian knew all too well that nothing at Acme could ever truly be that traumatic. No, Jennifer King was as sheltered as you could be in this day and age. If she hadn't been, she wouldn't have done what she did. Because of her inexperience, she had made a very bad situation a hundred times worse.

He got back in his car, shaking his head and gritting his teeth, infuriated by all of it. In years to come, he would wonder if he'd really made the right decision this day. He slammed the door and gunned the engine, dropping it into reverse. The tires dug into the hard-packed surface of the bulldozed lot. As he drove out he checked the rearview mirror repeatedly, hoping beyond hope that one of them would appear.

It didn't happen.

*   *   *

Mark was certain there'd been a mistake. He'd never received so many messages in his voice mail box—he didn't even know it was possible to fill a voice mail box.

Under the clear blue sky, standing in the middle of nowhere on one of the nicest days he could remember, he entered his four-digit code and waited.

"First message…" the pleasant woman's voice said.

"Mark, it's Jay. Hey, there's a tidal wave coming. I'm serious. Get out of there as fast as you can. Call me back if you get the chance. Hurry."

Mark's first thought upon hearing the words tidal wave was that it was a joke. Of course it was—how could it not be?

But, then, his photo editor at the *SandPaper* wasn't the type to joke. He had a sense of humor, but not of this nature. He wasn't a practical joker.

Also, what about the remaining forty-nine messages. Forty-nine.

That can't be right. There must be some mistake.

He went to the next one.

"Mark, oh my God…" It was Jennifer. His stomach sank. "Mark, there's a tidal wave coming. You've got to get out of there!" She was crying. *This is for real. Holy Jesus.* "Call me as soon as you get this message. I love you." Her voice rose to a strangled squeal at the end.

He kept the phone to his ear to hear all the messages, but he also knew it was time to get moving. He tried to call Jen back but was unable to penetrate the overloaded network. He grabbed the camera bag off the ground and slung it over his shoulder. Then he broke into a slow jog—first heading to his left, then right, then back again.…

"Oh shit," he said aloud as it occurred to him: *I don't even know where I am.*

He tried to remember the way he'd come in. He found his way back to the main trail, but it forked into two other trails, and they forked into others still. It was a maze, a goddamn maze.

I'm going to die, he thought, suddenly feeling sick. I'm going to die simply because I can't find my way out of here.

It was so depressing it was almost paralyzing. He had always been careful not to appear self-pitying to Jennifer, or to anyone else for that matter. He knew he lived in a world where self-pity found few sympathizers. But that didn't change the fact that he often couldn't help feeling sorry for himself—for having such a pathetic mother, losing his father at such a young age, and ending up with a scumbag for a stepfather. There were other problems, too, problems that weren't of his own making, strokes of bad luck that had kept him on the lower rungs of life's ladder. He didn't whine about them because he thought doing something about them was a more productive approach. But there were days when he just felt overwhelmed, when—even though he knew it sounded irrational and even a little ridiculous—he felt like there were unseen forces in the universe working against him, working to hold him down. That really seemed like the only way to explain it.

And here again was an example—the one day when he decided to wander aimlessly around the refuge, the one day when he almost purposely let himself get lost, was also the one day in a billion that Long Beach Island, New Jersey, was due to be struck by a goddamn tidal wave. What were the odds of that happening?

The immediate urge was to give up—drop to the ground, cry, and wait for the end. He was tired of fighting. He'd clawed and scratched for everything he had, and it still didn't amount to much. What would he be giving up? Did his life amount to anything? Would the future hold anything besides more struggling? Struggling to get nowhere?

But then he thought of Jen—his beloved Jen. The singular bright light in his life. She was so much more than just a girlfriend, she was the future. She represented everything he wanted—the stable home life, the pure and unaffected mind, the seemingly bottomless well of cheer and good nature. He was at a turning point, the transition from one chapter to another. Slowly, but surely, he was leaving the myriad old miseries behind and working his way toward a much better existence. All thanks to her.

He crouched down and studied the trail carefully. It was slightly concave, and the sugary sand had a way of consuming footprints as soon as they were made. But the trail to the right seemed more disturbed than the one on the left. The pine needles to the left looked as if they'd just fallen, whereas some of those on the right were crushed and partially buried.

I came from the right. Definitely.

At least I think I did.

He took a deep breath and, listening to the twenty-third message, began running.

*   *   *

Jennifer, while not as experienced in the wild as Mark, did manage to find her way back to the parking lot. When she saw that Brian's car was gone, she panicked. When she found the note he left on Mark's windshield, she began to cry.

Then she took out her own cell phone and tried to call her mother.

There was no getting through.

ELEVEN

00:43:00 REMAINING

*T*om Wilson, sitting behind Marie's desk, set the phone back in its cradle and scribbled in his notebook. He'd filled nearly ten pages in the last half hour.

"A Harrah's bus heading north to pick up people for an Atlantic City trip happened to be passing nearby, so I got it over the bridge and up to Barnegat Light to pick up those twenty-two people at the Lutheran church. The driver is a Vietnam vet and was more than happy to help."

Harper, behind his own desk but standing, nodded and gave the thumbs-up. "Excellent, Thomas, excellent."

"*Thomas*," Wilson thought. *How long has it been since I heard that?*

There was a time when he was dead-certain he'd never hear it again, a time when he considered Harper his greatest enemy, his arch-nemesis. Were those feelings ever reciprocated? In quiet, reflective moments, did Harper ever think of him the same way?

It was hard to tell because Donald Harper was very difficult to read. Wilson thought he knew him better than anyone, yet he never would have foreseen the scandal that had erupted and brought such a swift end to the man's political future. He was a complex individual, indeed, and perhaps that was what Wilson—who thrived on challenges—found so intriguing about him. Was it simply the urge to unravel the enigma of the man that had drawn him to Harper and fueled his devotion all these years?

Whatever the case, he was forced to admit he was enjoying the nostalgia of the moment. All the old comforts came roaring back, almost as if he'd never left. All the subtle "isms" of their relationship—the distinctive sounds Harper made when he walked (the right foot dragged just slightly, and the change in his pocket always jingled), the way he set his reading glasses almost on the tip of his nose and only wore them when he needed them (and never in public), and the somehow endearing fact that he still hadn't mastered the fax machine and cursed at it when it wouldn't do as he wished. He was so indirectly charming that Wilson began wondering just what he'd been so angry about in the first place.

The guy made a mistake—a stupid mistake, granted, but haven't we all made them? Are any of us perfect?

He had never explored this forgiving philosophy toward Harper before, and with it came something quite unexpected— a feeling of guilt. Was it acceptable to have judged Harper so harshly simply because he was a public official? You could hold him to a higher moral standard for that very reason, but it was impractical and unrealistic to expect him to be perfect.

The guilt came from the feeling that he had abandoned Harper during a difficult time. He could have helped, could have augmented and enriched Harper's defense, practiced a little damage control and put the right spin on things. Instead, he went on the offensive and became another attacker. (In fact, Wilson thought with a queasy feeling in his gut, there were times when he seemed to be spearheading the attack.) Why had he done it? What was his own motivation? Was it anything more substantial than the fact that he felt personally deceived? Yes, it was true Harper had disappointed him, but was that reason enough to sink his teeth into the man?

One of the phones on Harper's desk rang yet again, and the mayor pushed the button that engaged the speaker.

"Yes?"

"Mr. Mayor? It's Sergeant Howard."

"Yes, Bill."

"I wanted to let you know that the school bus that was stalled on Pike Avenue is moving again. It should be over the bridge in about ten minutes."

The sounds of other cars groaning along, honking horns, and cops shouting instructions provided the background. It was all happening less than two miles away.

"That's great, Bill. Thanks so much."

"We're more than halfway done, by our count."

"Good, good. Let's get the rest, and fast, okay?"

"Yes, sir."

There was a brief pause, during which Harper wondered if perhaps Sergeant Bill Howard—a friendly associate who wasn't sure what to do or say when the scandal broke but never flew the coop—had replaced his phone on his belt and forgot to turn it off.

Then Howard said, "If you don't mind my asking, Don, when are you planning to go?"

Wilson, pretending to be reading some of his notes, paid particular attention.

"Soon, Bill. Very soon."

"There's only about forty-five minutes left, if the estimates are correct."

"I'm aware of that."

Another pause, shorter this time.

"Don, don't do anything foolish, okay? It's not worth it. That kind of stuff only looks good in the movies."

Harper laughed. Wilson tried to read into that laugh, but he could not; he wasn't sure if it was manufactured or sincere. The few "blind spots" he had into the man's soul had bothered him in the past, but only mildly. Now they were maddening.

"Don't worry, Bill. I know this isn't a movie."

"Okay, good. I'll keep you posted."

"Thanks."

He pressed the button again, and the street sounds disappeared.

"Let's see now, what else...." Harper mumbled to himself.

Wilson got up, taking his notebook with him for some unknown reason, and went into the main office.

"Don?"

"Hmm?"

"You didn't really answer Bill directly."

Harper looked up from his desk as if startled. "What? Oh, come on, Tom. I'm not into martyrdom." He waved his hand and made a face as if it was the most ridiculous thing he'd ever heard.

"But what you said to Elliot before, about the captain going down with his ship. That was pretty ominous. And I have to tell you, I've been wondering when you are going to leave. It doesn't seem like you've made any plans."

Harper went back to sifting through the paperwork; there was considerably less than an hour ago. He was getting near the end.

He nodded. "I have an escape plan, Tom, if you want to call it that. You remember Gary Oberg, right?"

"Sure. National Guardsman, major. You've been friends for years."

"Right. He's arranged for a helicopter to come and pick me up." He checked his watch. "Should be here about ten minutes before the first wave hits. It'll drop me off on the other side of the bridge, about a mile in. From there I can continue coordinating the rescue effort and start working on what comes after." A moment passed in silence before he added, "If I'm still the mayor."

Wilson froze—not just on the outside, but inside. It was as though every bodily function momentarily paused. He read a thousand meanings into that comment and had no idea which one—if any—was the "right" one. Was it a shot at him? A cheap right-cross that Harper had been waiting for an opportunity to deliver? Or was it a genuine moment of self-pity that slipped out accidentally? Then again, it could have been a practical concern—perhaps he truly wondered how much control he'd have over the situation once the tsunami had come and gone. Would people even listen to him? Would he be a lame duck, or would his words still carry influence?

Whatever the intention, Harper wasn't showing it. Wilson stared at him for what seemed like a long time but was probably only a few seconds. The man simply went about his business as if he wasn't being watched at all. Another old feeling of Wilson's came to the surface—every day brought new surprises with this guy. Just when he thought he had him figured out, Bang!—something popped up that blew the formula to pieces.

Finally, Wilson broke the silence. "I'm sure the people of this community will continue looking to you for guidance, Chief," he said somberly. "Remember how it was with Guiliani on 9/11? He was caught up in a scandal the day before, and the day after it was forgotten."

Harper's reply was a noncommittal murmur and a nod. He had picked up some document and was reading it carefully.

Wilson lingered for another moment, then retreated to Marie's desk. He still couldn't settle Harper's comment in his mind. Even if it wasn't meant as a sucker punch, it rattled him. He refocused on the task at hand in order to push it aside.

The notion that Harper had injected it into the conversation solely to steer away from the subject of how and when he would leave the island never occurred to Tom Wilson.

* * *

Karen didn't like staring into the faces. She wished she could use her sun visor to block them out.

But she had no choice—as she zoomed over the Causeway, she had to keep an eye out for the Ericksons. That meant trying, at roughly sixty miles per hour, to identify every car she passed. They drove a white Taurus. She wasn't sure of the year, but it was a newer model. It was a plain, unremarkable vehicle, matching their personalities in a way—subtle, low-key, almost invisible. It would be easy to miss. The fact that there were three lines of cars instead of the normal two didn't help. She couldn't really see anything in the line farthest from her. She could've passed them already. What the hell happened to that cop who was supposed to go over to their house?

She reached the peak of the bridge and began down the other side. At the bottom, where the eastbound road forked and became 9th Street, she saw more military personnel. There were four stout men in the same camouflage fatigues and shiny jack boots as her corporal friend. On the other side of the road, two of LBI's finest were waving motorists along.

As she drew closer, all of them took note of her. Crazily she thought of the tagline in that old stockbroker TV commercial— "When E. F. Hutton talks, people listen." It was as if the whole world stopped. She could imagine the thoughts racing through their minds. *Here comes that crazy bitch Moreland radioed us about.*

As physical details became clearer she picked out the leader of the military clique—a man in his late fifties or early sixties with a rugged face, broad shoulders, and a barrel chest. Remarkable condition for his age. He had to be in charge, she thought. He was also the only one wearing a black beret. The rifle hooked to his arm looked as natural to his anatomy as the arm itself. The other three, all younger, were smiling and moving about restlessly in the way that younger people do. The black-beret guy, however, was rigid and expressionless. He watched Karen every inch of the way with a stare that could melt marble. For a moment her rage evaporated and fear took control again. *Please, God, please don't let them stop me.*

They didn't; they just watched her go by. She swallowed into a dry throat as she passed. A quick and quite irresistible glance into the rearview mirror showed one of the subordinates stepping forward and saying something to the black beret. The guy's face finally changed—a smile spawned on his straight-line frown. No doubt a cheap shot at her expense.

Rather than take 9th directly to Long Beach Boulevard, she made a right onto Central Avenue; Long Beach would be all but impenetrable right now. Central wasn't much better, but at least the shoulder was clear. More people honking, more yelling all sorts of pleasant things. She had begun to cry without realizing it. *I'm falling apart emotionally,* she thought. *I don't even have control over it anymore.*

As with any other time when she was stressed beyond her limits, Mike came to mind. She wished to God he was here. Would he even know what was happening? He was more in tune with world events than she was. He'd watch the news every night although he wasn't particularly political. He just liked to know what was going on. But he was in California on a business trip and it was possible he wasn't even awake yet. On the other hand he might already be in a meeting, sitting around a polished cherry table in a stuffy boardroom, crunching numbers or plotting strategies with a dozen other suited execs while she was trying to locate their children and outrace the first goddamn tsunami to hit New Jersey since time out of mind. Would he find out only after it was too late? Would he come out of that meeting to break for lunch and then, while sitting in some deli in an unfamiliar city, catch the report on CNN—"A tsunami, the result of a terrorist's bomb, struck the coast of southern New Jersey today leaving hundreds dead...."

She wished she could at least talk to him, get some assurance and advice. They'd always made a great team, compensating for each other's weaknesses while managing not to bruise one another's egos.

She realized she was still holding the cell phone. It had become moist from the perspiration in her palm. She flipped it open and dialed with her thumb.

"Sorry, all lines are busy right now. Please try your call again later."

"Oh, come on!"

As she reached the end of Central and made a left onto 28th, she tried again.

Same message.

"Dammit!"

She slammed the phone onto the passenger seat, wiped the tears from her eyes, and jammed the gas pedal. The engine roared, the car lurched forward. She doubted the cops would be issuing many speeding tickets today.

She reached Long Beach Boulevard and made a squealing right turn. As expected, she had to ride the shoulder again. More idiots honking, as if she was doing this for no good reason or had no idea which way she should really be going.

She checked her watch—just over forty minutes left, if their estimate's correct.

The fact that the tsunami's arrival was now being measured in minutes rather than hours was truly terrifying. Her heart began pounding, her breathing became heavier. Doubts, cold and cruel, began creeping in—

What if I don't find them? What if I get there and they're gone? And how will I get back out?

They'll end up without a mother. They'll live the rest of their lives knowing their mom came back to get them and died in the effort. What kind of scar would that leave? What seeds of guilt would that plant? God, why did this have to happen?!

There was still a little space between the gas pedal and the floor, so she took care of it. She was going almost eighty and climbing. She prayed that no one would step out between two cars onto the shoulder, or from behind a phone pole or something. She had no intention of stopping. She just wanted to find her boys and get the hell out of here.

If they're there and we can't make it back out, at least we'll all die together, she thought out of nowhere. Then an image followed—her two boys, floating dead as the tidal waters receded.

Struggling to keep her eyes on the narrow path ahead, she leaned her head down and vomited onto the floor.

* * *

BethAnn's car began smoking again.

"Dammit!" she squawked, pulling over so sharply that one tire ended up on the curb. The cars behind her immediately filled the void.

She scrambled out and slammed the door with all her might. She marched around to the front and threw the hood up. Steam hissed and billowed around her.

"Hey baby, wanna lift?" a voice asked.

She turned to see a guy leaning out of the passenger window of a brown van. He was maybe in his early thirties, with a Jesus beard and haircut. He looked skinny, almost to the point of malnourishment, and didn't have a shirt on. She thought he bore a slight resemblance to Dennis Wilson, the Beach Boys' late drummer, in his later years.

"What?"

"A ride? Need a ride? We got plenty of room in the back." He motioned with his thumb. BethAnn caught a glimpse of a tattoo on the inside of his forearm, but she couldn't make out the design. She also saw the shadowy figure of the driver. No beard, and with hair that was all over the place, as if he'd just woke up. He had a long neck and a goofy knob of an Adam's apple. He was smiling, she could see, but not really paying attention. This was probably his friend's fifth or sixth attempt at a pickup today. For all she knew, three other girls were already in the back, gagged and handcuffed.

"No." She turned her attention back to the radiator.

"Are you sure? Could be fun."

The line of traffic kept moving; slowly they were passing her by.

"Up yours," she said with a flick of the middle finger.

"Same to you, lard ass!" the weird beard yelled back as the van faded into the distance. She didn't react.

She looked around for another open house. She'd parked in front of a new three-story model with a balcony on the top floor. She hustled her bulk up the brick steps and found the door unlocked.

The contrast between this environment and the one in her trailer was so severe it struck her like a fist in the face. The air was light and sweet, as if some type of subtle floral freshener was automatically sprayed from recessed nozzles every day. Sun rays reached through skylights, giving everything a natural, almost exotic feel. The owners either had a maid or the wife didn't work, because everything was spotless—BethAnn took one awed look at the large tiles on the floor and was certain she could eat off them. The living room, immediately to the left, seemed to somehow capture the word "peace" in its furnishings and choice of colors—large and comfortable couches, as white as snow, combined with oak and glass tables and cabinets trimmed in gold. A bubble clock stood with silent dignity on an end table by a whitewashed fireplace, spinning out the hours. BethAnn had never even been in a home such as this, much less given any thought to someday owning one.

She ran up the brief flight of carpeted steps to the kitchen, which featured more oak cabinets, offset lighting, and an industrial-size, stainless-steel refrigerator. Everything was so perfect that she almost felt sorry the house would be destroyed in less than an hour. But the part of her that despised the wealthy and privileged suppressed any such sympathy. In fact a stronger part of her savored the idea with considerable delight. Bastards probably have maximum insurance anyway. Probably end up with an even nicer place.

She found another plastic container of milk in the fridge and emptied it. The chrome, hook-shaped spigot on the kitchen sink was so high she had to carefully "aim" the milk container under it. Once it was full, she turned and lumbered back out. On her way she noticed a wooden plaque in the distinct shape of a key hanging next to the cordless phone on the wall. Along the bottom was a series of brass hooks, and from two of them hung two sets of actual keys. I'll bet their cars don't have radiator problems, she thought bitterly.

As she re-emerged in the late-morning sunlight, she saw that the brown van containing her two hippie friends was much farther down. Good, at least the line is moving. She covered the radiator cap with the front of her shirt (she could still feel the heat of it underneath) and gave it a twist. A guttural wheeze came out as if the car was a living thing.

She poured until the fluid level reached the top, then waited for it to go back down to add some more. When the container was empty, she ran back inside to refill it. She did this three times before wondering why it wouldn't stay full. *How many gallons of water does this thing need?* It wasn't until that third try that she heard—really heard and registered—the sound of water spattering on the pavement.

Is that supposed to happen?

She thought at first it was simply runoff from her sloppiness—in her rush, she wasn't going out of her way to pour neatly.

But it kept running, even when she wasn't pouring.

She got down on all fours and peered underneath. Water was leaking not from one but three different places. Two of the leaks were steady but relatively minor; if they'd been the only ones, the car might have had a chance to make it up and over the bridge. But the third was a doozy—a steady stream about the width of a pencil, as if someone had shot a small-caliber bullet through the radiator shell. The damn thing looked like it was taking a piss.

She let go a rash of expletives as she reached over and put her forefinger into the hole. The flow of water stopped and she trolled her mind for a more permanent solution. I could tear off a piece of my shirt and stuff it in there.

And then, to her surprise, she heard the voice of her ex-husband—"No, the pressure will blow it right back out."

That's right, she remembered, pressure builds up in there. That's why fluid shoots out like a geyser when you open the radiator of a car that's running, especially a hot one.

So what was the answer? she wondered as her knees began to hurt from the sand and the pebbles they were resting on. She didn't know. Maybe there wasn't any answer. Maybe this was the end of the line.

Should've taken that ride, sweetheart.

"I think not," she said out loud.

You might've had to do a few favors for those two freaks, but at least you'd be alive.

"Yeah, uh-huh."

When she couldn't take the pain on her knees any more, she got up and brushed them off. Standing up and straightening them out was somehow even more painful, although only for a few seconds. The radiator continued to urinate at her feet.

With her mind racing and her breathing growing heavier by the second, she considered the idea of just getting back in and driving the damn thing until it was stone-cold dead. Once this nightmare was over, she was sure she could wrangle a new car out of her insurance company. She did still have insurance on it—not because she wanted to, but because you had to, regardless of what a flagrant rip-off it was in Jersey. Maybe she'd even get something nicer, like the people in the house in front of her no doubt had....

That train of thought carried her to the solution to this problem. It was like a light had been turned on.

The keys. The ones hanging in the kitchen.

The image of them flashed through her mind, followed by a second—Wasn't there a garage around the back?

She was sure there was. Sure enough, at least, to invest a few seconds in checking it out.

*   *   *

Bud Erickson grumbled as he stood in his sunny kitchen, cutting up an apple with his penknife. He'd had the knife for more than fifty years; the relief image of the infantry division's emblem on either side was worn down like the face on an old coin. He grumbled because he didn't particularly care for apples, or oranges, or salads, or pretty much anything else that was good for your health. But he didn't have much choice anymore—a cholesterol level of 277 caused his doctor to declare sundown on his glory days of eggs and sausage in the morning, pork roll and cheese for lunch, and kielbasa—split up the center and soaked in butter while frying—for dinner. He ate like a female gymnast now and hated every minute of it. He thought about getting another doctor's opinion, but he knew it wouldn't be any different.

As he sliced the apple in his particular way—into eighths and carving out the seeds, all the while leaving the skin on because he simply could not get the hang of peeling—someone hammered on the front door. It made him jump, which annoyed him. It wasn't Nancy, as she didn't do things like bang on doors, and the boys didn't, either. Maybe it was the UPS guy.

He set the knife down with a groan and went out. His knees were killing him today; two trips up and down the cellar stairs had done it. As he passed through the living room, the banging came again.

"I'm coming!" he growled, sounding angrier than he'd intended.

He pulled the door open and found Jerry Logan standing there, looking red-faced and sweaty. He and his wife Denise lived a few doors down. Jerry was slim and wiry, with wispy gray hair that thinned a little more each year but still managed to cover everything. At the moment it was sticking straight up on one side, like an open lid on a beer stein.

"Jerry, what the hell—?"

"Why are you still here?"

He was out of breath, and Bud noticed two unusual things: first, he had a small cardboard box under his arm, and second, his car was parked and running at the end of the driveway, with Denise behind the wheel and leaning over to see what was going on.

"What do you mean?"

"Why haven't you left yet? Where's Nancy?"

"She's out back. What do you mean, left yet?"

Logan stopped panting, seemed to stop everything.

"Don't you know about the wave?"

"What wave?"

"The tidal wave!"

Now Bud froze.

"What?"

"There's a tidal wave coming, and you and Nancy need to get out of here, right now!" He looked down at his watch, a cheap black plastic thing wrapped around his bony, tubular arm. The extra length of band stuck out like the tail of a capital 'Q.' "You've only got about a half-hour left! Get moving—now!"

Bud put his hands up. "Wait a minute, wait a minute. A tidal wave here?"

"Yes!"

"That's impossible."

"It's not impossible, Bud. Get moving!"

Logan turned to head back to the car, and when he did Bud saw that his trunk was half-open, filled with boxes and bags, the lid tied down with an old piece of rope. It all looked hastily done, as if....

As if he was telling the truth.

Bud Erickson felt something like a narrow lightning bolt with many branches and forks flash through his body. It was something he hadn't felt in a long time—genuine fear.

"Holy God, you aren't kiddin', are you," Bud called after him.

"No, I'm not. Bud, you have to go now."

Bud was already turning around. "Thanks, Jerry," he said hoarsely.

Logan didn't hear this. He was already climbing back into his car.

TWELVE

"*T*hat's right, Governor, one of the biggest in recorded history," Sarah Collins said into the phone. "That comes not only from me, but from Dr. Daniel Kennard—probably the world's leading expert on tsunamis."

"What about this theory some have proposed—that the continental shelf off New Jersey is so shallow that the wave should break well offshore, rolling in as a white water bore from a long way out. Is that a possibility, in your opinion?"

"Dr. Kennard and I have discussed this scenario, sir. While we'd like to hold out some hope, we're convinced that, given its magnitude, not one but several destructive waves will in fact reach the coastline."

"Can you give me a rough assessment of the likely damage?"

"Well, I can tell you this for sure—anything standing on the beachfront won't be there an hour from now. I wouldn't be surprised if most of the buildings behind it were wiped away, too."

"Good God."

"I'm not dramatizing, sir. This is an historic occurrence."

"All right, thank you, Dr. Collins. Your good work is greatly appreciated. Your early phone calls will no doubt save thousands of lives. If we hadn't heard from you...."

He trailed off. No sense finishing that line of thought.

* * *

Nancy was trimming the rosebushes in the backyard, and the boys were playing in a tent she'd set up for them. She was thinking about her sister, Frannie, who lived in Scottsdale, and that she would call her this weekend. The last time they'd spoken, Frannie had mentioned she'd been having mild dizzy spells and was going to see her doctor. Nancy was concerned and hoped to hear something soon.

When she saw Bud emerge from the back porch, she smiled. In spite of his aches and pains, he was determined to stay active. She admired him for that; she'd always admired his strength of will. The fact that he seemed to be in something of a hurry, at least in context, didn't register. When he gave her the news, she looked at him as if he was joking. When he said he just checked it out on NJN, she dropped her clippers, stripped off her gloves, and ran to the boys.

"Come on, we have to go," she said.

"Why?" Patrick wanted to know.

"I'll tell you later," she responded. "But we have to go now." She hoped she didn't seem too alarmed, as she didn't want them to be frightened. It wasn't easy, though, considering her heart was banging like a drum and her hands were starting to shake.

As Bud went out to get the car ready, Nancy went to the phone and dialed Karen's work number.

"Tarrance-Smith Realtors. This is Scott Tarrance."

"I'm looking for Karen Thompson, Mr. Tarrance. It's Nancy Erickson, her babysitter."

A pause, then, "Karen left for your house well over an hour ago, Mrs. Erickson. You haven't heard from her?"

The complications this presented to Nancy were so numerous her mind couldn't keep up with them. "No. My God...."

"She should have gotten there by now," Scott Tarrance said. "Would you like me to try her cell phone?"

"No, I'll try it."

Scott paused again, then said, "Okay, Mrs. Erickson. Good luck."

Calling Karen's cell phone produced a recorded message stating that service was currently unavailable and that she should try her call again later.

"Are you going to take us where Mommy works?" Patrick asked. Nancy barely heard it.

"What?"

"Are you going to take us where Mommy works?" the youngster repeated.

"Oh...yes. Maybe. Um, do you have everything? Did you get all your things?"

"Yeah." Patrick was looking at her strangely. He was only four, but he was old enough to know something wasn't right.

Sensing this, Nancy smiled. She wanted to stroke his hair, too, but he might notice that her hand wasn't steady. "Okay, good. What about your brother? Does he have everything?"

"Everything!" Michael said happily, holding up his blue SpongeBob Squarepants backpack. His emotional sensors weren't as developed as his brother's. Pure ignorance, pure bliss.

"Good boy."

Bud was at the door. "Okay, everybody ready to go?"

Nancy looked at him, her eyes wide. She walked over to put some distance between them and the boys.

"I've got bad news," she said quietly.

"Worse than a tsunami?" he asked, keeping an eye on their young charges.

Her lower lip trembled. "Karen's on her way here."

"What?"

"I just called Tarrance-Smith—she left there over an hour ago."

"Did you try her cell phone?"

"Yes. No service."

Bud ran both hands through his hair. "Everyone in the county's probably on the line."

A small single tear rolled down Nancy's cheek. "What are we going to do? We can't leave now."

Bud said, "Okay...okay. I think I've got an idea."

"Is it a good one?"

"I hope so."

She touched his arm near the shoulder. Not a grab or even a pat—just a light brush of the fingers. "Okay," she said feebly, more air coming out than sound.

"I'll be back in two seconds, no more."

"Make it one."

"Right."

He walked past the boys, gave them a quick everything's-fine smile, and went out into the backyard.

* * *

Her heart pounding inside her considerable chest, BethAnn grabbed both sets of keys that were hanging next to the cord-less phone in the kitchen, then found the back door and went out. The lawn, like everything else on this property, was perfect, absolutely perfect. *They probably spend more on this grass than I make in a year.* She felt the urge to kick at it, create divots with every step, but didn't bother. It'd be underwater shortly.

And so will I if I don't get my ass moving.

She got to the garage door and threw it up, the rollers rattling angrily in their runners. This revealed an awe-inspiring sight—a 1964 Jaguar XKE convertible, pearl with dark blue trim, and in absolutely mint condition. It had been backed in and parked diagonally for maximum showroom effect. With the exception of a handful of basic tools, a few rags, and a couple of jars of wax, the garage was otherwise empty; the Jag had the place all to itself. It even looked as though the garage had been built exclusively for the car; the wood—just bare studs on the inside—not only looked fresh, it smelled fresh.

BethAnn gasped. She also managed a smile for the first time all day—*It's mine*, was her first thought. *This car is mine.*

She ran around to the door and squeezed herself inside. It was tight, no doubt about that—this model Jag wasn't designed for someone of her bulk. The steering wheel was just inches from her chest. This would not be a comfortable ride by any stretch of the imagination.

She began trying the keys, which was all guesswork because neither set had any identifying marks—no little leather Jaguar key chain or Jaguar logo stamped into the metal. One set had a die-cut Yankees' logo hanging from the ring, the other had what appeared to be a pewter bottle opener with the word "Budweiser" carved in decorative script. Big help.

She tried all the keys in the first set, wheezing as she was forced to lean over the unforgiving steering wheel, her boobs pressed against it and barely letting her breathe. None of them fit. There were five keys on the second set, and after the third didn't work she began to get nervous. A thousand pounds of worry slid off her shoulders when the second-to-last key slid neatly into the ignition and turned.

The engine rumbled to life, low and guttural, like a bear waking from its winter sleep. Everything shook; she could feel the raw power. This little car was a demon, a warrior. She didn't know squat about the internal assets of an older Jaguar, but she bet this one zipped around like a dragonfly.

"Mine, all mine," she said, clapping and howling. Down the end of the long driveway she could see the ever-moving line of cars heading toward the bridge. It was only about a mile away— one more mile and she'd be free. As she sat there waiting for the engine to warm up, she formed a plan in her mind—*get over the bridge, bypass the gathering point at Home Depot, get on the Parkway and head straight to Forked River and Sharon Leggett's house.* Leggett was a friend she'd met a few years earlier when she and her husband were still barhopping on Friday and Saturday nights. Sharon's husband, Vince, worked as an auto mechanic in Waretown. *They'll love this*, she thought. Vince could probably help her get it painted and remove the VIN numbers.

Suddenly excited, she decided the engine was warm enough; time to get this baby—her baby—on the road. She reached down and grabbed the shifter, but it wouldn't budge.

"What the...."

She tried it again. Again nothing happened.

Just what the hell is the prob—

When she saw that the bald head of the gear shifter had little numbers and a simple five-point diagram etched into it, her newfound excitement evaporated.

"Oh no...."

A manual transmission.

"No WAY!!!"

She slapped the dashboard hard; she had no idea how to drive a stick. Her ex had tried to show her a few times, but she never got the hang of it, mainly because she wasn't really interested. She figured she'd always have an automatic, so there was no reason to bother.

Her immediate urge was to scream until her voice was gone, then grab anything nearby that was heavy enough and slam it through the goddamn windshield. (*If* I *can't have the car, then no one else can, either....*) But then she made a fairly intelligent decision—*I'll try to drive it. I've got nothing to lose, and the clock is ticking away here.*

She knew that getting a stick into gear had something to do with coordination of the feet. Something about releasing one pedal while depressing another. But which pedals did you use?

She opened the door and swung her bottom half out. Now she saw that there were three pedals. The one in the center, she was certain, was the brake—it looked like a brake pedal, and that was where all brake pedals were, right? The one on the right had to be the gas, as most people were "rightfooted." So the only one left, which was on the left, had to be the...the....

"That's the 'other' one," she said to nobody, pointing to it. "The 'gear' one or whatever."

I think....

She wiggled back into position, shut the door, and released the emergency brake. Then she put her right foot on the gas pedal, and her left on the "gear" one. She wasn't quite sure which one got pressed first, so it was time for a quick test.

She engaged the gas first, pushing it down until the engine sounded downright angry. Then, very slowly, she began pressing the other one. She pushed the stick into the "one" position then let up on the pedal. For a second nothing happened. Then the clutch reached the point of engagement, and the car jumped forward. BethAnn's head snapped back like the top of a Zippo lighter. She grabbed the steering wheel out of pure reflex and jammed the brakes with both feet. The car screeched to a halt, stalling about ten feet from where it had been, and about three inches from the corner of the garage door.

The sudden halt brought her forward with such force that, as her torso more or less consumed the steering wheel, she felt like she was going to explode out the sides. Her mouth dropped open and her tongue shot out—both involuntary movements — and for a fleeting moment she was sure she was going to coat the dashboard with vomit. She pushed the door open and spilled onto the neat cement floor in one fluid motion, gasping for air.

She got back up, wiping her hands together, and gave the car a murderous look. It was the look she'd given to other objects in the past just before reducing them to rubble. How badly she wanted to; how very badly.

"All right, you bastard, you better not try that again."

She climbed back in, determined to take a different approach—clutch first, then gas, releasing the former slowly. This time, before starting the car, she moved the shifter into the "R" spot (at least what she thought was the "R" spot—it was so hard to tell). Her nerves frayed as she brought the clutch up—slower...slower.... When nothing happened, she thought she was simply doing it wrong again. Then the car jerked back, and again her feet went to the brake pedal before her brain engaged.

"GODDAMMIT!" she screamed, sending dots of spittle onto the glass. "COME ON! COME ON!" She launched into a bizarre visual symphony of shifting and pedal-pressing that had no focus, no intent. The idea was to "try everything."

Miraculously, it worked—at some point during the fit, the car started forward slowly and easily. BethAnn quickly identified what she had done—clutch down, shift into gear, then clutch up while the gas pedal was pressed gently.

Clutch comes up as the gas goes down.

She heard this in her ex-husband's voice and could actually picture him sitting there with his red-checked flannel jacket,

212

looking at her earnestly, hoping to God she might start paying attention and actually care.

She let go of everything in order to start fresh, then pressed the clutch all the way to the floor. Studying the baldheaded gear shifter for a moment, she set it into first, gripped the wheel, and began pressing the gas while bringing the clutch up at the same time. In her mind she pictured them passing each other at the halfway point.

As the transmission engaged, the car lurched—but only slightly. It was working now.

Clutch comes up as the gas goes down, clutch comes up as the gas goes down.

She had to stop when she reached the end of the driveway. The Jag leaned down, ready to enter the flow. BethAnn noticed her old car sitting on the shoulder to the right. The junk food was still in there, as were the tapes. She wanted desperately to get them—just jump out and grab them. It would take all of five seconds. But someone would see her—someone who knew damn well what she was up to. The tapes were the symbolic sacrifice she was required to make.

She rolled the window down, manually, and put on her best wide-eyed "please-let-me-in" face. The first person who saw this stopped to let her in. She smiled and waved, trying her best to appear casual, i.e., in a car that she drove all the time, every day. She prayed to no particular God that she could get it moving again. *Clutch comes up as the gas goes down.*

She tried engaging the gears again, and the car jumped like a jackrabbit. She was unable to keep her foot off the brake, and the tires screeched on the exhaust-stained pavement. She gathered her nerves and tried again. This time the results were a bit more satisfactory—the Jag hopped slightly, then ran smooth. As she straightened out to take her place in the line, she realized the steering was also manual, and quite an effort. For an instant she wondered if perhaps it would be best just to sell this thing because of all the work required to drive it. If it came to that, at least she'd get a good piece of change for it. The fact that she didn't possess the title was a detail that could be ironed out later.

She stopped about a full length from the vehicle in front of her in order to provide a safety buffer; she had no doubt she'd need it. Her heart was pounding, her face covered with sweat, her senses sharper than they'd been in years. She felt like every set of eyes was on her, that every driver around her was somehow aware of her thievery. She imagined roadblocks and police with rifles and mirror sunglasses waiting for her, their faces blank. Far from the truth, she was sure, but she couldn't help feeling that way.

She let the car in front of her get a little farther up, then moved up as well. More jerking, more halting, more abuse to the ancient transmission.

She was getting the hang of it.

*   *   *

Officer Jeff Mitchell knew they were running out of time. In fact, he was all but certain they wouldn't be able to get back.

Even if we find these two kids waiting for us at the entrance, we'll have to turn around, race back, and hope all the cars ahead of us make it over the bridge in time.

He glanced at the dashboard clock. If the estimates on the tsunami's arrival were accurate, they had less than a half hour left. About twenty-seven minutes, in fact.

We won't make it. There's just no way.

He took the microphone and called in to the dispatcher, praying to God Terry was still there.

"Go ahead," she said after the longest pause of his life.

"Terry, it's Jeff. Look, I'm still with Mrs. King, and we're almost to the refuge, but we're going to run out of time. I need some help."

"Like what?"

"Something in the air. A helicopter, preferably. Didn't they say the National Guard and the Staties were sending a few?"

"Yes, they're all here already."

"Can you ask them to send one over there?" He disengaged the button, then pressed it again and added, "I don't think we're going to make it, Terry."

"I understand. I'll ask them right now."

"Great, thanks."

He hoped Mrs. King didn't pick up on the noncommittal nature of her response—"I'll ask them right now." That, Mitchell knew, translated to, "I can't make any promises." Which, of course, further translated to, "If I can't get one, you're dead."

He spied his passenger from the corner of his eye again. She was sitting there with her back straight, eyes forward, hands folded neatly in her lap, acting every bit the proper lady. Twenty minutes ago he would've translated this impenetrable facade as coldness, detachment, and a bit of superiority. Now he was thinking it was more the case that she had trained herself to be like this for the benefit of her children, to set an example— *Always be strong*, she'd tell them. *Especially when the chips are down.* Like any good and decent parent, she was always teaching them, giving them the tools they needed to survive in the world. What he had earlier sensed as lack of emotion was in fact her way of dealing with every emotion in the book.

"Thank you for making that call," she said suddenly.

It pulled Mitchell out of his trance, the one that had formed while analyzing her. "Huh?"

"For the helicopter. I'm very grateful."

He smiled. "I promised you we'd get her, didn't I?"

She smiled, too, although she kept her ever-hopeful eyes on the road. She also nodded. It was a quick, happy gesture, almost like that of a little girl who's just been asked if she'd like an ice cream cone. In that instant Mitchell saw the real Carolyn King, or at least the one who had been in control of her personality at some point in the past.

"You have children of your own, don't you, Jeff?"

"Yes, two," Mitchell replied.

They kept talking.

* * *

Tom Wilson set the phone back into its cradle after making his last call from this building. He knew that, too; he knew his work here was finished forever.

Harper was in his office, doors wide open just as they were in the old days. (Wilson couldn't help but think of his time at Harper's side as "the old days" even though, technically, they had ended less than a year ago.) Wilson rose and went in, hands in his pockets. Harper was seated at his desk, scribbling something. It looked like ordinary paperwork on an ordinary day.

Wilson checked his watch, then said, "I think it's time to head out, Chief."

"Huh? Oh, is it?" Harper checked his own watch, a gold Rolex. Wilson couldn't help but wonder if he'd acquired it honestly.

"The damn thing will be here in less than a half an hour. We really should go."

Harper got up, dropped his glasses on the desk, and rubbed his eyes with two fingers.

"Yeah, staying any longer would be cutting it a bit too close."

Wilson noticed he didn't specify who shouldn't be staying any longer—him, or them. Words were crucial to a politician, he had learned through the years. Every syllable meant something. And not just the words themselves, but how they were delivered. Subtleties such as body language, inflection, rhythm—elements so minute that ordinary people wouldn't be able to distinguish variations—became so definitive between politicos that they might just as well be transmitted with a bullhorn.

"Then let's go," Wilson said, forcing the issue. "You've done everything possible."

Harper said, "I plan to, Tom, don't worry about that. Not right at this moment, but I will."

"I don't understand...."

"I've got that chopper coming, remember? Gary's sending it for me. It's due to land in the lot in about twenty-five minutes."

"That's a bit of a gamble, don't you think?"

Harper came around, clapped him on the shoulder. "I trust Gary to save me in time," he said with a laugh. "He doesn't owe me any money or anything."

The next thing Wilson knew, he was being led back out. Classic handling; he'd seen his old boss do it a million times.

"Are you sure you'll be okay?" he asked. It sounded whiney, but he couldn't help it; the time for finesse was running out. He cursed himself for not checking up on the helicopter claim earlier. "If I know you, you'll stay here and let the ocean sweep you away." He paused, carefully considered whether or not he should actually say what came next in his mind, then decided to risk it. "I mean, what with everything that's happened recently...."

To his surprise, Harper laughed again—that casual, boisterous guffaw (largely manufactured, Wilson felt) that sent the message, *Oh please, be serious.*

"Tom, that kind of stuff only happens in books and movies. Besides, suicide isn't my style. Now stop all the nonsense and get going. You've got less than thirty minutes to reach that bridge."

He began leading again, his arm still firmly around Wilson's shoulders.

"Besides, I've got to help coordinate the rescue efforts in the aftermath. Believe it or not, it looks like I'll still be useful around here." They reached the double doors that led outside.

"Of course you will. But—"

"Come on, get moving. No more bullshit. I'll meet you on the other side."

"Where?"

"I don't know. Somewh—"

"No, Don. Where?"

Harper studied him for a moment, a look of uncertainty glimmering faintly in his aging brown eyes. Wilson knew he didn't like to be cornered, didn't like answers forced out of him. A politician to the core.

Then he smiled again, putting every ounce of charm he had into it.

"How about Howard Breidt's office?"

"Breidt's?"

"Uh-huh."

Wilson appeared to consider it, as if it was a negotiable point. It wasn't, of course.

"Okay."

"Good, now get the hell out of here."

Wilson paused briefly, wanting to say more, but didn't. Harper returned to his office, slumped into his chair, and sighed heavily, running a hand through his carefully combed and sprayed hair. This made it stand up in spots, which looked ridiculous, but right now he couldn't have cared less.

How in the name of God that guy read so deeply into him was always a mystery to Donald Harper. No one else had ever been able to do it—not Jane, not Marie, not anyone. Just Tom Wilson. It was as if he had been born with some kind of internal radio tuned to Harper's bandwidth. Harper could still block him out at crucial moments, throw him off the airwaves when it was necessary. But he never felt like he could completely fool Wilson. There were times when the guy just knew.

This was one of them—he had sensed Harper's inner conflict, picked it up like a dog picks up the scent of a soup bone or a shark smells blood from a half a mile away. Wilson knew he couldn't decide what was right—stay and hope for the best, or leave and hope for the best.

From a political standpoint, both options had their risks and their rewards. If you went down with the ship and survived, your heroism would be beyond question. Certainly all would be forgiven if that happened. Maybe he'd have trouble getting re-elected because the scandal would still be there, but at least the family name would be cleansed. The trick, of course, was getting through a tsunami in one piece. Harper knew the odds were against it, but there just might be a way.

The second option—wait until the last possible moment and get the hell out of town—was obviously the safer bet. Unless his friend's helicopter crashed on the way down, his survival was all but assured. Would this cast him in a cowardly light? Probably, in some people's eyes. But many would appreciate the fact that he'd stayed until there was virtually no time left. In Wilson's words, they would know he had done everything possible.

On the other hand, considering that he was already embroiled in a scandal, if he survived while other residents perished it would be impossible to overcome that politically. The mere fact that he'd be flying away to safety on some sort of "private ride"—furnished through a personal favor, no less—as other residents drowned below, would be regarded in many quarters as nothing short of a sin. Harper would valiantly coordinate all emergency efforts, but once things began getting back to normal, his career would wash out with the tide along with the rest of the corpses.

Making decisions, he knew, was what leadership was all about. And up until now he'd never had any trouble. But this one was the toughest of his life. Not just his career—his life. Because that was exactly what would be on the line.

He stared blankly into space, hoping the answer would appear out of nowhere...and soon.

* * *

Bud hurried down the slope of the backyard as quickly as his arthritic legs would carry him. This section of his property was enclosed by a stockade fence that had been installed the previous year. The unpainted and unstained pickets still had a new look to them. In one corner, the lawn gave way to a serpentine line of bricks that acted as a border between the grass and a tasteful ground scape of small, glassy stones and larger, rough-hewn patio stones. The latter were arranged in a quaint footstep pattern leading down to a gate, which Bud pulled back. The step-stones continued a short way to the very edge of the property, where it met the waters of Little Egg Harbor Bay. There, tied to a piling, bobbing quietly in its homemade skirt on this otherwise postcard-perfect day, was Bud's 120 Impact Boston Whaler.

He'd had it for two years, used it only for fishing, and kept it in immaculate condition because he planned to resell it and upgrade. It was just over eleven feet long and five feet wide, with a 40 ELPT FourStroke Mercury engine, a white canvas sun top, a cushioned aft bench with underneath storage, and a self-bailing cockpit sole. Bridge clearance was two feet ten inches, fuel capacity fourteen gallons, and it was rated to carry four adults.

As he jumped into it, the shock in his knees was like a heat explosion and he almost screamed on impact. As the pain subsided he got behind the console and fished the key from his pocket; it was attached to an orange floating-buoy key chain with a tiny waterproof compartment that held one dose of his pain medication. He jiggled it into the ignition, and the Merc roared to life without hesitation.

Whether the boat would start or not wasn't what concerned him—he was more interested in the fuel gauge. The needle wavered for a moment, then settled a hair above 'E.' That was what he thought—he wasn't planning on taking the boys out until tomorrow, when he could get down to Jingles' Bait and Tackle and get some fresh night crawlers. He also needed to mix a fresh batch of gasoline and two-cycle oil.

He would have to do it now.

He turned the motor off and climbed back out. He could hear the joints popping and feel the ligaments pulling and stretching in his knees. He ran up and across the yard again, trying to ignore the fact that the beautiful landscaping he and Nancy had worked on for so many years would be gone shortly. It all seemed so surreal.

He went into the garage and flicked on the light. The worktable was to his immediate right, against the back wall, and the red plastic gas container was on the shelf underneath. Thank God I keep things organized, he thought, and remembered a guy he knew in high school named Artie. Most disorganized sonofabitch Bud had ever known. He once blew an afternoon helping the guy search for his wallet. What would he be doing if he was stuck in this situation? "Sorry, kids, we won't be able to get off the island in time. I have no idea where I left the gas container, so I can't fill the boat...."

The container—a five-gallon job—was about half full. He hefted it onto the table and unscrewed the cap. A number of stubby cans of four-stroke oil stood neatly on the shelf overhead, lined up like soldiers. He took two down, peeled off the aluminum lids, and poured in their black, syrupy contents. Then the gas cap went back on, and he took the container out. His knees were screaming as he made his way back to the boat, lugging the heavy, sloshing container with both hands. He tried not to think about it, thought instead about those two boys inside—with so much to look forward to, so much of life left to live.

Once the engine was filled, he restarted it. This time he would leave it running; they'd be ready to go at a moment's notice. He checked his watch—11:10. About twenty minutes left.

He hustled back to the house and went inside. The boys were sitting on the living room couch, watching television, their backpacks on the floor at their feet. For the moment they looked content. They had their windbreakers on and were watching the Cartoon Network. Wile E. Coyote was riding a rocket—which was, of course, completely out of control—in his interminable efforts to catch the Roadrunner.

"Well?" Nancy asked, standing in the kitchen.

He was so out of breath he could barely speak. "We'll take the boat," he said. "I just started it up and put some gas in it."

"Are you sure that's the best way, Bud?" she asked. "Are you sure?"

"Yes, definitely. We'll cut across Little Egg Harbor Bay right to Tuckerton. It should take about ten minutes. Once we're there, we'll have to beg a ride. I don't see any other way. If we try to drive out of here, we'll hit all those cars trying to get over the Causeway, and we'll be at the back of the line. As time runs out, people'll start getting nastier—there'll probably be accidents and fighting. And the first car that stalls or stops, everyone behind him will be screwed. I wouldn't be surprised if that's already happened."

It was a dark, pessimistic prediction, and one that, years ago, Nancy would've dismissed as her husband's natural cynicism. But, as with all good marriages, the couple had learned from each other, and one thing she learned from him was that sometimes—sometimes—human beings really were prone to doing horrible things to one another. Not everybody was good and decent deep down inside. Some people were just plain bad.

"Did you get hold of Karen?"

"I tried again, but I still can't get through."

"Okay, keep trying. We can't leave until she gets here." He paused, thought about the inevitability of the forthcoming disaster. "At least not until the last possible moment. How are the boys doing?"

"They're okay. I think Patrick is feeling a little frightened. He keeps looking at me like he knows something's up. Michael doesn't suspect a thing."

She paused, then said, "Oh, Bud" and slipped her arms around him.

He returned the hug and kissed her on the temple. "Okay, okay. Take it easy. We're going to get through this. What's important here is that we survive. You, me, and those two little boys out there. The insurance will take care of the property. There's nothing here we can't replace."

"There are some things," she countered in a choked voice. "Some things can't be replaced."

"I know, I know, but even if we had more time we couldn't bring any of it. The boat only holds four adults, so when Karen shows up we won't have any room to spare."

They separated but still held each other. "Do you think she will?" Nancy asked, a tear running down her cheek. "Do you think she'll make it in time?"

Before he had the chance to answer, his wife buried her face under his chin, trying to mute her sobs so the boys wouldn't hear.

"I hope to God she does. Like I've never hoped for anything before."

He let her cry for another moment, then patted her back and said softly, "Okay, let me get the boys' bags into the boat. And if you have something light you'd like to bring, we can work that in, too. Maybe that box of letters in your closet."

Nancy brought her head up. Her eyes were red and puffy, her cheeks glossy and damp. But she wore a smile—a tiny one, but a smile nevertheless. She massaged her husband's cheek and kissed him. "I love you, Bud."

"I love you, too, sweetheart."

He went into the living room, asked the boys what they were watching, then told them they were all going on a boat ride in a few minutes. They hooted and hollered like lunatics. Bud told them to stay put until he called to say the boat was ready, then took their backpacks.

As he headed back down to the slip again, his own fears finally began to penetrate. A litany of harrowing scenarios marched through his mind. As was his habit, he simply pushed them out of the way and focused on the task at hand: Get the boat ready to go, and get the hell out of here the moment Karen arrives. Nothing else matters right now—nothing.

He got in and lifted the seat of the bench, exposing the storage area underneath. Most of the items inside would have to go—a few containers of boatwash, the steel anchor, a spare battery. All extra weight that would slow them down. He threw them out quickly, straining his back as well as his knees. They went on shore and would stay on shore until the water came to claim them.

When he turned to get back out, he found two people standing there, watching him. His heart jumped.

"My God, you scared the hell out of me!"

He barely knew the names, only faintly recognized the faces. But when he saw what one of them was carrying, he knew why they were there.

THIRTEEN

00:24:00 REMAINING

*D*r. Kimberly Benton, associate professor of oceanography at Texas A&M, was on FOX News explaining to anchor Jackee Welcher the tsunami's progress with the aid of a diagram showing the radiating waves as concentric circles. Benton pointed out that LBI and the surrounding communities would be struck by not one, not two, but at least four separate surges, each more destructive than the last. As she spoke, FOX created a slick computer-generated simulation of the strikes, replete with generic homes and commercial properties that were remarkably close in form and proportion to LBI's actual municipal layout. It was evident to some viewers that there was no human element—the simulation lent a speculative vision as to what kind of material destruction would take place, but there was no mention of casualties. This was a conscious decision on the part of the network.

FOX then went back to its field journalist, Rob Little, who by this time had been asked to move farther inland by the gradually retreating National Guard. He stood at the edge of Home Depot's parking lot, which was filled with thousands of displaced LBI residents. Some were crying and embracing, others seemed calm, even bored. A few were trying, in vain, to use their cell phones. A small police cadre attempted to create some semblance of order, but the general impression was that nobody was really in charge.

"What's the latest word, Rob?"

Little, with one hand covering his ear, said, "It's pretty chaotic right now, Jackee. I've tried to find out who's running the show, but no one seems to know. I've counted roughly 2,000 people so far, but that's not an accurate representation of Long Beach Island because so many cars are not stopping here—they're going further inland."

A crying teenage girl with her hand over her mouth entered the screen and bumped into Little. Seemingly unaware of what she'd done, she disappeared from the frame. Her three seconds of fame were over.

"Do you know if the authorities managed to get everyone off?"

He looked away for a moment. "I'd say no, because I can see cars still coming over the bridge. They're moving pretty smoothly, but they're still coming with less than a half hour left. Right?"

The host checked the digital clock that viewers saw in the lower left-hand corner of the screen.

"Yes, about twenty minutes according to our experts."

Little shook his head. "I don't know what to say, Jackee, except pray."

Jackee assured him that she would, then went on to tell the viewers that hundreds of thousands of people were now following the story—crowds huddled in offices and supermarkets, pausing in their daily lives to catch the details on whatever television set was nearby. Humanitarian aid programs had been arranged; a team from the Red Cross was on its way. Suddenly it seemed all of America cared deeply about the fate of tiny Long Beach Island, New Jersey. And in response to the belief that this disaster was the result of a new phase of terrorist attacks, the stock market, which had seen healthy gains in previous months, began once again losing altitude.

About fifty yards from the Causeway, in an '89 Chevy pickup in the left lane on the westbound side, a heavyset man in a flannel jacket was running out of patience. Bobby Gorman wanted to kill the old bitch in front of him, wasn't even sure what had kept him from doing it already. She was acting as if she was on a friggin' Sunday drive. She had to be at least eighty-five, and her head barely rose above the steering wheel. He'd been stuck behind her for fifteen, maybe twenty minutes. The cars ahead of her would go, and she wouldn't. Half the time he'd have to honk to get her moving. Cars from the right lane would slip in and fill the space she left. It was driving Gorman mad.

Gorman's girlfriend of six years, in the passenger seat, made sure to keep her mouth shut. Efforts to soothe him in the past had usually resulted in a violent physical response. When he started mumbling, "I'm gonna kill her, I'm gonna fucking kill her" she pressed herself into the corner of the cab to get as far out of his reach as possible. When the old lady hesitated again and someone in a minivan slipped into the spot ahead of her and then waved gratefully, she actually waved back. That was it for Gorman. He slammed the transmission into park so hard the truck rocked, and threw the door open. His girlfriend pleaded with him to come back, but he ignored her.

He reached the door of the elderly woman's car and smacked the window with his open hand. The woman jumped and turned to look at him, eyes wide with horror. He began screaming at her, while drivers of vehicles stopped behind his truck started honking. Another man—about Gorman's age and general size but without the beer belly and five o'clock shadow—appeared from out of nowhere and began cursing at him. In less than ten seconds the confrontation became an all-out fistfight.

One LBI resident who had decided not to leave was Marion Edward Hartley. A resident of High Bar Harbor, Hartley was thirty-seven, six-foot-four, overweight with narrow shoulders, and lived with his aging mother. He was also an active, although relatively monogamous homosexual. His mom was already off the island, having been picked up earlier in the day by some church friends bound for the Columbus flea market. She had called a number of times to make sure her only child was able to make his escape. He assured her that a friend—that was how he described his lovers to her—was coming to pick him up.

Hartley's actual plan, however, was to record this amazing event for posterity via the digital video camera he'd bought a week earlier. He'd been fascinated with natural disasters since boyhood—earthquakes, hurricanes, and tornadoes. They had relatives in Kansas, and he'd visited them almost a dozen times in the hopes of seeing just one twister, though, unfortunately, none had ever materialized. There was no way he was going to miss what would probably be the only tsunami to strike this area in his lifetime. Aware that the best way to survive this phenomenon was to get to high ground, he decided to pack up his camera equipment and climb to the top of Old Barney, the famous lighthouse located on the island's northern edge, not more than four hundred yards from their home. As Barney was made of reinforced concrete, Hartley felt sure it could withstand even the force of the driving Atlantic. When it was all over, he'd sell the footage to the highest bidder.

In North Beach, as the precious seconds ticked away, two men reached a backyard shed at exactly the same moment, both with the same intention—to get at the dirt bike inside. After a brief and uncomfortable pause, they began fighting to get the door open. When one of them finally did, and they saw the bike waiting for them with its gleaming chrome hardware and orange plastic mudguards, they went after each other like kids in a playground fighting over a baseball. Then, with remarkably good sense, one of them pointed out that they could ride it together, and suddenly they were best friends. A moment later they were zooming across the backyard of the bike's anonymous owner, throwing up chunks of lawn in their wake.

At the base of the Causeway, on the island side, officer Nick Albano, standing by his squad car with the lights swirling, checked his watch one last time. Fifteen minutes left, and time to get the hell out of here. Climbing into the car, lights still swirling, he blended into the moving line. With his radio's microphone in hand, he used the car's external speaker to instruct the people in front of him to keep moving...keep moving.... As he began the ascent up the bridge, he realized he was going to make it. He closed his eyes and offered a silent prayer to the God he'd believed in his whole life. Then he offered another for all those behind him, hoping for the same good fortune.

In an empty parking lot in Haven Beach, an Army helicopter landed for the third time to pick up a load of passengers. The pilot, a Captain Holbrook, saw that the group had grown since the last time—there were fifteen then, and twenty-two now. Knowing his limit was twelve at a clip, pushing it at that, he stepped out and, waving, yelled, "Let's go! Twelve more!" His voice was hoarse, almost gone, from screaming over the powerful din of the rotors for hours.

As he had feared, the entire group began to move forward. "I can't take more than twelve!" he said, holding a hand up. He knew how much time was left, and he knew that they knew, too—and that they would understand this was likely to be his last trip. Now Holbrook would have to make the most difficult decision of his life. Starting with the women and children, by age, youngest to oldest, he made his instructions clear. An elderly woman who wanted to remain with her husband was the sole female not to board. After the lucky ones were all seated, he shouted to those still on the ground, "I'll be right back!" and headed toward the cockpit.

As he was about to climb in he heard someone scream, "You're not going to make it!" He turned to face a medium-built man in his late thirties or early forties, with short-cropped hair and glasses, dressed in jeans and a white golf shirt with a little blue Polo logo on the left breast. Probably an accountant, the pilot thought. "Yes I will!" he yelled back. The man in the Polo shirt grabbed his arm, hollering, "No, you won't! I timed your last trip—almost twenty minutes! We've got less than fifteen minutes left before the wave hits!"

"The arrival time of the tsunami is only an estimate," Holbrook said. "But the longer we stand here arguing about it, the more time we lose!" As he turned away and began to climb in his antagonist grabbed him by the shirt and yanked him back.

"You're not leaving me here!"

Holbrook spun around with remarkable speed, jamming the heel of his hands into the man's chin, the force of the blow knocking him off his feet. Holbrook climbed into the cockpit and, without closing the door or fastening his belt, lifted off. The man in the Polo shirt scrambled to his feet and, charged with rage, leaped up and wrapped his arms around the bird's skids. It tilted crazily to one side, and Holbrook, caught off guard, very nearly spilled out.

"Let go, you crazy lunatic!" the pilot yelled as he stabilized the chopper, continuing to gain altitude. "Let go now!"

"No!" the man screamed as Holbrook reached for his sidearm, knowing he wouldn't face disciplinary action for shooting the guy, though he would try to hit him in an arm or leg. In that instant, the hanger-on managed to get one leg over the skid. The chopper dipped sharply downward and, before the pilot could react, drove into the unyielding macadam. Those on the ground, who moments earlier had felt like losers in a very dark lottery, watched in stark terror as the chopper first crumpled like an aluminum can, then exploded into a ball of orange flame.

* * *

Bud Erickson knew their names—Walter and Violet Carson. He knew that they lived on nearby Magnolia Avenue. He was fairly certainly the husband used to work in the garment district in New York City, back when they had a home somewhere in the northern part of the state. He knew less about her. He saw them on Sundays, walking to the bus stop in their dress clothes, though he didn't know what church they were headed to. Occasionally he would see them at the Acme, an aging couple on a fixed income, forced to clip coupons and assess the relative value of every item they put in their cart. He'd never seen either of them driving a car. He'd never heard Violet speak. In fact, he could not remember a time when he'd thought of them as anything other than "one of the old couples who lives nearby."

But here they were, standing in front of him in their pressed Sunday garb—Walter in that same cheap brown suit, Violet in an understated, patternless dress. A suburban New Jersey variant of Grant Wood's *American Gothic* without the pitchfork. Instead, Walter was holding a tiny suitcase that appeared antique.

"Have room for two old carpetbaggers?" he asked with a smile. His voice was scratchy, sandpapery. And while it was polite, it was also pleading.

Bud already knew the answer—no, he didn't. Between himself, Nancy, the two boys, and Karen, they'd be maxed out.

"Hang on a second, Walter, okay?"

He walked back up and into the house, where Nancy was watching out the kitchen window, waiting for Karen to magically appear.

"Nancy?"

"Hmm?"

"We've got a new problem."

Her shoulders sagged. "Oh no, what now?"

"The Carsons are outside. They need a lift."

"Who?"

"The Carsons, from over on Magnolia."

"Can we make room for them?"

"No, not if—" Bud leaned over to see if the boys were still in the living room. "—not if Karen shows up. There's no way."

Nancy shook her head. "My God...."

"Still no word from her?"

"I haven't been able to get a call through."

"Try again. We can't wait more than a few more minutes."

Nancy took the phone and dialed the number. Once again a recording told her there was no service available and that she should try her call again later.

"Well?"

"Still no service," she said.

Tears welled in her eyes as she looked at Bud helplessly. The expression said it all—*Does this mean we'll have to leave her behind?*

"All right, let's get them on the boat," he said. "We'll wait until the last possible minute."

The boys bounded through the kitchen and out the door, yelling, "Boat ride! Boat ride!" When they reached the slip and saw the elderly strangers, they paused.

"Hello, boys," Walter said. The smile was warm and genuine in spite of his crooked teeth, yellowed from years of pipe smoking.

"Hello," Patrick said. Michael only stared.

"Patrick, Michael, these are the Carsons," Bud said. "They live over on Magnolia Avenue. They'll be coming with us."

"Hi," Patrick said with a distinctly friendlier tone this time.

"Hi," Michael echoed, his brother having confirmed the situation.

"How come you're bringing a suitcase?" Patrick asked.

The Carsons and the Ericksons exchanged glances. Bud waved his hand in the hope of conveying the message, *They don't know.*

Walter looked back to the boys and said, "I bring it with me wherever I go. You never know when you're going to need something, right?"

The boys appeared to be confused by this alien idea, but confusion was good enough for all adults involved.

Bud checked his watch again. "We need to get going." A light spray of perspiration had broken out on his forehead.

Nancy, nodding her agreement, shepherded the boys in first, then stepped in and helped Violet. As Walter came up to Bud, he said quietly, "Are you sure we can join you?"

Bud's expression—a mixture of uncertainty and discomfort—said it all, and Walter Carson, while no rocket scientist, had been on God's Earth long enough to recognize trouble in a man's eyes.

Bud's eyes shifted briefly to the front of the house, hoping beyond hope that he would see Karen running toward them. No such luck.

"We were expecting someone," he whispered, "but it looks like she's not coming."

"Who is it, Bud?" Walter asked, his remarkable calm communicating that there was no point in evading the truth any longer.

"Their mother," he said, nodding in the direction of the boys. "She left work some time ago, on her way here, but there's been no word from her and we can't get through to her cell phone."

Walter closed his eyes and, so slightly that it was almost imperceptible, shook his head. It was the gesture of a man who had seen his share of pain, death, and loss, and still, after so many years, could not understand why life had to be this way.

Bud added quickly. "If she doesn't come, we should be able to take you. We'll be over the boat's weight limit, but I think we can handle it."

"Bud..." Walter said. He did not finish the thought; it didn't need finishing.

"Come on, we've got to go. Now."

Walter lingered for one more moment, staring hard into Bud's eyes. Then, with no trace of outward emotion, he allowed the younger man to help him board.

Bud unwound one of the two satin ropes that moored the boat and threw it in. He left the second one tied for the moment. Nancy was staring at him, on the verge of tears. No one else could see this, but he knew.

"I almost forgot something," Bud said to no one in particular. "I'll be right back."

Reaching the yard, he closed the wooden gate behind him and ran up the slope to the back door faster than he had in years. His knees were shooting bolts of pain into his brain that, under normal circumstances, would have caused him to collapse like a rag doll. He barely gave it a thought.

He went into the kitchen again—realizing with a touch of surrealism that this was the last time he'd ever see it—and then into the living room. The TV was still on, now halfway through an episode of SpongeBob Squarepants. Bud opened the front door and looked up the street. Nothing—no cars, no people, no signs of life at all. *Come on, Karen, where the hell are you?* This part of the island, he felt in his gut, was deserted.

A thought, as cold and as solid as a bullet, entered his mind at that moment—*It's time to get the hell out of here.*

He went back into the kitchen, and grabbed the cordless phone from its wall-mounted base. It was a very modern phone that seemed out of place in their retro household—the LED screen with caller ID was the reason they'd bought it, in the interest of fending off telemarketers in the days before the government enacted the do-not-call list. It seemed to be working because the solicitations had significantly decreased since they stopped answering.

He pressed redial with his thumb and brought the phone to his ear. When he got the "no service available" message, he hung up and went out the back door.

Opening the gate to his slip, he found the Carsons sitting silently at the back of the boat, huddled together. The boys, clad in their bright orange life jackets, were leaning over one side, drawing shapes in the water while Nancy, eyes trained on his, waited for an answer. The wait was a short one.

"Let's get going," he said solemnly. He moved to the other rope and unwound it. Then he climbed in, glancing at his wife from the corner of one eye. She had turned away from him, from everyone. *Please don't start crying, Nan. Not now, not in front of the boys.*

He got behind the wheel and said, "Everybody ready?" Only his two youngest passengers responded.

He shifted into gear and, after a deep breath and a fleeting moment when he felt his own grief climb up into his throat, throttled the engine. The tiny craft groaned out of its water-filled box and into the sunny warmth of the bay.

*   *   *

The bridge was only a few hundred feet away now. BethAnn knew, deep down, that she was going to make it. Her nerves were still frayed to the point of madness, but the knowledge that safety was within reach helped soothe them to some degree.

She'd fallen in love with the Jag in the last fifteen minutes. Hopelessly, helplessly in love. It wasn't just a machine, it was a divine creation. She'd never known such luxury in any form. The control panels weren't simulated wood—they *were* wood. The dials didn't have some classy, understated look to them— they were classy and understated. The seats weren't that cheesy plastic copy of leather often called "pleather"—they were leather. It was simply unbelievable. She figured that a person driving a car like this every day couldn't help but start feeling pretty good about herself.

She'd learn the proper way to drive a clutch. It would take some doing, but dammit, she'd do it. She decided this tidal wave was a blessing in disguise, at least for her. Symbolically, it would wash away the old BethAnn, enabling the new one to emerge. This was the turning point in her life, the moment that Lady Luck started to smile on her. By the end of this day, all the "bads" would be long gone—the trailer, working at the Acme, living on LBI. She'd never felt at home here, never felt welcome. She'd only moved here because of her ex, and since he'd left she'd always wanted to go, too. Now Fate was giving her a nudge, with the Jag the symbol of all that lay ahead—better times, a better standard of living. She'd try to keep everything on the same level. No more sitting around all day watching television. She'd land a better job, work her way up, start getting used to the good things in life. Yes, this was what the powers that be wanted her to do. That's why she was given this dazzling ride—it was a down payment on her future.

The late model Buick ahead of her moved up again, so she moved up, too. Her shifting and accelerating skills hadn't improved much in the last quarter hour. The stick still vibrated wildly, sometimes to the point where she had to let it go. And that noise—that horrible grinding, screeching noise. She was sure it wasn't a good thing in any case, but as long as she got to where she needed to go she'd live with it.

She reached the point where she had to make the turn off Long Beach Boulevard and, just as she straightened out, she caught the distinct scent of something burning. Then she noticed a fine wisp of smoke undulating from the nose of the car like a ghostly serpent.

Her shoulders fell. "Oh Jesus, no. Not the radiator again!"

There was no chance to stop for water this time, she knew. She'd just have to live with it. She just hoped the car could.

As if on a roller coaster, she began the ascent up the bridge. She rolled the window down and yelled to nobody and everybody at once, "Come on, let's go!" She peered at the clock on the dash and saw she had less than fifteen minutes left. "Move it!"

BethAnn was on the left side of the roadway—normally used by eastbound, incoming traffic—in the right lane, as the left had been designated for incoming emergency vehicles only. She watched in surreal detachment as two cops abandoned their posts, jumped into one squad car (leaving the other behind, its red and blue lights swirling) and sped like demons up the emergency lane. Her heart jammed itself into her throat—she was certain that the moment they reached the peak another vehicle would come screaming from the other direction, causing a spectacular head-on collision. A part of her—the part, no doubt, that hungered for the kind of negativity that only shows like *Springer* could provide—hoped this would happen. She'd love to see it just once in her life. But another part of her—the part that possessed enough reason to remind her that such an accident

239

would very likely bog down this entire road and thus leave her stranded with a lifespan of some twenty minutes—was relieved to see that nothing of the sort occurred. When the cops reached the top, they both put their arms out the windows, motioning the traffic to follow. Then they disappeared into oblivion.

The race to get into the now-accessible lane was like the one between consumers waiting on endless checkout lines at Christmastime when a new register suddenly opens up. The mystery became: Who would take the risk of causing an accident by swerving into the "new" lane, and who would play it safe and remain where they were?

BethAnn was part of the latter contingency. She deduced—and quite accurately—that the bulk of the increasingly nervous drivers would take a shot at getting to safety as quickly and as effortlessly as the two cops just did. She watched in delight as the line in front of her seemed to melt away. Cars that were previously behind her sped by. In a matter of mere seconds, as she had expected, the left lane became packed and sluggish, and those who'd had the common sense to remain where they were suddenly found wide open spaces in front of them.

She gunned the gas and zoomed up to close the gap. The people who had passed her now watched in burning frustration as she regained her lead. She'd gone from the base of the bridge to halfway up in the blink of an eye.

The fact that a car with a manual transmission will drift lifelessly backward if the driver is not careful was previously unknown to BethAnn Mosley, but she learned it fast enough—before she had the chance to hit the brakes, she met with the vehicle behind her. It was a maroon Lexus sedan, and it looked pretty close to new.

"Oh, shit!"

The Lexus's owner—a tall, thin man wearing expensive glasses that adjusted their tint automatically (at the moment they were in dark mode)—got out and quickly surveyed the damage to his car. The bumper had been badly dented and would obviously need to be replaced.

"What the hell's the matter with you?" he said, gesturing angrily with his hands as he walked up alongside the Jag.

"I'm sorry, I'm sorry," BethAnn said quickly, eager to avoid conflict at the moment. "I'm just very nervous."

"We all are, but that doesn't mean you can drive like an idiot!"

"I know, I know." She moved the stick around to make it seem as though she was regaining control of the situation.

"You're going to cover the damage to my car...."

"Of course," she said, lying through her teeth. "Meet me in the Home Depot parking lot. I'll give you all my information and we'll work it out." She couldn't wait to floor the Jag on 72 and leave this asshole in the dust. "I'm really sorry."

Others had begun honking at this point. The car in front of them was pulling away. This was not the time to be arguing about a fender bender.

The Lexus's owner lingered for another moment, staring at her as if he couldn't believe morons like this really existed. He made a short, snotty sound through his teeth and retreated, stopping to assess the damage one more time. He got back in, shaking his head, and slammed the door mightily. In the rearview mirror BethAnn could see a woman in the seat next to him. They began discussing what had happened. He was very animated, using his hands for emphasis. The woman, on the other hand, simply nodded.

The last thing in the world BethAnn wanted was to nail him again. She had to pull away cleanly, as if she'd been driving this car all her life. The trouble was, she had no idea how to make that happen.

As she fiddled desperately with the stick, praying for a miracle, the burning smell returned. More smoke appeared and drifted over the hood. Some came through the vents on the dash. The gap between the Jag and the car ahead of her was widening. The honking began in earnest and quickly heightened to a bizarre automotive overture. The man she'd just struck joined in, leaning on the horn rather than tapping it, producing a single, ear-splitting tone that bore into her brain like an ice pick.

Convinced she had somehow suddenly "lost" the skills she'd developed in the last twenty minutes, she tried every clutch-stick-gas combination imaginable, and all within the span of about ten seconds. All four limbs were in motion, creating a series of semi-hilarious octopusian gestures. Nothing worked; nothing happened. The Jag didn't lift off the Lexus's bumper, didn't even "hop" forward like it had back in the driveway. Her heart was pounding like it was about to explode. Cars in the left lane were swerving back to the right, populating the space in front of her. Others couldn't get to it, as she was blocking them.

She heard the Lexus's door open, glanced fearfully into the rearview mirror and saw the guy coming toward her again. He was moving quickly and decisively, the way you walk when you're really pissed. She could only see his torso and his legs down to his knees. He was wearing jeans and a denim shirt that matched perfectly.

"What the hell's the problem? Come on!"

She continued with her octopus aerobics while the guy waited. She suddenly had the feeling he knew she couldn't drive this car. He watched her like an impatient teacher giving a student one last chance to prove herself before throwing in the towel.

"Well?"

The honking overture now included the angry shouts of others.

"I'm trying, I'm trying!"

"I don't think you have a clue about driving a stick."

"Of course I do—"

Smoke started leaking around the hood as if something was being barbecued underneath.

"Ohhhh," she groaned.

"Your clutch is burned out!" the man said, throwing his hands up. "You have no idea—this isn't even your car, is it?"

"Push me!" BethAnn pleaded.

"What?"

"Please get back in your car and push me over the bridge!"

"Screw you, honey. Get this piece of junk out of the way, now!"

BethAnn heard other doors opening. A quick check in the mirror confirmed her fears—a small gang of irritated-looking people had formed and was heading in her direction.

"What's the problem?" someone shouted.

"She doesn't know how to drive a stick," Mr. Lexus informed them. "She just cooked the clutch."

"Yeah? Then let's move the damn thing! There's no time for this!"

A face suddenly appeared in her window—brown hair, bushy beard, sunglasses. It was the face of someone you might see at a roadhouse bar or an Allman Brothers concert.

"Get moving, lady."

"Fuck you!" she screeched, and the moment she did she knew she'd made a mistake.

The Allman Brothers guy's face turned bright red. In a singular fluid motion he reached in, popped the lock, and opened the door. Then he hooked his hand under BethAnn's arm.

"What are you doing? Get your hands off me!"

His strength was unbelievable. He lifted her out of the seat and flung her onto the road like a doll. Her first instinct upon hitting the pavement was to get back up, jump on his back, and scratch his eyes out. What halted her was pure instinct—she had a feeling, in fact was damned certain, that this guy was as accustomed to violence as he was to breathing. He'd be able to handle whatever she threw at him.

"You asshole!"

"Hey, give me a hand!" he said to the others who'd gathered around. He shut the door and leaned down, grabbing the Jag at the edge of its undercarriage. It looked like he was trying to hug it.

At first BethAnn had no idea what he was doing. But when five or six other men, including the Lexus driver, joined him, the realization struck home like a missile.

"Okay, on three...."

"Oh no, don't you dare!" she squawked, scrambling to her feet. Futile or not, she was going to make him think twice. She leaped on him like a monkey, wrapping her arms around his neck and pulling backward.

"What the—?"

He staggered back, barely able to maintain his balance with this 250-pound woman attached. Others from the crowd rushed to help. The pair went down in a heap, and it took four people to separate them. BethAnn squirmed and kicked like a rabid animal in a net. Two more people were enlisted to subdue her. The man she'd attacked, much to her surprise, did nothing in retribution. He didn't even acknowledge her, really—he simply got back up, hair running crazily in every direction and a slight trickle of blood oozing from one nostril, and went back to the Jag. The entire incident consumed no more than ten seconds, but it seemed like an eternity.

Hurriedly taking position again, he said, "Okay, ready? One..."

"No!" BethAnn screamed.

"Two..."

"Don't you dare!"

"Three!"

"NO!!!"

They rocked the car back and forth a few times, just to build some momentum. It was surprisingly light, but then perhaps that was just the psychology of the moment—under less stressful, less urgent circumstances, it might have felt much heavier.

They got it onto its side first, then leaned it against the guard rail. The crowd of onlookers had grown, and the Allman Brothers guy hastily recruited another bulky male or two to help with the final effort.

BethAnn lost what little control remained and went berserk in a desperate final attempt to free herself. At one point she kicked one of her captors in the side of the face. All that did was double the guy's determination to hold her down.

A combined groan came from the heaving team, who slowly but surely lifted the Jag up and onto the steel-tubed guardrail. It hung there for one brief but fascinating instant, balanced like a dinner plate atop a pool cue in a circus act. Then it finally gave way to gravity and tipped over, slipping off the rail at a 45-degree angle.

Most people ran back to their vehicles, but a few couldn't resist standing there to watch the Jag's descent. It whistled quietly through the warm spring wind, its sooty black underside fully exposed, then slammed mightily into the bay. The gentle current carried it for a few seconds before it slipped below the surface.

BethAnn was released, the people responsible fleeing to their cars.

"You assholes!" she screamed, picking up a little stone that was lying nearby and chucking it at one of them. It missed by a mile.

The line started moving again, and she had little doubt they'd run over her if she didn't get out of the way. She got up on the sidewalk that followed the guardrail. A quick look over the side confirmed that the Jag—her symbolic entrance into a better world—was lost forever. The spot where it had gone down was bubbling and fizzing like seltzer, but even that wouldn't last long.

With an open road in front of them, the cars zoomed over the bridge. Turning away from the Jag's final resting place, BethAnn was suddenly struck with the realization that she now had no way of getting to the mainland besides walking.

Actually, running might be a good idea.

She couldn't remember the last time she had run anywhere. Probably not since gym class in high school. But now wasn't the time to be thinking about this. Traffic was racing by, and she figured there was a fat chance of anyone stopping to pick her up. Percolating with a combination of rage, despair, and more helplessness than she'd ever known, she turned and began jogging up the incline. The peak looked like it was a million miles away. She didn't look back because there was no reason to. She wasn't just running from the tidal wave, she was running from everything she'd known over the last ten years. That thought didn't eclipse the physical strain she was already feeling. After only a few minutes she was huffing and puffing. She paused to catch her breath, leaning against the rail for support and hoping her heart didn't explode. One of the things I would've done if I'd been able to keep that Jag is get into shape, she told herself. Slim down, maybe look for a man again. But it was all academic now. The Jag was gone. All she had left was herself, and saving her ass was the priority.

When she felt better, she began jogging again. She'd only gone a few steps when she heard a voice—"Excuse me, miss?"

She turned to find an elderly man leaning out of a maroon minivan. Wispy white hair covered all but the very top of his head and added contrast to a remarkably deep tan. His mouth was small and upturned in a warm, grandfatherly smile.

"Do you need a lift?"

The man kept the vehicle moving, slowly. BethAnn, although she barely realized it, kept moving, too.

"That would be great."

"Then hop in—but quickly, please. I don't want to hold everyone else up."

The side door slid back automatically, revealing a handful of other passengers. They were all very young—no more than teenagers—and they all wore white crewneck T-shirts with red trim. "Highway Holiness Church of Jesus" was printed on the front.

The little group moved back to make room for her. After a moment's hesitation, she climbed in. The door slid shut again.

As they reached the top of the bridge and began down the other side, the priest glanced into the rearview mirror and said, "I'm Father Brad, leader of the Highway Holiness Church. What's your name, dear?"

The others waited for her response with what seemed like unusually high anticipation.

* * *

Karen was sure the car was going to flip—she'd never gone into a turn so fast. The tires squealed, just like in the movies. At least the two on the driver's side did—the other two lifted a few inches off the pavement. What amazed her, though, was that the car didn't flip. She had to be doing at least eighty.

What's the difference? I'm dead anyway.

As she straightened out on the Erickson's street, she checked her watch—less than ten minutes now. This was an exercise in futility; she'd known that for some time. What did she think, she'd pick up her children and then fly away? Did she really believe she'd have time to go all the way back?

Those damn soldiers, if they just hadn't slowed me down.

Would her death weigh on their minds? Would it keep them up at night? Would they even speak of it? Probably not. The men responsible would keep it locked inside. If the topic ever did come up publicly, they'd cover for each other. That's what people like that did. *Those thirty minutes I wasted.* Then a corrective thought—*No, those thirty minutes they wasted.* They were playing with your time, and it's so much easier to play with someone else's time.

"Bastards," she mumbled, tears rolling again.

As soon as she reached the house, she pulled over crookedly and jumped out, leaving the car running. Halfway up the front walk she noticed the Erickson's car still parked in the driveway.

Oh Jesus, no. Don't tell me....

The nightmare scenario came rushing forward—they were all in there, in their little vacuum, blissfully unaware. She would have to die with them, would have to see their faces, explain to them what was about to happen. No chance to say goodbye to their father.

She ran to the door, yanked it open, and bolted inside.

"Nancy? Bud? It's me!"

She paused for only a moment, and upon receiving no answer began opening other doors. First the bedroom, then the sewing room.

"Patrick? Michael?"

The notion that they were still here was unnerving for all the obvious reasons, but the idea that they weren't was, to her surprise, equally harrowing. If they weren't here, where were they?

In the backyard, gardening?

She opened the back door and scanned the fenced-in landscape that sloped down to the bay. As beautiful as ever, green and brown and meticulously maintained.

"Nancy! Bud! Are you out here?"

Her reply came in the form of birds chirping and a light breeze rustling the trees; the soundtrack of a peaceful spring day. But the feeling that she was alone—completely alone—suddenly entered her system and spread itself around, the way a drop of food coloring spreads through a glass of water.

"Patrick! Michael!"

My God, they're already gone.

She went back inside, and the tears started again. She cried openly, leaning back against the sink, covering her nose and mouth with both hands.

There's nowhere to go. No way to get back in time.

She thought of trying to call Mike. Maybe it would be easier getting through on an ordinary phone. He always left his cell on, in fact he made a point of doing so when he went on a trip—in spite of the absurd roaming charges—so he'd always be accessible.

What should I say? "Thanks for the memories, darling. By the way, I couldn't find the kids, so I'm finished. Have a nice flight back."

The distance from where she stood to the phone was maybe four steps, but in that journey a million thoughts surged through her mind—about death, about what came after, and about all the things she would miss in the land of the living. Patrick and Michael's growing up, going to college, getting married. What would their wives be like? What about their own children? How would they fare professionally? Would one of them become a

Nobel prizewinner? Find the cure for AIDS? Become a wealthy entrepreneur? She would never know. She'd always believed in God and the concept of an afterlife—some form of afterlife. But what if it was all a farce? What if someone, or perhaps a group of someones, had invented all that to provide peace of mind? What if this really was the end of everything?

She removed the phone from its base without really thinking about it. The plastic "click" and the ensuing electronic beep brought her back to reality. Half-dazed from a hail of uncommonly profound ideas, she entered Mike's number and waited.

The call went through.

After two rings, she heard his voice—"Hi, this is Mike. I'm not available at the moment, but if you'll leave—"

"Dammit!"

"—a brief message, I'll get back to you as soon as I can. Thanks."

"Mike, it's me. Look, there's a lot going on over here at the moment. If you turn on the TV you might see something about it. There's a tsunami coming. I'm at the Erickson's house right now. I don't know where Bud and Nancy are, but I assume they left LBI with the boys. I'll call you back as soon as I know more."

The whirl of horror and worry and other emotions in her mind suddenly came to a halt as one bright and shiny thought drifted forward.

"I love you, Mike," she said, her voice wavering. "No matter what happens, I want you to know that I love you and the boys more than anything in the world. I always have, and I always will."

Grief overwhelmed her, shattering the courageous facade she'd been working so hard to maintain.

"I'll call back as soon as I can," she said, barely able to shape the words.

* * *

Dr. Sarah Collins scribbled the last set of numbers on the clipboard, then handed it back to Dave Dolan, who was now so pale he looked as though he'd died and been drained by an embalmer.

"Will it reach us here?" he asked, his throat dry.

Collins seemed at first not to hear the question, but a moment later she replied, "It might."

"It could pass over the island and then cross the bay?"

Collins was nodding. "I can't believe how big it'll be. Holy God...."

Dolan took a quick look around the room—there was nothing that belonged to him other than the knapsack with the textbooks.

"The fourth one should be more than twenty feet high," Collins added grimly. "Only takes a ten-footer to wipe out a town." She gestured to the east-facing window. "Take a good look, Dave, while you still can."

Dolan went over. LBI stood majestically along the horizon, a postcard-picturesque scene on any other day. What must it be like, he wondered, to be over there right now? To know that your life would end soon and that escape was impossible?

He decided he didn't want to find out.

"I think it's time to boogie," he said, turning away and heading toward his knapsack. "Don't you?"

"Yeah," Collins said hollowly, staring dreamily into space. "Is everything packed?"

"Everything important."

Sarah Collins took one last look around. Her heart was going like a drum.

"Let's go."

FOURTEEN

*W*ith so little time left, Donald Harper decided his future.

It would play out like this: The helicopter would arrive only moments before the tsunami, and he'd get on it. (He was actually intrigued by the possibility of watching the giant waves strike as he flew overhead, but he didn't have the stomach to witness that kind of destruction knowing there were people dying down there.) He'd take the short trip to the mainland, manage the rescue effort, and then, once the island's infrastructure was up and running again, he'd step down. He didn't want to be remembered as the guy who got to keep his job because he was "lucky" enough to be in office when disaster struck. He also knew his detractors wouldn't stand for it—they'd be back on him as soon as they were able. All would be forgiven for awhile, but not forever.

And, of course, eventually they'd find out everything.

His day of judgment would surely come if he clung to power. The longer he stayed, the harder he would fall, and the greater the humiliation. If he stepped down gracefully, admitting he had made mistakes and sparing the residents the details, and the despair, he might—might—be able to salvage the family name. Yes, he would be regarded as the black sheep, the one who screwed up. But at least he would be regarded as the exception, the dark chapter in an otherwise shining history. He would have to disappear, find some other way to make a living.

Maybe, just maybe, he could survive.

As he sat there behind his desk, elbows on the blotter, folded hands resting against his lips, the urge to cry was overwhelming. Just a year ago he and Tom had begun to plot—seriously plot—his road to Washington. Everything seemed perfect, could not have been going better. It was all within reach. He found himself wondering what it was like to be a United States Senator. Real power and influence, making decisions that determined the course of a nation. Your effort affecting millions of people—millions. He saw it, like a bright light along the horizon. It was still a good distance away, but it was there. All he had to do was stay the course.

And then the light had gone out. Nothing but darkness and uncertainty lay ahead. The fragility of it was so...so pathetic.

You make a few mistakes in your private life, you ask God for forgiveness and move on. You make a few in public life, you're finished.

The career of a politician, no matter how charismatic or successful, was as delicate as the wings of a butterfly. He hadn't realized that. Or maybe he did and chose to ignore it. Whatever the case, he would've given anything for the chance to go back to that day one year ago and do it all over. But human beings weren't permitted the luxury of going back in time and fixing things. You could only go forward. And that option didn't seem to offer much for him at the moment.

He stood, took his jacket off the back of his chair, and slipped into it. I'll never sit here again, he thought stupidly, hardly able to believe this moment had really arrived. *Next time it'll be someone else.*

Maybe a different chair, maybe even a different building depending on the extent of the destruction. But the same chair in the figurative sense. It wouldn't be him in it.

Who'll be the lucky S.O.B.? he wondered. It wasn't the first time he'd mulled this over. Davis? Surely not—he was never in the running. He doesn't have what it takes. No way. Maybe Naughton, or Phillips. Maybe even Valerie Pruitt. She's about as bright as they come.

One thing he knew for sure was that he would not have an official say in who his successor would be. No one would want that. Maybe the election committee would make some kind of grandiose gesture in public, just to seem forgiving and decent. A feel-good move designed to show a little mercy. But offstage his input would be about as welcome as a vial of anthrax.

He stepped to one side and slid the chair under the desk. A futile gesture, he realized, as everything in this room would be swirling in a billion gallons of water very shortly. It was more a symbolic gesture, and for some reason it made him feel proud of himself. He was at least still trying to carry himself with class and dignity.

He turned off the green banker's lamp, leaving only the sunlight through the windows. He went to the doorway, turned for one final look, and mumbled, "Thanks for the memories." Then, out of nowhere, he thought, *Maybe I can lose some weight, grow a beard, dye my hair, and run again.* An utterly absurd notion, but it gave him a chuckle.

There was a kitchenette on the other side of the main room, directly across from Marie's desk. On the shelf above the sink was a coffeepot and a police scanner. The former was already off. He didn't drink coffee, and Marie had only a cup in the morning. The scanner, however, was on and very active. Harper liked having it on when he was here; it made him feel more in touch. The downside was that you got so used to hearing it after awhile that it gelled with all the other background sounds and became meaningless. Acoustic wallpaper.

He went over to turn it off, but just before he got there he heard a voice, troubled with static but clear enough—"Terry, it's Jeff. Look, I'm still with Mrs. King, and we're almost to the refuge, but we're going to run out of time. I need some help."

He knew that voice—it belonged to Jeff Mitchell, one of LBI's best cops. *What the hell is he still doing here?*

The dispatcher's voice immediately followed—"Like what?"

Mitchell: "Something in the air. A helicopter, preferably. Didn't they say the National Guard and the Staties were sending a few?"

Dispatcher: "Yes, they're all here already."

Mitchell: "Can you ask them to send one over there?" A pause, and then he added, "I don't think we're going to make it, Terry."

"Oh, shit," Harper murmured.

He went back to Marie's desk and picked up the phone. He knew the direct number to the dispatcher's office by heart (along with all the other municipal numbers, including those he rarely used—his memory for phone numbers was legendary). It rang five times before it was picked up.

"Long Beach Police Department, Dispat—"

"Terry, it's Don Harper. I just heard Jeff on the radio. What's going on? Why is he still on the island?"

"He's out at Forsythe looking for some kids."

Harper's heart skipped a beat. "You've got to be kidding."

"Carolyn King insisted he take her. Her daughter apparently went over there looking for her boyfriend—Mark White, the *SandPaper* photographer. No luck finding them so far."

"Jesus Christ. They'll never make it now."

A pause, and then, "I'm trying to get a helicopter to them, but they're all tied up." She started crying. "I've got to go, too, Mayor Harper. I can't...I...."

A plan formed in Harper's mind in a span of milliseconds. "Look, Terry, get out of there. There's no point in staying."

"But what about Jeff and the others?"

"I've got an idea. I'll take care of it, okay?"

Another pause, and then, "What can you possibly do?"

"Trust me, Terry. Get moving."

He hung up without waiting for a reply.

Harper knew Carolyn King, knew the whole family. The Kings were among the wealthiest people on the island. Burton King, Carolyn's husband, owned an engineering firm in Parkertown and made his fortune with government contracts. He designed and manufactured the small parts to military equipment that most people never noticed—custom nuts and bolts, hooks and levers, locks and frames. He held over a dozen U.S. patents and was a bonafide millionaire, not just on paper. He was also one of the straightest, most upstanding human beings Harper had ever known. As far as he knew, Burt King didn't drink, smoke, cheat on his wife, or fudge his tax returns. In fact, in the nearly twenty years Harper had known him he'd never once seen the guy lose his temper or say a bad word about anyone. Back before the scandals broke, Harper played Friday-night poker with a few friends about twice a month, and sometimes King would join in.

How his daughter, Jennifer, had gotten mixed up in this mess was a mystery; she certainly wasn't a problem kid. Whatever the case, there was no time to puzzle it out now.

He ran outside just as the chopper came into view. He waved, and it moved toward him. It landed in the parking lot, spraying sand and pebbles everywhere. The pilot pushed the door open as Harper ran over.

"Ready to go?" he shouted, more of a statement than a question.

As Harper stepped in, the cardiac beat of the machine networking its way up his legs and into his ribcage, he said, "Actually we have to make a quick stop first."

The pilot's face went blank. "Where?"

"The Forsythe Wildlife Refuge." Harper got into his seat and slipped on the belts. "Do you know where it is?"

"No! Not far, I hope!"

"It's not. Let's get going and I'll show you."

"You sure about this?"

"Yes! Go—head south!"

Without another word the pilot lifted out of the parking lot and into the spring sky.

It was the last time Donald Harper would ever see the building where he had spent the most important twelve years of his professional career.

*   *   *

Jennifer tried her mother three more times on the cell phone before giving up. Thinking it might have something to do with her mother's phone, she tried Mark again, then her father at work. She got the same recorded "No service available" message each time. She rarely lost her cool, but the urge to smash the phone on the ground was so powerful she had to struggle to suppress it.

So what now?

She looked at her watch—less than ten minutes left.

A moment of paralysis came and went. The notion of death was vague and unformed in her mind. She really hadn't seen much of it in her brief life, nor for that matter any of its cousins—suffering, pain, misery, etc. Her parents had successfully shielded her from the darker aspects of human existence. An aunt in Colorado had died of pancreatic cancer, but Jennifer hadn't seen her during the illness and in fact had not known her well—she'd only met her once, during a family trip when she was six years old, before the cancer formed. She remembered Aunt Janet as vibrant and lively, which was symbolic of the way her parents were bringing her up—let in the light, filter the dark.

And now she found herself staring death in the face. Facing the end of everything. Everything.

I was so stupid, she thought, unable to restrain the tears. *I never should have come. I should've called the police. They would've sent someone—someone trained at finding missing persons.*

And Brian...that jerk, leaving her here. No way of getting back now. She'd been stranded, plain and simple.

That bastard.

She looked at Mark's car, the old, beat-up clunker. It barely ran, spent more time in a mechanic's garage than in his own. The sight of it made her cry even harder.

He never had anything, ever. He had an awful life from the moment he was born. It's so unfair, so goddamn unfair!

She'd thought about getting him a better car, somehow. Her parents had more than enough money, but they wouldn't do it, so she never bothered asking. Deep down she knew her mom didn't really like him because he came from the "wrong kind of family," and her dad barely knew he existed. It wouldn't happen. But she could've used the money she made at the supermarket. She wouldn't be able to get him something great, but at least it would've been reliable. The guilt that arose from the fact that she lived so much more comfortably than he did often inspired ideas like this. She felt bad for him. He was a good person who deserved much more than he'd been given.

She opened the door and got behind the wheel. For a moment she wondered if maybe he left his keys somewhere. She checked the ignition, but no luck. Then she realized, *If you find them, what are you going to do? Take off and leave him here?*

She couldn't. She knew she'd never be able to go another sixty or seventy years carrying that kind of guilt. Just wondering if Mark might have come back to make his escape and found his car gone—stolen, essentially—would be enough to land her in the laughing academy, under constant sedation and fed through a tube.

She checked the trail through the windshield. "Come on, Mark, where are you?" She'd never felt so helpless.

She checked her watch again. Then, realizing the situation was now utterly hopeless and the chance for escape lost forever, she made a heroic decision—*I'm going to go down that trail, find the man I love, and die with him. Maybe we'll get lucky and find a way to survive this thing.*

She got back out, slammed the door, and headed toward the trail. No sooner had she done so, however, then she caught the distant sound of a police siren. She paused, thinking perhaps she'd imagined it. It grew stronger, clearer.

It's coming this way.

She turned toward the road. Seconds later a Long Beach squad car zoomed up, its lights swirling madly. She had little doubt it was here for her—perhaps her and Mark—but the sight of the person in the passenger seat made her stomach drop.

"Oh my God, mom...."

The car pulled up just a few feet from her, doors already opening on both sides. Jennifer ran over, the two embraced. Fresh tears rolled down her cheeks.

"Oh, mom, I'm so sorry. I'm so sorry."

Her mother stroked her hair. "I know, I know. It's okay, sweetheart. It's okay."

"Carolyn," Mitchell said quietly but firmly from the other side. "We don't have a lot of time."

Without turning to face him, Carolyn King said, "There's a helicopter coming, isn't there? Didn't I hear you ask for one?"

"I can't say for sure. No one radioed back to confirm." He looked at his watch. "They might all be gone by now."

Mrs. King looked into the endless blue of the late spring sky. "Will we make it?" she asked, struggling to stay calm on the outside.

"We might," Mitchell replied. "But not if we stand around here talking."

"Okay, let's go. Jen, get in the back."

"But mom, what about—"

"You heard what the officer said. There's no time left."

"Mom, I can't just leave him here!" Her eyes reddened and she shook slightly.

"Jennifer, there's no time for this! Get in!"

The sharpness of her voice—the undeniable command of it—made Mitchell's heart jump. He'd never used such a tone with his own kids, but then he had never been in a situation like this, either.

A moment passed when nothing happened—Jennifer and her mother were locked in a staring contest while Mitchell watched with rapt fascination. No more than two seconds passed, but it felt like hours.

"No, I'm not going," Jennifer said flatly. It came out pouty, almost childish, as if she was refusing to leave a toy store. But the face was a different story—cold, glaring eyes full of anger, the kind you associate with the courage of a person who stands by their convictions. Mitchell thought distantly that he was witnessing a measurable step in Jennifer's evolution—for what was probably the first time in her life, she was standing up to her mother, afraid, and yet willing to deal with that fear for the sake of a principle.

Carolyn King had similar thoughts, and instead of simply raising her voice higher as she would've done in years past, she decided on a new tack—reason. A part of her felt the deepest pride and respect for the inner strength that had begun to bloom. But now was not the time to show it.

"Jennifer, I know how you feel about this, about Mark, but we have no time left. No time at all."

"I can't just leave him here!"

"But you can't stay."

Jennifer turned away from her, in silence, and it was more than her mother could take.

"If you think I'm going to stand here and let you die, Jennifer, you're wrong. It'll never happen, and I'm ordering you to get into that car right now!"

Jennifer turned back to face Carolyn, and for a moment Mitchell feared the girl would start into Round Two. At that point he'd have to step in and take action. Carolyn was right that there was no time left for this. None at all.

Then, to his great relief, Jennifer grabbed the handle of the rear door and yanked it. As the tears rolled from her eyes, Mitchell thought, *This will stand between them forever. This damn wave is going to destroy a lot more than real estate.*

Jennifer slammed the door shut mightily; her mother did likewise up front. With two angry women inside and the race of his life ahead of him, Mitchell made the mental comment that this ride should be a real laff-riot.

He saw the helicopter before he heard it, a tiny white shape in the otherwise cloudless sky. If he'd gotten into the car a moment earlier, he probably would've missed it.

"Let's go, Jeff," Carolyn King said matter-of-factly, leaning over just far enough to make eye contact.

"Couldn't agree more," Mitchell countered. "But we may be in luck. Look."

She got back out. As the chopper drew closer, she took her rosary beads from her pocket and kissed them.

Mitchell waved vigorously. The pilot spotted him after a few moments and landed about fifty feet away.

The passenger door flew open and the familiar figure of Donald Harper emerged, waving them on.

"Come on! Let's go! There's no time left!"

The three of them started over, then Jennifer stopped, turned—

"Mark!"

She was beyond ordinary grief now, bordering on a breakdown. She trembled violently, her face red and twisted.

Harper rushed over, put a hand on Carolyn King's shoulder. "He never came out, I guess?"

"No."

"Mayor!" the pilot called.

Harper hustled back. "What? What's up?"

The pilot—late thirties, wearing a headset and sunglasses—said, "I have some bad news. We can't carry this many."

Harper shook his head. "I don't think the other kid is coming. It looks like he's still—"

"No, I mean even with what we have now! It's too many!"

Now Harper paused. "You're kidding."

"I wish I was, but there's no way I can take four people. Even if there were enough seats, we couldn't handle the load."

"Can we toss anything off?"

"I already did that—there's nothing left to toss."

Harper, hands on the doorway and arms spread wide, dropped his head. What a day. *What did any of us do to deserve this?*

Then he had a sudden inspiration.

"Take these people, I'll stay here!"

"What?"

"There's a flush pipe on the western side of the refuge, big enough for a person to crawl into. I should know—I put it there. The DEP had a fit, but we had to do it. It doesn't connect with the ocean, so I should be able to hide in it. If I find Mark I'll take him with me."

"Are you sure?"

"What choice is there?"

The pilot nodded, then put his hand out. "Good luck, Mr. Mayor. I'll be back to get you when it's over."

Harper smiled and shook his hand firmly. "I'll watch for you."

He turned back to the group, waiting nervously. Jeff Mitchell kept glancing at the Atlantic. It was so calm, so peaceful, so... ordinary. He wondered for the umpteenth time if this was all some elaborate gag, like Orson Welles's 1938 "War of the Worlds" radio broadcast. If it turned out to be a hoax, Mitchell, at heart a peaceful, forgiving man, would track down the people responsible and make their lives miserable.

"What's up?"

"You guys have to get on, now."

Jennifer, her eyes trained on the trail, said in a wobbly, choked voice, "I...I can't leave without Mark."

"I'm going to find him," Harper said.

Everyone turned.

"What?" Mitchell asked.

"All four of us can't fit on the chopper, so someone has to stay."

"I'll stay," Mitchell said quickly. "I can—"

Harper shook his head. "I'm not intending to die, Jeff. I'm hoping to find Mark and take him to that flush pipe. Remember, two years ago? We put it in and the DEP blew their top? It's the one with the pressure lock."

"I remember," Jeff said. "The one by the cove."

"Exactly. If we reach it, we should be able to survive this thing."

"Let *me* go," Mitchell countered.

Harper gave him a look that enlisted so many different emotions it was hard to register all of them—sadness, desperation, the struggle of a repressed ambition, a plea for mercy. In that instant Mitchell understood. This is his chance to redeem himself. Maybe, just maybe, if he finds this kid and they both survive, the people will forgive him. This could be the closest thing to salvation he'll ever have.

"Jeff, you've got your family to think about," Harper said, giving Mitchell his escape route. "And this is something I need to do."

The cop thought for a second, then nodded. "I understand, sir." He put his hand out and Harper took it. "Good luck."

"Thanks, Jeff. You too."

Carolyn King had been following the exchange. "Good luck, Don," she said.

"Thank you, Carolyn." He put a hand on Jennifer's shoulder. "Take care of her."

"I will."

Harper turned and jogged off down the trail. The others watched wordlessly for a moment, then Mitchell said, "Okay, let's go."

They started for the helicopter, Jennifer pausing for one last moment before finally and fully resigning herself to the situation. She stumbled toward the chopper, every molecule of her body pulsing with emotion. Suddenly she felt like someone else, and no longer part of reality. The scene was dreamlike, disconnected, and abstract. Her mind became a slow-moving blender of words, phrases, and broken images. There was no black or white, nothing solid.

They loaded in, Mitchell up front, the Kings in the back. Carolyn went first, then she and Mitchell guided Jennifer to her seat. They secured her belts for her, as if she was an invalid. When Mitchell pulled the door shut, a fresh wave of the girl's grief poured forth. Wordlessly, her mother wrapped her arms around her daughter and held her tight.

The chopper lifted into the sky and turned northwest. Toward the mainland, and safety.

* * *

Karen ran outside, hoping and yet not hoping that she'd find them all out there, maybe working in the garden. She wanted to see her boys again—more than anything in the world—but to see them now would also mean their fate was sealed. There was simply no time left.

She called their names several times, but got no answer. She had regained some of her focus, and an equal amount of grief had returned to the shadows. But it remained close by, waiting.

She stopped, allowed herself a moment to think. The car was still here; she'd spotted it on the way in. So if they weren't here, how did they leave? Someone else? One of the helicopters? Or did they take a—

Boat. Bud's boat.

She ran down the hill toward the slip, thinking about how Bud loved his boat, how he kept it in perfect working order. How he washed it, waxed it, lubricated it. It was probably in better condition now than the day it rolled off the assembly line.

She pulled the gate back and found the empty slip.

Gone.

But had they reached a point of safety? She wanted to see them, wanted to know they were safe. That was impossible at the moment. She had to take it on faith.

Now, what about saving yourself?

It was the first time since she'd heard about the tsunami that this crossed her mind. She checked her watch, saw that there were less than fifteen minutes left, if the reports on the radio were accurate, and realized with a sickening feeling that there was no way she could drive back to the bridge in time. At best she'd make it to the end of the traffic line. That wouldn't be good enough.

Oh God, please help me. Please give me the answer. What do I do? Is this how it ends for me? Didn't all those years of going to church and saying my prayers at night mean anything? Haven't I always been a good person? Haven't I at least always tried? Doesn't that count for something? What about my children?

The grief came forward again. She battled to keep it back, but it was a struggle. She stood on the edge of the property, the bay water lapping at her feet, and scanned the horizon. There wasn't a boat in sight, not even a dot speeding toward the mainland.

Where the answer came from, she did not know. At that moment she attributed it to a kind and merciful God, because she was sure it hadn't come from inside her—

The Erickson's neighbor has a boat, too.

She went through the yard, out the other gate, and across the front lawn. The temptation to check her watch again itched like a rash, but she fought it. What was the difference? The M.O. here was "move as quickly as you can, period." The hour of day was irrelevant.

The neighbor's house was built from the same plan as the Erickson's. Karen had met him once, last summer. His name was Ralph Bokowitz, a retired dentist from Passaic, widower, and father of two. Nice enough guy, the Ericksons had said, but not terribly social. Karen reached the garage door and tried to pull it up. It didn't budge, so she cursed at it.

Then she realized the handle simply needed to be turned. When she did this, she heard the rods slide back neatly. The door, on well-oiled runners, slid up without further effort.

And there it was.

Bokowitz's little aluminum boat was, like everything else in his garage, in immaculate condition. It sat on a shiny new trailer, ready for action. The engine in the back had been pulled up and was tilted forward.

Now for the hard part.

The trailer was kept upright by a single cinder block, which had been positioned vertically under the hitch. With a mighty effort, Karen lifted the hitch and nudged the block away with her foot. Then she set nose of the trailer down and moved the block aside to clear the path. These few simple actions left her winded.

Mustering all the strength she had, she lifted the hitch again and started pulling. It was a struggle just to gain the first few inches until momentum kicked in. Halfway down the driveway she drew the trailer to the left, dragging the reluctant rubber tires across a lawn that would be submerged very shortly. Her arms burned with pain, turning first to wood and then to stone. Each time she felt like she couldn't go any further she thought about her family. She knew dropping the trailer here would be the fatal, final error. There was no way she had the strength to get it up to speed again; not on the soft grass. It was already moving and she had to keep it moving.

She glanced briefly up the street, half-expecting to see huge gushes of water crashing around the barrier of houses on Long Beach Boulevard. If that happened, she decided then and there, she'd drop the trailer and run for it. She had to pull left again to get the trailer through the front gate. In a moment of pure good fortune, it fit through the opening with maybe an inch to spare on either side.

The pain in her arms had reached where she could barely feel them anymore; they were so numb it was as if they weren't even there. She propped the trailer's forward beam over her shoulder and turned, pulling it Viking-style so her legs would bear the brunt of the load for awhile. Once she hit the downhill part of the yard her problem was to keep from being run over by the trailer. As she slowly inched it down the steep slope, she was becoming exhausted.

By the time she passed through the gate and reached the shoreline, the weight of the boat and trailer had become too much for her. Every muscle had frozen as if she'd been hit with a stun gun. She didn't even have the strength to lower the trailer's nose onto the ground. Instead, she simply stepped to one side and let it fall from her shoulder.

Unfortunately, the rest of her body did not move as swiftly as it needed to and the galvanized steel tubing landed on her right foot like a sledgehammer.

The scream that emanated from Karen's slender body echoed first through Little Egg Harbor Bay, then around the rest of the country, then the planet, and finally throughout the deepest reaches of outer space. In her shock she tried to yank the foot free, which only served to tear the gash even further. She dropped to the ground, squeezing her ankle in an attempt to dampen the zillion-watt bolts of agony that were shooting into her brain.

When she finally mustered the courage to look squarely at the wound, she saw more blood than she'd ever seen in her life—and that included the birth of her two boys. The moment became surreal, dreamlike; she felt detached from it. She was looking at someone else's foot, not hers. She was aware of the pain, but it was somehow muted and distant.

Then she tried to wiggle her toes, just to make sure the foot wasn't broken. Although she felt like she was wiggling them, they barely moved. Something else did, however—something bloody and shiny. It was visible through the opening in her shoe. She wasn't a medical expert, but she was pretty certain it was either a ligament or a tendon.

And it was moving.

She vomited so fast and so hard that her throat seemed to catch fire. She turned her head just far enough to puke on the ground and not her foot.

Then the adrenaline hit her. Suddenly, alongside terror and extreme anxiety came wild rage unlike anything she'd ever experienced. She'd lost her cool a few times in the past—felt the sting of anger and the rumble of hatred—but those instances were always understandable: the shooting death of a close friend, a news story about a child being raped and murdered, the 9/11 attacks. But now, for the first time in her life, she felt like there was some unseen force working against her, some being other than God—perhaps Satan himself—trying to throw up barrier after barrier in order to seal her fate. To make sure she perished on this island with the other unlucky ones.

To keep her from her children, and they from her.

This was at the core, the very heart of her fury. Something was out there trying to keep her from her kids. Some Thing wanted them to be motherless, wanted them to suffer the anguish of losing a parent, bear the scars of that loss for the rest of their lives.

She had no intention of letting that happen.

She wiped her chin with her sleeve and got back up. The pain in her foot was intense, but she ignored it. She lifted the nose of the trailer again and dragged it to the water's edge. She detached the boat and went around to the back. Pushing it off, she figured, would require another Herculean effort, but the little craft rattled along the tiny black wheels almost on its own, sliding quietly into the bay.

As she stepped into the salty water pain shot through her foot again. She dropped to her knees, grabbing the side of the boat as dizziness threatened to deliver the knockout punch.

"No," she said, out of breath and staring at her reflection on the rippling surface. "This isn't where it ends for me. Not a chance."

She hauled herself into the boat, landing on her back and remaining motionless for a long moment. She was so weary now that she felt thoroughly drunk. Everything was moving, swirling. Somehow she remembered that the engine needed to be lowered in. She got to her knees and crawled aft. She could feel her hands moving over the intimidating solidness of the machine, heard it splash when the prop hit the water. But she was barely aware that she was doing all this. She set her head onto the top of it; actually her head put itself on top of it. All she wanted was to sleep.

She had to get the engine going.

Her fingers felt around for the starter. First one side, then the other. Where was it?

And what was that noise in the distance?

It was coming from the direction of the beach. Louder than anything she'd ever heard before.

Hope became sorrow.

Day became night.

Darkness closed in.

* * *

Mark heard the helicopter in the distance, had a feeling it might be for him. By the time he actually saw it, it was heading the other way. It grew smaller and smaller, and with it went his last hope of survival. He watched it numbly, thinking about what his life might have been. About his life with Jen.

This is how it was meant to be, a voice told him. It wasn't his normal mind-voice, but just as clear. *People like you never really get to be with people like her. It's not in the cards.*

He ran—not just in the direction of the chopper, but away from that voice. He waved his hands and screamed. He deduced that the aircraft was heading off the island and toward a safe area, which meant it was traveling northwest. If he headed in that general direction he should run into the parking lot.

Then what? Get in the car, head for the bridge, and get off the island—all in the next five minutes?

He checked his watch. Not even five. Less than that. Maybe two. Maybe none. Even if the wave-strike estimates weren't dead-on accurate, how much time could there be? Ten minutes? Fifteen at the most? It still wasn't enough. Not even close.

Time has run out for you, Mark White, the voice observed. *Life never really worked for you in the first place. Maybe this is for the best.*

"Fuck you," he said, still running.

He and Donald Harper never came within hearing distance of each other, but Mark did find the parking lot. He managed to get his car keys out of his pocket just before he heard something. A loud roar, coming from the East.

He turned to see what it was.

The voice said, *Are you really that surprised?*

FIFTEEN

he beaches of LBI were deserted—no sunbathers, no swimmers, no surfers; not even a lone ship drifting drowsily along the horizon. Lifeguard stands lay on their backs, exposed to the brilliant morning sun, and plastic garbage bags billowed up over the rims of rusted steel trashcans. Sandpipers scurried along the edge of the surf in search of food, squawking angrily at one other.

At precisely 11:33, the tide began falling. A normal tide cycle takes roughly six hours, but this one was complete in less than eight minutes. The sea withdrew as if someone had yanked out its rubber plug, then began to reverse course, swelling violently as it sucked the remaining water from the surf to empower itself. Crabs that had been comfortably concealed only seconds before now found themselves scurrying for cover. Millions of tiny stones and shell fragments rolled downward in a tinkling, rattling cacophony.

Then the wave surged forward. It was not a "surfer's curl" with a little crest at the top. It was as ugly as the destruction it promised—a hurried, disorganized rise, as if the Atlantic Ocean was being pushed forward by the hand of God. The deafening roar that accompanied it was like something from another universe. The wave climbed the slant of the beach with no effort, enveloping and moving swiftly over the dunes.

The first line of resistance came in the form of an eighteen-mile row of homes. Many were large and majestic, and far too old to put up any kind of a fight. The wave slammed into them with an intensity their designers had never anticipated. A beautiful Victorian in Loveladies, built in 1911 and lovingly maintained by all three of its owners, folded as if it had been gut punched. In Beach Haven Terrace, a modest Cape Cod that had been purchased a few months earlier by a 62-year-old widower rose off its foundation and cruised into the home next to it, immediately reducing them both to a chaos of shattered boards. In Holgate, a spidery construct of studs and windowless frames that would have been a three-story home in a few more months bent forward in a respectful bow, creaking and groaning before it disintegrated.

Water gushed down access paths and alleyways. It poured onto Atlantic Avenue and Ocean Boulevard, wiping out thousands of Japanese black pines that had been planted soon after the storm of '62 in the hope that their fast-spreading roots would hold the ground firm in the event of some future catastrophe. Telephone poles snapped like twigs, leaving behind jagged stumps. A rusted pickup truck on Passaic Avenue in Harvey Cedars was scooped up and carried some seventy feet before first striking a flagpole then rolling side-over-side until it landed on someone's front porch. In Brant Beach, the observation deck behind the Mancini Municipal Building exploded in a shower of timber, with one lengthy, creosoted four-by-four effortlessly impaling the windshield of an unmarked police car.

In Ship Bottom and Surf City, hundreds of residents watched in terror from their vehicles as the Atlantic Ocean rose up and over homes, businesses, and roadways. Suddenly it was no longer theoretical, no longer merely a news report—it was here, and it was real. No cameras, no reporters, no fifteen minutes of fame. Just tons of water rushing at breakneck speed and filling every available opening.

The first wave would not reach these unfortunates, but that didn't stop the fear from escalating out of control. Cars at the back of the line swerved to the shoulder and accelerated, colliding with others who had the same idea. Tempers flared and obscenities were screamed, but there was no time for confrontation. Some drove onto the sidewalks as the scene degraded into a bumper-car mentality, property damage no longer a concern. A man in a silver Volkswagen Jetta who had deviated from Long Beach Boulevard to take Central Avenue cut a path across nearly a dozen lawns before finally colliding with a mailbox at the intersection of Central and 2nd. It was a federal crime, but he couldn't have cared less. In spite of the damage to his crumpled front end, he kept going.

Inevitably, through a combination of horror, adrenaline, and paralysis, the already sluggish traffic came to a near halt in the confusing layout where Long Beach Boulevard met Route 72 and headed west. As the bone-chilling sight of homes and businesses being consumed by the sea unfolded behind them, many people abandoned their useless vehicles and began running. Those who still maintained an ounce of consideration pulled over first, some into the Mobil Station or the Ron Jon, others into the Eckerd or the B & B. One woman, small and mousy-looking with pulled-back hair, got out of her car and stood crying in the road. The man stuck behind her, with his very pregnant wife in the passenger seat, opened his window and hollered at her to get back in and keep going. When it became clear she wasn't listening, he got out, ran over, and slapped her across the face. Rather than snapping her back to reality, this caused her to crumple to the pavement as if she'd been shot. She curled up in the fetal position, crying even harder. The enraged man shook her violently. When she didn't react he dragged her to the grassy margin on the shoulder, then returned to her car and, depressing the gas pedal, sent it into the parking lot of the Quarterdeck Inn.

As the first wave receded, it brought miles of debris with it. Couches and tables floated alongside books and toys, mattresses and boxes. Strips of aluminum siding and sheets of paneling drifted like tea leaves, intermingling with nondescript chunks of sheetrock and splintered pine studs. Priceless personal items, on their way to being lost forever, bobbed on the surface—photographs, greeting cards, letters. A silver cigarette case made in 1827, passed down in one family through six generations, would tread water throughout the day until finally, shortly before five o'clock and almost ten miles out, it dipped under the surface and see-sawed lazily through green-tinted space, past the reach of the stippling sunlight and downward into eternity.

As the second wave arrived, it brought the debris back with it. The shattered glass and broken timber became weapons—projectiles as deadly as anything the world's armies had in their storehouses.

This wave was considerably larger than the first, and it rolled over the beaches with even greater ease. It smeared all remaining structures from the first line, then went to work on the next. The old Coast Guard Station at Barnegat Light trembled violently, as if it were a living thing wracked with fear, before breaking apart in hulking sections. In North Beach, a recently built, multimillion-dollar home with dozens of skylights held out with considerable valor, flooding all the way to the second floor before imploding from the sheer weight of the acquired water.

Businesses along the main strip were not spared. The concrete building that housed Murphy's Market in Beach Haven managed to remain standing, but the monstrous gush that blew through the back forced the store's contents out the front, pouring them into the street. A few doors down, Kapler's Pharmacy spewed its contents in similar fashion, decorating the intersection with vaporizers, toothbrushes, and plastic peroxide bottles.

The water-wall slid across Long Beach Boulevard and into the parking lot of the Acme where BethAnn Mosley and Jennifer King worked. It toppled light poles and flipped dumpsters, driving one of the latter into the glass front of the Beach Theater next door. A lone trailer that had been parked alongside the supermarket tipped over slowly, crashing through the cinder-block wall. In Ship Bottom, Pinky Shrimp's Seafood Company, not much larger than a two-car garage, folded like a figure in a child's pop-up book. Its chimney, with the word "seafood" printed in bold white letters down one side, collapsed almost gracefully into the raging current.

The second wave claimed the first human casualties. An elderly couple who had heard about the oncoming disaster only fifteen minutes earlier gripped each other in wordless terror as their Impala was plucked from the road and driven sideways into a rocky outcrop featured in a miniature golf course. The car crumpled like a beer can, squashing the occupants and, mercifully, killing them instantly.

Closer to the Route 72 intersection, an unemployed man in his early thirties who had been a thorn in the side of local police for years and, on this day, had tried to clean out as many cash registers as possible was running for his life, his pockets dribbling loose change and bills of various denominations, when he was swept off his feet. He was a strong swimmer and tried desperately to follow the movement of the current, but he went under after becoming entangled in a stray fishing net. As he tried to free himself he was struck by a wooden pallet that moved through the water like a torpedo. It removed his head in a messy, bloody explosion; his decapitated body would never be found.

At precisely the same moment, a woman who had taken a motorcycle from a neighbor's garage found herself in the wrong place at the wrong time as the Ship Bottom water tower buckled and fell onto the gas station through which she was taking a shortcut. One resident who would ultimately escape to safety and had witnessed her gory end would spend almost a full year in therapy in an attempt to purge the ghastly image of her body being flattened, then cremated when the station's pumps exploded in flames.

When the second wave finally withdrew, it dragged more debris into the ocean along with nearly forty bodies. The pandemonium that ensued was near apocalyptic. Those who'd retained some hope of reaching the mainland via their cars and trucks up until now threw the doors open and hit the ground running. A young mother who had suffered two harsh pregnancies and was about as thin as a whip clutched her bawling children under her arms, stumbling every few minutes from the physical demands for which she simply was not equipped. She begged for help but received none. There were no civil authorities left, and no helicopters dared risk landing, for they would be swamped in seconds. She and the others were on their own.

With almost all the structures between the Atlantic Ocean and Long Beach Boulevard gone, the third wave traveled forward unabated, tearing up miles of roadway and smashing homes and businesses with sickening efficiency. The man who had made the fateful decision to climb to the top of Old Barney for the purpose of filming this historical event lost control of his bladder as the famous structure shuddered violently. Dropping to his knees, the digital camera clattering as it fell from his pudgy hand, he prayed in earnest to a God he had long ignored. A few hundred yards away, the gift shop known simply as

"Andy's" was pushed off its foundation and into the bay, where it sank like a wounded ship. The death of the nearby Mole Hole was considerably less dramatic—the agitated ocean simply overwhelmed it, erasing it as if it hadn't existed in the first place.

Rick's American Cafe split in half horizontally—the pink bottom was washed aside, leaving only the light blue top to float for a few moments before going under. In High Bar Harbor, the Viking Village disappeared in a matter of seconds. At the Harvey Cedars Marina, the five remaining boats slammed together and shattered into small pieces. Back in Ship Bottom, three people squirmed their way onto the floating roof of what had been the Drifting Sands Motel, hoping to ride it out until the horror was over. Instead, the third wave flung the roof through the giant, pastel-colored facade of the Ron Jon surf shop.

At the southern end of the island, the wave struck the trailer park that BethAnn Mosley had called home for so many miserable years. The homes were broken off their flimsy foundations and swept together in a macabre domino effect. Adelaide Foster, the elderly woman BethAnn had left behind, was polishing her beloved carnival glass with a cotton cloth when she heard something. Her knees popping painfully, she shuffled across the beaten carpet to the east-facing window by the door and parted the curtains just in time to see the Hudsons' trailer, which had been on the other side of the dirt road, riding crookedly toward her, roof first, atop seven feet of pale, churning water. She opened her mouth to scream, then was abruptly cut off.

The third wave pushed on greedily, tearing apart thousands of homes on the island's overdeveloped geography. Back on Route 72, the wave reached the base of the Causeway. More terrified residents found themselves caught up in the raging flow, paddling madly. They would learn the hard way that a great percentage of tsunami victims perish from drowning after being struck by objects pulled loose and carried by the wave.

A heavyset, balding man managed to reach the surface before a spear-shaped strip of wood from a telephone pole shot through his neck. Another man, a lifelong fitness buff in his late fifties, managed to make his way halfway up the first segment of the Causeway, to Cedar Bonnet, before a wrought-iron guardrail was thrown from the water like a Frisbee and met the back of his head, knocking him unconscious. Moments later the ever-progressing current found and claimed his body.

The third wave also triggered hundreds of explosions. The saltwater ignited power substations, massive transformer boxes, and python lines with 11,000-volt charges running through them. Hundreds of propane tanks feeding houses and barbecues popcorned all over the island. An underground fuel reservoir at Harvey Cedars Auto somehow caught a spark and blew through the water like a miniature bomb, sending up a sixty-foot flame column along with two pickup trucks and a '69 Mustang whose transmission one of the mechanics was rebuilding in his spare time. The force of the blast left a crater thirty feet in diameter; no trace of the building that once marked the location would ever be found.

One by one, the other stations went, along with gas lines and more above-ground propane tanks. The water spread burning fuel everywhere; cars, homes, even the floating debris were suddenly ablaze.

The third wave retreated at exactly 12:04. Six minutes later—at 12:10—the fourth and most deadly wave rose over LBI. Smaller waves would follow in the coming hours, but with relatively little effect. This was, in every sense, the moment of truth.

The wave was more than an ocean swelling; it was like a life force created in Satan's workshop for the sole purpose of obliteration. From Barnegat Light to Holgate, the island was first shadowed and then hammered by a 27-foot-high mass of churning green fluid. Within it, like chunks of fruit in a Jell-O mold, was the wreckage of what once was Long Beach Island.

The wave reached over the previous killing fields as if they weren't even there. The man who had idiotically gambled his life on the safety of Old Barney screamed until he could scream no more, his bulging eyes frozen on the sight of the colossal wall of water carrying a yellow bulldozer, obtained from God-knows-where. As the wave tossed it into Barney's base, the grand old structure lingered for a final, defiant moment, then gave a slow bow and crashed into the water.

Next the wave leaped across the main island and engulfed High Bar Harbor, tackling the homes as if they were cardboard boxes. More sparks, more explosions, more cars tumbling into Barnegat Bay. Meantime, at the island's other end, the Forsythe Wildlife Refuge was completely submerged, killing thousands of Piping Plovers and destroying their nests. Nearby, TC's Surfside Deli had disappeared, as had almost every home in Holgate. The house Bud and Nancy Erickson had happily occupied for so long was now nothing but a water-filled basement and a few stubs of foundation block. Million-dollar homes in Loveladies and North Beach were no more. In Beach Haven, the consumer Mecca known as the Schooner's Wharf had been reduced to floating piles of junk. LBI T-shirts and hats drifted through the water with seashell nightlights and necklaces.

For all intents and purposes, the intersection of Long Beach Boulevard and Route 72 was history. The road was still there, but the traffic lights, the gas stations, and the businesses were all gone. The Eckerd Pharmacy, a modern structure of rein-forced concrete, still stood, but its interior had been gutted. The Quarterdeck, which began to crumble during the third strike, finally went down.

The last wave gobbled up cars like candy. It clustered them together and used them to pound the Causeway. At first it appeared the bridge would survive the beating, bending and flexing beyond its engineered limits in order to compensate. Then, at exactly 12:14, the first cracks appeared on the eastern side. After that, piece by piece, the bridge began to crumble. Giant hunks of concrete, steel strands curling out of them like stray hairs, fell away. Cars and trucks fell with them. Those who had been lucky enough to survive until now found that their luck had run out. Some chose to dive off the bridge before it disappeared beneath them in a bid to swim to the mainland. Others kept running. The last wave reached for all of them, flattening the infamous "clam shack" in the process and putting to rest once and for all the question of who really owned the damn thing.

Eventually, the last of the Causeway bridge—a striking feature of LBI—fell away. Once it was gone, the fourth wave—as if destroying the bridge was its central objective all along—departed as well, carrying with it the spoils of its victory.

SIXTEEN

*T*he footage of the Causeway first swaying and then crumbling was played and replayed across the country on every major news channel. The cameramen who'd filmed it had been forced back by the National Guard for their own safety, but not so far that they could not record the harrowing images of cars and trucks tumbling into the bay like toys.

While being interviewed on CNN, Dr. Daniel Kennard pointed out that a tsunami wave reaching more than ten feet in height was considered unusually powerful, so this one would make the record books. "Considering the destructive nature of such a giant wave and the fact that there was only one way off the island, it's a miracle more people didn't perish." He added that this one was more than twice as large as the one that struck Newfoundland in 1929. It was, without question, the most devastating oceanographic disaster ever seen along the eastern seaboard.

The damage extended well beyond the boundaries of Long Beach Island. In Atlantic City most of the boardwalk was destroyed along with nearly two hundred small businesses. Most of the casinos—modern structures with reinforced steel running through the concrete like veins and arteries—survived with only cosmetic damage. The relatively new parking garage at the Claridge Hotel and Casino, however, crumbled for the second time in five years, killing two people and leaving a pile of rubble that would take nearly four months to remove. North of LBI, waves reached as far as Point Pleasant, nearly 50 miles away, pulling tiny beach houses into the sea that had previously survived gales, hurricanes, and other forms of nature's wrath since their construction in the booming postwar era.

As the nation followed the story on TV and the Internet, details began dribbling out about the "accident" that caused it. Khalid Sheikh Mohammed, the al Qaeda mastermind of the 9/11 attacks who had been captured in Pakistan in March of 2003, revealed to CIA interrogators that Sayed Zaeef was carrying out his plan to detonate a dirty bomb from a commercial airliner as it landed in Washington DC. According to Sheikh Mohammed, he had lost touch with Zaeef prior to his arrest and assumed he had been captured at some point, too. He insisted there was never a plan to create a tsunami, but he said he was "warmed" by the idea and hoped, now that it had happened, that operatives still in hiding would consider trying to precipitate similar natural disasters. He praised Allah for his "bountiful justice" and theorized that attacks gone wrong but still resulting in the deaths of Americans provided proof that God was on the side of his cause.

Shaken by this latest sign of continuing life within the terrorist organization, American society responded in a familiar way. By mid-afternoon the Dow had fallen more than 300 points, the NASDAQ by more than 80. The President, eager to calm jittery nerves and maintain an economy that had finally begun to bloom again, gave an impassioned speech from the Rose Garden. Working from early intelligence reports, he pointed out that the wave resulting from the downed airliner was not part of an al Qaeda design, but in fact the unfortunate result of an otherwise heroic effort on the part of the plane's crew to thwart a larger and more sinister plan. He reminded the nation that the majority of the terror network's infrastructure had been dismantled, and that its leader, Osama bin Laden, was dead. Only a handful of isolated individual terrorists remained, the President said, but they were still dangerous and needed to be rooted out. He promised with characteristic conviction to hunt them until every last one was captured or killed.

Back in New Jersey, Atlantic and Ocean counties were declared federal disaster areas, which opened the floodgates for relief funding. Meanwhile, FEMA began sending critical supplies to the area—food, water, generators, cots and blankets, and so on. Governor Jim Mayfield ordered the rebuilding of the Causeway to begin immediately and earmarked nearly $75 million in state funds for the purpose. In the meantime, all boats in the area—private and federal—were required to ferry residents back and forth so they could begin cleanup operations and tend to their personal affairs as soon it was safe to do so.

No one seemed to know when that would be.

*   *   *

Thousands of now homeless LBI residents were packed into the Home Depot parking lot on Route 72. Lights swirled above ambulances and police cars. Blankets and drinks were handed out. Some people were given oxygen, others sedatives. Dozens of doctors and nurses were on the scene, many of them from Southern Ocean County Hospital. Others were nearby residents wanting to lend a hand. People with clipboards were taking names, trying to get a rough head count. At one point a sooty old bus with a Philadelphia Eagles logo on either side groaned in and parked. The driver, a devoted fan and veteran tailgater, quickly set up two long grilling tables and began cooking. As it turned out, he was also a wholesale butcher and ended up giving away more than $4,000 worth of ribs, chicken, beef, hot dogs, and hamburgers. He would later receive a personal commendation from the governor for his actions.

About an hour after arriving, BethAnn Mosley spotted a pay phone. It appeared to be one of the few that were working, as about thirty other people were waiting to use it. With nothing else to do, she went to the end of the line. She had managed to escape what she quickly decided were a bunch of religious loonies and possibly an unpleasant foray into the dark world of gang rape. She'd sat on the floor of the van, smiling and nodding until they passed the Home Depot, then feigned what she believed to be a pretty convincing epileptic seizure (she'd seen a few on TV through the years and had the gist of it). The moment the van came to a halt, she'd thrown the door open and rolled out. The other passengers started squealing like little girls (although they were all male, and pretty young at that), and one had managed to get a hand around her ankle. She pulled it free and hit the pavement chest-first just as the driver gunned the motor in an attempt to scare her back in. Without looking back, and certain she would be chased, she ran faster than she ever had in her life. Now, an hour later, still physically drained from the incident, she was anxious to call her friend Sharon in Forked River to come get her.

Carolyn King got in line next, her makeup and clothes still perfect, looking every bit the upper-class woman she was. She crossed her arms and gave BethAnn a quick appraisal, then just as quickly looked away. In that singular instant she had summed up the girl and made her judgment—white trash. *Something my kids will never be.* BethAnn caught the look and wanted to say something, but decided not to bother; a few hours from now she wouldn't have to worry about that shitty little island or the people who'd lived on it ever again.

Carolyn needed to speak to her husband, let him know what was going on. She also wanted him to contact that psychiatrist friend of his. She was certain Jennifer was going to need a lot of therapy to get past this. It would change her, she had no doubt, but with a lot of care and attention she'd be okay. As Carolyn waited, she glanced over at her daughter, sitting on a blanket with another one wrapped around her, still red-faced and occasionally crying. A policeman, a friend of the King family, tended to her. He was on one knee with his arm around Jennifer's shoulder, trying to be comforting. She didn't seem to notice.

Next in line was an older couple looking haggard and stressed, along with two young boys clutching their backpacks tight against their chests and continually surveying the chaos that surrounded them. They had been dropped off by an older woman who had offered them a lift in Tuckerton. Neither of the boys had spoken much in the last few hours beyond an occasional "Where's mommy?" Bud and Nancy kept reassuring them that she'd be along shortly. But now, truthfully, they were beginning to wonder. The current plan was to get to that phone and try her cell number again. Worst case scenario, they'd try to reach Mike in San Francisco.

Bud had asked the police on the scene if they had any information about Karen, but there was no news of her. Now, as they stood in line, an officer came up and asked if they were the Ericksons, and if the two boys were Patrick and Michael Thompson. The officer was young and serious, and he spoke in the steady tone of one who has been given the unpleasant task of delivering bad news. Nancy began crying immediately, no longer able to maintain the "everything-will-be-okay" facade for the boys. When Bud confirmed their identity, the officer calmly informed them that the boys' mother had been found in a small motorboat that crashed into a moored rescue boat along the mainland. She was unconscious—probably from the collision, he said—and had suffered an injury to her right foot. But she was going to be all right. Nancy squeezed the boys with all her might and continued to sob openly as the officer led them to an idling squad car that would take them to the hospital.

When the Ericksons left, Tom Wilson moved up in line behind Mrs. King, hands in his pockets. He wanted to call his parents up in Brielle to let them know he was okay. Then he'd put in a quick call to his on-again-off-again girlfriend Melanie, who lived in Staffordville.

After that he would try every number he knew in an attempt to contact the man he had spent years worshipping. There were almost a dozen possibilities—offices, residences, even the home of his estranged wife who was now living in Ringwood, in North Jersey. Between calls he would stand in the parking lot, amid the crowd and the chaos yet somehow feeling alone at the same time as he scanned the skies for Harper's helicopter. It wouldn't be until much later that the pilot who'd left Harper at the Forsythe Refuge recognized Wilson and told him what had happened.

Numbed by this news, Wilson found a quiet spot behind the Home Depot, sat down with his back against the building and cried. He cried for the man who had given his life in an attempt to save another, and for the loss of a modern hero in an age when heroes were as likely to be vilified as celebrated. He wept for the loss of a friend, one who was most certainly flawed, who had committed his share of sins, but was willing to acknowledge his shortcomings and regret his transgressions. He had made the ultimate sacrifice, and for that his sins would be forgiven.

Tom Wilson felt certain of it.

SEVENTEEN

*T*hat first night, thousands watched from the fringes of Route 72 as the vacant island burned on the horizon. Every now and then the steady orange flames would be interrupted by the explosion of a propane tank or a gas line, and many commented that it looked like a scene from Hell. By the third day the fires were under control, thanks not only to the valiant efforts of fire companies from thirty-two different communities, but also those of the U.S. Air Force, which sent a dozen C-130s into the area to drop nearly eight-thousand gallons of a pinkish fire-retardant chemical used to snuff out woodland blazes, colloquially known as "Sky Jell-O."

By the end of the first week, 204 people were assumed missing or dead. Two days later that number dropped to 183, and by the end of the second week 154 bodies had been recovered. That left a total of 29 individuals unaccounted for including Mayor Donald J. Harper. The general theory was that the waves had simply pulled them out to sea, a common occurrence in tsunami scenarios. For the families of those 29, there would be no closure, no bittersweet assurance. They would have to live

289

with the nightmarish thoughts of their loved ones' bodies slowly decomposing in the open waters until, finally, they became a part of the food chain, courtesy of whatever life forms were lucky enough to encounter them.

While few could imagine anyone remaining on the island and surviving, several miraculous stories emerged. A professional diving instructor, who had spent nearly his whole life on LBI and most of that in the water, chained himself to an old wreck a few hundred yards offshore and waited until the waves subsided. He later sold his story to SCUBA World for $10,000. A very lucky woman in her early twenties was found unconscious in her 2001 Volkswagen Beetle, atop a pile of rocks somewhere near what used to be the Causeway. She was at a complete loss for an explanation, as her last memory was of waiting in a slow-moving line of traffic on Long Beach Boulevard. Then there was the unconfirmed report, by the pilot of a fire-fighting plane, of a man walking on the beach near the Forsythe Refuge less than an hour after the fourth wave had subsided.

One of the bodies recovered—on the third day of searching—was that of Mark White. It had washed ashore within a hundred yards of the Forsythe Refuge and was spotted by a passing Coast Guard vessel shortly after sunrise. Due to the detrimental effects of the elements on the corpse, the coffin was kept closed during the wake. Jennifer King attended, but she broke down during the service and had to be supported as she was led out by her father and two brothers. Mark's mother, conversely, seemed to be in deep denial, humming tunelessly to herself and communicating with no one. She would end her own life six years later, hanging herself in a squalid efficiency apartment in southern Florida.

Sixteen days after the disaster, LBI residents were allowed to return to the island via boats, albeit in controlled numbers and only for brief periods. Even those who had managed to regain their emotional centers found it difficult to look at the thousands of personal items scattered along the sand-covered streets, tangled in miles of seaweed, and lying broken along the beaches. One of the saddest sights was that of pets laying twisted and dead in gutters. Most of the homes that were still standing were badly damaged, and too dangerous to occupy. All but twenty-four were declared uninhabitable and would have to be rebuilt. Insurance claims on residences alone would total more than $13 billion, and the loss to businesses would reach even higher. Many residents took their insurance checks and fled, never to return.

* * *

On the one-year anniversary of the tragedy, Long Beach Township Mayor Valerie Pruitt stood at the eastern base of the new Causeway, where the Quarterdeck Inn once stood, and dedicated a memorial to those whose lives had been lost. "We turned a corner on that day," she said. "And although we began down a new path in misery, we moved forward with bravery together." Indeed, the majority of the survivors stayed and saw to the rebuilding of their community. The island had undergone a fundamental paradigm shift, a redefining of its persona. Whatever was before was gone, and whatever was to come had yet to be built. It would never be the same.

Once Pruitt was finished, she stepped aside so Tom Wilson could speak. The crowd of more than 4,000, including members of the media—many of whom had covered the disaster the year before—waited eagerly. Wilson had taken part in the rescue efforts for the first few weeks, then disappeared into seclusion and had not been seen or heard from since. He was known and liked among the residents, the loyal soldier of a fallen general who, it was generally accepted, had paid for his mistakes and was now, slowly, attaining folk-hero status. In most people's eyes, Wilson was one of the few remaining links to Donald J. Harper.

In a choked voice, Wilson began by saying how proud Harper would be of "his people" if he were alive today. He said that Harper was as given to temptation as anyone but that, in the end, he "displayed his true self by displaying true selflessness." There were sobs from the crowd; tissues and handkerchiefs came out. At the end of his speech, Wilson helped Pruitt uncover the memorial—the only jetty boulder that had been jarred loose, found on Seabreeze Drive in Peahala Park. It was chosen to symbolize the community's resolve—a small part had been loosened and cast off, but the greater whole remained intact. A heavy bronze plaque had been riveted to the boulder, bearing the names of all 183 who had perished, including the 29 whose bodies hadn't been recovered. Donald Harper's did not hold a special place or even bear the title of "Mayor"; it was simply listed alphabetically with the others.

The dedication ceremony ended just before noon that Saturday. Some left right away, but many lingered for awhile to gaze at the new memorial and remember. They spoke of their friends and loved ones and reflected upon the delicacy of life. Some commented that they lived in dangerous times, and the deaths of those 183 people was evidence of that. But others maintained that life was always precious and fleeting. There was no such thing as complete safety; security was merely an illusion, an idealistic dream. Even here, on this tiny island that few people on the planet had ever heard of, the darkest forces in the universe were closer than one might think.

The sky was blue and clear that day, as it had been precisely one year earlier. A few light clouds brushed the otherwise shimmering canvas, and an early summer sun was shining cheerfully overhead. Little by little the crowd dissolved. The people returned to their lives as residents of Long Beach Island, New Jersey. Tomorrow would arrive soon enough and would have to be faced and conquered.

By two o'clock they were all gone. The sun remained for awhile, then moved west until it, too, disappeared over the horizon.

AFTERWORD

*T*he story in this book is, of course, fictional. But true tsunami disasters occur all over the world. The most recent, in southern Asia in December 2004, has claimed more than 150,000 victims as of this writing—many of them children. It was a tragedy of inestimable proportions and depthless sorrow. *Wave*, it should be noted, was *not* inspired by this event. The pages were undergoing final proofing when it happened.

As we grieve every day for those who perished, we must continue to help those who survived. I urge you to contribute to any of the fine charities involved in the relief effort. You can make a difference.

MORE GREAT FICTION AND NONFICTION
FROM PLEXUS PUBLISHING, INC.

WRONG BEACH ISLAND
By Jane Kelly

When the body of millionaire Dallas Spenser washes up on Long Beach Island with a bullet in its back, it derails Meg Daniels's plans for a romantic sailing trip. As Meg gets involved in the unraveling mystery, she soon learns that Spenser had more skeletons than his Loveladies mansion had closets. The ensuing adventure twists and turns like a boardwalk roller coaster and involves Meg with an unforgettable cast of characters.

From the beaches of Holgate and Beach Haven at the southern end of "LBI" to the grand homes of Loveladies and the famed Barnegat Light at the north, author Jane Kelly delivers an irresistible blend of mystery and humor in *Wrong Beach Island*—her third and most deftly written novel. Meg Daniels, Kelly's reluctant heroine, may be the funniest and most original sleuth ever to kill time at the Jersey shore.

Hardbound/ISBN 0-937548-47-2/$22.95

KILLING TIME IN OCEAN CITY
By Jane Kelly

"*Killing Time in Ocean City* is a unique, riveting, engaging mystery that all fans of the genre will find immensely satisfying."—*The Midwest Book Review*

After being jolted from a sound sleep by police early in her vacation, Meg Daniels discovers that her former boss has turned up dead near her rented beach house in Ocean City, New Jersey. Along the way the action shifts from Ocean City to Atlantic City to the Pine Barrens, with Meg frantically hunting for answers while she herself becomes a target of the killer.

The familiarity of the author to the shore areas of South Jersey brings a fun, real-life dimension for the local reader to this suspense-filled "whodunit."

Hardbound/ISBN 0-937548-38-3/$22.95

CAPE MAYHEM
By Jane Kelly

"Lots of local color, a memorable cast of characters, a fast paced plot, and an irresistible heroine."—*Herald Newspaper*

Temporarily unattached, Meg Daniels arrives in Cape May for what should have been a romantic off-season holiday, but instead finds herself in the middle of a mystery. Overnight, a certain female guest at the Parsonage Bed & Breakfast has undergone an impossible transformation. Suspecting foul play, Meg enlists a hunky investigator in the local DA's office, as well as the B&B's spunky co-owner, to help her figure out a killer of a question: "Who was that lady who checked in with Wallace Gimbel?" The weather is frosty, but the trail is hot as Meg and friends unravel the truth behind a scheme marked by imposters, infidelities, and—if she's right—even murder.

Hardbound/ISBN 0-937548-41-3/$22.95

PINELANDS
By Robert Bateman

In a compelling blend of history and fiction, Robert Bateman examines the seductive legacies of the past and how they are used by many to resist the abrasive realities of modern life. With its startling conclusion, *Pinelands* brings the reader full circle through decades of ambition, violence, love, and decadence to a present that is, perhaps, all too familiar.

"A riveting story, written in a style to catch and hold the reader's attention." —*Barnegat Bay Banner*

"Bateman has written an elegy for one section of New Jersey and for all the places that have been devoured by progress without vision." —*The News and Observer* (Raleigh, NC)

Hardbound/ISBN 0-937548-27-8/$21.95
Softbound/ISBN 0-937548-28-6/$12.95

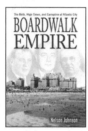

BOARDWALK EMPIRE
The Birth, High Times, and Corruption of Atlantic City
By Nelson Johnson

"This is the best book I've read on Atlantic City ... extremely well researched and documented ... reads like a novel."—Robert Peterson, *Egg Harbor News*

Atlantic City's popularity rose in the early 20th century and peaked during Prohibition. For 70 years, it was controlled by a partnership comprised of local politicians and racketeers, including Enoch "Nucky" Johnson—the second of three bosses to head the political machine that dominated city politics and society. In *Boardwalk Empire*, Atlantic City springs to life in all its garish splendor. Author Nelson Johnson traces "AC" from its birth as a quiet seaside health resort, through the notorious backroom politics and power struggles, to the city's rebirth as an entertainment and gambling mecca where anything goes.

Softbound/ISBN: 0-937548-49-9/$18.95

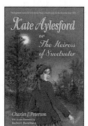

KATE AYLESFORD
OR, THE HEIRESS OF SWEETWATER
By Charles J. Peterson
With a new Foreword by Robert Bateman

"Plot twists, colorful characters, timely observations, lyrical descriptions of the Pine Barrens, and ... an unusually strong and well-educated female protagonist."—Robert Bateman, *from the Foreword to the new edition*

The legendary historical romance, *Kate Aylesford: A Story of Refugees*, by Charles J. Peterson, first appeared in 1855, was reissued in 1873 as *The Heiress of Sweetwater*, and spent the entire 20th century out of print. As readable today as when Peterson first penned it, *Kate Aylesford* features a memorable cast of characters, an imaginative plot, and a compelling mix of romance, adventure, and history. Plexus Publishing is pleased to return this remarkable novel to print.

Hardbound/ISBN: 0-937548-46-4/$22.95

GATEWAY TO AMERICA
World Trade Center Memorial Edition
By Gordon Bishop
Photographs by Jerzy Koss

Based on the acclaimed PBS documentary, Gateway to America is both a comprehensive guidebook and history. It covers the historic New York/New Jersey triangle that was the window for America's immigration wave in the 19th and 20th centuries. In addition to commemorating the World Trade Center, the book explores Ellis Island, The Statue of Liberty, and six other Gateway landmarks including Liberty State Park, Governors Island, Battery City Park, South Street Seaport, Newport, and the Gateway National Recreational Area. A must for history buffs and visitors to the area alike.

Softbound/ISBN 0-937548-44-8/$19.95

OVER THE GARDEN STATE & OTHER STORIES
By Robert Bateman

Novelist Bateman (*Pinelands, Whitman's Tomb*) offers six new stories set in his native Southern New Jersey. While providing plenty of authentic local color in his portrayal of small-town and farm life, the bustle of the Jersey shore with its boardwalks, and the solitude and otherworldliness of the famous Pine Barrens, Bateman's sensitively portrayed protagonists are the stars here. The title story tells of an Italian prisoner of war laboring on a South Jersey farm circa 1944. There, he finds danger and dreams, friendship and romance—and, ultimately, more fireworks than he could have wished for.

Hardbound/ISBN: 0-937548-40-5/$22.95

NATURAL WONDERS OF THE JERSEY PINES AND SHORE
By Robert A. Peterson with selected photographs
by Michael A. Hogan
Additional photographs by Steve Greer

"*In capturing the beauty and uniqueness of southern New Jersey, Natural Wonders makes it clear why so many people have worked so hard to save its treasure of nature and human history. This extraordinary book will inspire readers to cherish the Pine Barrens and coastal estuaries anew.*"—Carleton Montgomery, Executive Director, Pinelands Preservation Alliance

In this exquisite book, fifty-seven short yet informative chapters by the late Robert Peterson celebrate a range of "natural wonders" associated with the Pine Barrens and coastal ecosystems of southern New Jersey. The diverse topics covered include flora, fauna, forces of nature, and geological formations—from birds, mammals, and mollusks, to bays, tides, trees, wildflowers, and much more. More than 200 stunning full-color photos by award-winning photographers Michael Hogan and Steve Greer bring Peterson's delightful vignettes to life. For South Jersey aficionados—young and old alike—this is a book to treasure.

Hardbound/ISBN: 0-937548-48-0/$49.95

THE UNDERGROUND RAIL ROAD

By William Still

"The Underground Rail Road is a masterpiece ... a powerful and triumphant work that demands our attention." —Bill Cosby

Originally published in 1872 and out of print for many years, this landmark book presents firsthand accounts of slaves escaping north via the human support network known as the Underground Railroad. The narratives were painstakingly documented by William Still (1821-1902), a son of emancipated slaves who helped guide untold numbers of fugitives to safety in the mid-19th century. Based in Philadelphia, he corresponded with, interviewed, and recorded the stories of hundreds of fugitives at great personal risk. The 2005 edition features the complete 1872 text, including more than 200 slave narratives, 60+ black and white illustrations, hundreds of letters and newspaper clippings, and biographical sketches of abolitionists and other contributors to the cause of freedom. By turns heartbreaking, horrifying, and inspiring, *The Underground Rail Road* is a remarkable reading experience.

Hardbound/ISBN: 0-937548-55-3/$49.50

DOWN BARNEGAT BAY
A Nor'easter Midnight Reader
By Robert Jahn

Down Barnegat Bay is an illustrated maritime history of the Jersey shore's Age of Sail. Originally published in 1980, this fully revised Ocean County Sesquicentennial Edition features more than 177 sepia illustrations, including 75 new images and nine maps. Jahn's engaging tribute to the region brims with first-person accounts of the people, events, and places that have come together to shape Barnegat Bay's unique place in American history.

Hardbound/ISBN 0-937548-42-1/$39.95

WONDERWALKS: THE TRAILS OF NEW JERSEY AUDUBON
By Patricia Robinson

Wonderwalks is the first book to present all of the accessible trails, sanctuaries, and nature centers owned by the New Jersey Audubon society. This delightful guide explores the 34 New Jersey Audubon nature preserves and sanctuaries throughout the state. Both casual hikers and seasoned naturalists will enjoy this one-of-a-kind, top-to-bottom environmental tour of the Garden State. The book includes dozens of photographs, seasonal lists of birds and butterflies, trail descriptions, driving directions and much more.

Softbound/ISBN: 0-937548-53-7/$19.95